# DARKEST
# VENGEANCE

# DARKEST VENGEANCE

*Night Hunters Book 3*
*A Contemporary Vampire Series*

T.M. KEHOE AND JOSEPH HAGEN

*Darkest Vengeance* - Night Hunters Book 3  A Contemporary Vampire Series
T.M. Kehoe & Joseph Hagen

Join our mailing list here:  https://BookHip.com/PMBGPMM

# DEDICATIONS

T.M. Kehoe

To everyone who believes.
Stay aware!

Joseph Hagen

To our readers who have traveled this dark trilogy with us and survived.
I am happy T.M. and I kept you entertained.
I dedicate my portion of this book to each of you.
Thank you!

Our website and social media pages are cited below. Please meet us there to learn more about us and our spin offs which are being polished even as you read this.
https://stlouisauthors.com
facebook.com/stlouisauthors

Join our mailing list here: https://BookHip.com/PMBGPMM
We look forward to meeting you!

# PROLOGUE

Drawn with her vampire Sisters to the vagrants' cavern, Sharon's eyes narrowed as she focused on the man called Britt. Moments before, he'd escaped the cavern, shouting to his co-conspirators. Now, he stood at the partially blocked entryway as she and her sisters followed, intent on feeding — also on removing their greatest threat.

The vampires' movement through the cavern had stirred the propane leaking from the surrounding tanks, but Sharon ignored the odor and focused on her nemesis. Tonight, the Order would have their revenge.

Again, she was thwarted as Sharon's Sisters, betrayed by their Arithmomania, an irresistible impulse to count items, shuffled, heads down and shrieking around her. Counting the brightly colored jelly beans scattered by the humans, her Sisters would not continue their attack until they satisfied this compulsion. Sharon turned from them and glared at Britt. Even without the help of her sisters, the danger from these humans would end tonight.

With a leer evil enough to curdle blood, Sharon reached into her pocket. Her enemies had focused their energy on weapons used against the supernatural, but she did not suffer that limitation. There were many simpler ways to deal with those opposing her order. Holding the .38 pistol she had taken from an earlier victim, she walked closer, intent on hitting her target.

Eyes glowing green with rage, Sharon aimed, and fired. Britt screamed and crumpled when the bullet tore into his shoulder. Instantaneously, the spark from Sharon's gun ignited the propane — her world exploded in hellfire. The flames filled the cavern, causing the blood of the vampire Sisters to combust as well, bringing new bright flares of destructive heat.

The explosions threw Sharon aside. Writhing in pain, she cowered as her Sisters burned. When a wall near her collapsed, she crawled through. Moaning in pain, she rolled away from the heat and through the weeds. When her flames were finally extinguished, she lay still, anguished and exhausted. Hidden in a scree of high weeds and brush, blood trickled from her wounds as she cowered.

She heard the hateful intruders shouting. At least one was dead, another injured. That was a balm to her heart. She only wished it could soothe her burned skin and broken shoulder. Blistered, peeling, completely raw and bleeding in places, she listened as these humans whined over their meager losses.

For hours Sharon lay in the weeds, shivering and biting her lips to keep silent. She waited through the wailing sirens, the arrival and departure of the EMTs, and the extinguishing of the fire. She heard other sections of the cavern collapse as she lay still and quiet.

Near dawn, a single officer was left to secure the scene. He propped himself on one of the sawhorses at the original cavern entrance. Soon, he was engrossed in his cell phone, leaving Sharon the freedom to move.

First, she tried to stand, but pain made that impossible, so she instead crawled toward deeper cover in the cavern.

She whimpered as sharp rocks and other objects gouged her tender, blistered skin. Gasping with shallow breaths, she entered, using her one good arm. The other, with its broken shoulder, was a great source of pain.

With agonizing slowness, she dragged herself through the cavern, praying that the rear passage remained open. Relieved to find that it was, she paused to breathe.

Startled, she awoke. She didn't know how long she'd been unconscious, but the time had allowed her preternatural blood to ease her pain. Her injuries, however, were no less severe. She was grateful for the blood Mother Eugenia and other ancients had allowed her to drink over the years as it had allowed her to survive her current injuries. As she lay on her back contemplating, she realized that the three ancients who were unable to leave their berths to join the hunt might remain among the living. Their blood should heal her.

With a great moan, she stood. Looking back toward the cave entrance, she was relieved to see the officer had moved away and had not heard her.

The vampires' passage at the back of the cavern was intact but damaged. Stones had come free from the walls and ceiling. With less pain but great fatigue, Sharon stepped over and around them to reach the door to her dark convent.

The door was scorched, but two-hundred-year-old oak was thick, hard, and tough. It was a struggle, but she grasped the ancient knob and pulled. The old wood and hinges groaned, but slowly opened.

The room was dimly lit by the lantern still shining beside her cot. She half-sat, half-fell onto one of the empty tables.

Lining both walls of the cavern, the tables echoed the placement of the steamer trunks in the basement at St. Eugenia Ravasco Academy, their former home. These ancient wooden tables had served as her Sisters' resting place.

Sharon's face pinched as she felt a new pain, at what she was planning to do. Blood-stained tears welled in her eyes as she looked to, then moved toward three tables containing three sacks.

Standing over one, her strength left her, and she fell beside it. Clinging to the sack and the table, she wept. After several minutes, she wiped away her tears reached for the rope binding the sack. With the burned fingers on her functional hand, she awkwardly worked until the ropes came free. Her pain returning, desperation drove her as she pulled the cloth away.

Folded inside the sack, knees tucked against her chest, was an ancient vampire in a decaying nun's habit. When the sack opened, the body squirmed slightly, too weak to do more. Sharon thought of the many nights she'd prayed for that sign of life. A green glow from beneath the dry lids was all she'd received. Now, the sign pierced her heart as she, and the ancient one, knew Sharon's plan.

Flinching at the effort, Sharon reached into the sack and pulled out the withered body. Limp, wrinkled, it was a cursed rag doll. Again, the body squirmed. Sharon hissed, "Stop!"

Using her dagger, Sharon pierced her Sister's jugular vein. She bent over, sucking, slurping, careful not to waste a drop. Sharon gasped as the blood flowed into her.

First, the blood reawakened her pain, mirroring its intensity during the fire. Weeping now for herself, Sharon continued until she had drained her Sister dry.

When finished, all that remained was an obscene ball of skin and bone. Turning away, Sharon stood beside the table. Conscious of renewed energy, her burned skin now only stung. She moaned in relief. "It's working."

Moving more easily, she left the first body without another thought. Again, with one hand, she opened the next sack, pulled out the revenant and once more used her dagger to open the font of life-giving blood. As she drank, there was a sudden sharp pain and pop from her broken shoulder. Her face didn't react, however, as she fed until this second body was dry.

Again, she stepped back. Stretching her back and legs, she reached to touch her face, then realized she was using the arm with the broken shoulder. It was broken no longer. Feeling stronger, she paused, noting the lack of pain. Instead, she felt a strange hunger. She stepped over, tore open the third sack, and wrenched the body out. Lifting it, she stood, joyous in her strength, as she bit into its neck, using her newly grown fangs.

Finished with the third Sister, she tossed aside the empty husk with none of the sadness displayed toward her first ancient sister.

Sharon's eyes suddenly widened as she lurched forward, convulsing with powerful cramps. Her body was sloughing off its human tissues, as her blood was replaced with vampiric blood. With a grunt, she vomited explosively, flecks of tissue and fluids spraying over the last ancient she'd fed upon, as she shed the last of her humanity.

Struggling to a table, she slumped in a faint and lay unmoving for over an hour. When her eyes opened, she could see every detail in the room perfectly. Her old lantern was no longer needed.

She flexed her arms, feeling supple skin moving easily, with no pain. Focusing her preternatural eyes, she listened and identified a worm crawling in a corner of the cave. She inhaled deeply, smelling each odor around her distinctly. Sharp and bright, as if each was a different neon color, splashed over her senses.

She felt exceptionally well — except for her stomach. Faint hunger pains stirred in her gut, each wave growing stronger. She thought of the officer at the entrance to the cavern, and her mouth watered. She laughed and spoke, enjoying the new timber in her voice. "He is a lucky man, for he is safe from me. I will not give myself away. Not yet. The fiends who've brought this all about will not be warned before I am ready."

But revenge was for later. Soon she would need the warm, fresh blood of a human.

Sharon wrapped her arms around herself in exultation. She believed she'd done it, but there was one final test. The night had ended. Even though still deep in the cave, she knew that dawn's light was already blushing the horizon. She walked through the crumbling tunnel and the disaster of the vagrant's cavern. Avoiding the officer at the only previous exit, she moved to one of the several openings now providing access to the outside.

Still inside, she stopped, suddenly anxious of that opening. After several moments, she stepped closer. The early light burned her eyes, which streamed with painful tears. She extended her hand, and saw dawn's early light fall across her new perfect skin… and jerked it back into the shadow. In pain, she retreated to the tunnel. Her skin was blistered where the sunlight had touched it. It was raw, burned once more. There was no longer any room for doubt — she was a vampire.

# 1

The days following the cavern fire were busy ones at the riverfront. Although most evidence had been incinerated, the investigation went on. Despite the vagrants' denials, the presence of propane tanks was blamed on them. Britt's bullet wound was blamed on the homeless as well. Frank's testimony was that he was there following his Captain's orders, and that a single man protecting his meager belongings released the gas and demanded that Frank leave. Seeing Frank being threatened, the team stepped in and Britt was shot. Frank's corroborating testimony was accepted by the authorities as negating any doubt. With the shooting and the origin of the propane tanks resolved, attempts to investigate the interior of the cavern were abandoned as pointless and dangerous. It was presumed the remains of the shooter were bound to be unidentifiable and sections were continuing to crumble. The threat of the unstable cavern prompted additional explosives being brought in to complete the collapse.

Nikki and the team remained anxious, concerned about the possibility that any of the vampires had survived.

The origin of the instructions given to Bolden to secure the cavern, which appeared to be signed by Bolden's Captain, remained a mystery. Detective Frank Bolden, who had fought the vampires alongside Nikki and the others, attempted no explanation. "I found it in my e-mail and followed the Captain's orders. The order gave me the authority to assign men to close off the area but no support to secure it. That's why I was there alone."

Frank and Ladso had actually generated the false document, giving them the cover they needed to destroy the vampires. It was, in Frank's opinion, a pleasant side effect that it put his Captain in the hot seat. The normally grumpy detective was left with a temporarily elated disposition.

Frank's wide smile had dissolved as the team gathered in Britt's hospital room. Nikki sat closest to the bed, as Britt continued to rest under the influence of pain killers, antibiotics, and healing fatigue. Nikki's eyes were nearly spilling tears as she attempted weak opposition to the team's suggestion that she and Frank stay with the still unconscious Britt while Ladso and Pi open the back door to the vampire's lair and investigate the possibility of survivors.

Eyes focused on Britt, Nikki said, "He'll be asleep anyway. Chances of his awakening while I'm gone…"

Ladso interrupted her. "Excuse me Nikki, your mind would be here, on Britt, as it should be. To enter the lair, everyone must be fully focused on the danger that may be…"

Pi spoke over Ladso's words, recognizing that they were only going to increase Nikki's worries about her friends going into danger without her. "Besides, our plan worked perfectly. Those ugly women were stumbling over one another, counting jelly beans and surrounded by hissing tanks. They didn't survive and we know that damned Sharon was with them. We're just going to verify the obvious." Seeing Ladso move to object, Pi said, "I know it needs to be done, but none of us really expect to find any of Sharon's creeps down there."

Nodding, Ladso added, "It does seem unlikely, but we will be carrying torches and burning everything in our path…"

"Whether it moves or not!" Pi put her hand on Nikki's shoulder. "We don't want Britt to wake up alone and yours is the face he'll be looking for first."

Nikki deflated, acknowledged their words and hoped that Pi was right about the back of the cavern being empty.

All the trouble had started for Nikki and her band members, Bryant and James, when they'd arrived in St. Louis and moved into Saint Eugenia Ravasco Academy, or SERA, as it was commonly known. The school was closed as was the adult day care which had been housed there. In the basement, there were apartment-like quarters with a kitchen and laundry. There was also a magnificent, old chapel which the school had used as a music room. The band loved this space and used it for their rehearsals. Amazing acoustics and a rent they could afford left them feeling far luckier than they actually were.

Nikki was the first to be uneasy and Britt Blasengane, a customer at the bistro where she worked shared stories about the school and neighborhood which increased her anxiety. Anxiety, it turned out, that was well founded as the band settled into their space and added a bass player, Wayne, to their trio.

Strange happenings came to a culmination when the band held their debut concert on Halloween Eve. The audience had come wearing costumes. Britt judged the costume contest during the band's intermission. On stage he called his first prize winner, a woman dressed as an ancient-looking nun … only to be attacked by what turned out to be a real vampire, in a nun's habit.

Chaos ensued, and while Britt, Nikki and her friend, Pi escaped, the rest of the band were not so lucky. Some of the vampire nuns also escaped. Their Reverend Mother, Eugenia, and many others burned, either in the fire, or when the sun came up the next morning and they had no cover.

Britt and Nikki went to Chicago seeking the help of Britt's friends, Murray and Ladso. The two had spent decades pursuing and destroying dark creatures of all sorts. As soon as they could, the group returned to St. Louis, to hunt down and kill the surviving vampires.

While staking out the burned remains of SERA, the group met Detective Frank Bolden, who had been assigned to the burned school's case in which arson was suspected. Suspicions were high on both sides initially, but Frank quickly became a welcome and integral member of their team.

Nikki's friend Pi, whose sister Delta had died in the school several years earlier, supposedly by suicide, joined the group as well. Her bravery and snark enriched and strengthened the team.

After a difficult hunt, they found the vampires hiding in the cave systems underneath St. Louis. With that knowledge, they set a trap using propane tanks which was successful, but they paid a high price.

Their guide and dear friend Murray died of a heart attack as the tanks exploded. And almost simultaneously, Britt was shot, resulting in the loss of his left arm.

While Nikki and Frank waited anxiously at Britt's bedside, Ladso and Pi armed themselves with flame-throwers and tools, and went to the second access to the vampire's lair. They'd previously secured the door in an attempt to prevent the vampires' escape until their trap could be sprung.

In the bright sunlight of late morning, the two worked to remove the screws, nails, rebar, and two by fours they'd attached to the door of the outhouse sized structure which they were confident led to the vampires' resting place.

Once they finished the removal of their efforts to secure the doorway, they were now faced with breaking through the door which they'd been unable to open when last tried. Both were shocked and anxious when it opened relatively easily now. Ladso shot flame into the opening and down the spiral staircase behind the door. Confident there was no immediate danger, they stepped in and flinched upon seeing the discarded lock on the ground and the gouges in the old wood on the back of the door.

"They must have attempted to leave," Ladso surmised.

"But was it before or after we sprung our trap?"

Turning on their head lamps, Ladso, his flame-thrower ready, took the lead as they advanced downward. Every few steps, he launched flame down the narrow spiral staircase. They paused, listening for the screeches of a burning vampire before they continued.

Before reaching the bottom, they detected a stench. Pi tied a bandana covering on Ladso's nose and mouth and then did the same for herself. The bandanas' assistance was minimal, but after another burst of flame, they advanced. At the bottom, they found a pile of dried bodies. Ladso and Pi did not try to imagine how much worse the stench would have been if the victims hadn't been drained of blood before being left to rot.

The space before them was large with curved arches. A short search revealed a passage off to their right. Pi flooded the tunnel with flame before they followed it to a closed door which was unlocked. Opening it just a crack, Ladso prepared his flame-thrower, kicked the door open and sent flame into the darkness beyond for several seconds. He released the trigger and heard nothing but Pi's breathing and his own. He whispered for her to wait while he went in.

"Like hell I will." She held her flame-thrower ready. "If they're in here they aren't going to let me escape. We're safer together."

With a nod, Ladso accepted her words, and they entered.

"As we'd feared." Frank looked sadly at the little creamed pig floating on top of the cappuccino Pi had made for him. The bit of art floating on what he called a Cop-achino didn't improve his mood as he listened to Ladso's description of his excursion with Pi into the SERA vampires' lair.

Gathered back in Britt's home after visiting hours ended at the hospital where Britt continued his recovery, the entire team minus Britt was present, including Trooper, Britt's dog that he gifted to Nikki when she lived at SERA. Ladso took a sip from his own hot drink, then spoke. "Yes, they had clearly been expanding the range of their feedings and bringing the bodies to that old tunnel to hide their activities."

Nodding, Pi said, "There were easily thirty bodies, piled like garbage." Her eyes teared as her thoughts shifted to her sister who she believed the vampires had also killed. Seeing her tears, Nikki put her arm around her friend and hugged.

Ladso nodded. "The number of bodies is horrific. It also demonstrates again how different these vampires are from any Murray and I ever dealt with." As the others looked at him and waited, he explained. "None of the others did more to hide their victims than leave them in the desolate areas where they killed them. Truly, there was no effort at all to hide victims. They simply left them where they killed them, whether in a field or a home. Once emptied of blood, they lost all interest in their victims."

Standing, Ladso held his cup. "Of course, these vampires did more than just hide their dead. They placed several of them as decoys, to be found and, theoretically, lead us away from their lair. If the ones at SERA were found earlier it might have worked."

"What do you make of the dead vampires you found?" Nikki asked.

"They were ancient. The slashes over two of the jugulars, and the punctures on the third's, along with the almost complete lack of fluid in their remains, imply several possibilities." Again, his team waited. "It is all theory, but… Sharon used a dagger to inflict the wounds she made on her victims." The team stirred uneasily. "Sharon led the others through the cavern. The others were distracted by their Arithmomania, but I saw Sharon continuing forward."

"It feels like contradicting facts." Frank set down his cup. "That is, if you're thinking Sharon fed on those ancient vampires."

"Only if she fed on them before our attack." Frank's brows rose as the ladies frowned. "It seems very unlikely that Sharon survived the explosion. Her luck would have to have been extraordinary." He studied the teams' eyes. All appeared hopeful for his conclusion. "She was not in their lair when we entered. The authorities collapsed the cavern two days ago. The tunnel that connected the lair to the Vagrant's Cavern had also collapsed." Still, the team frowned in silence. "There were guards there every night until the explosions that collapsed the cavern. None of them were attacked. The only other way out was the door we used to enter. It was unlocked from the inside, but our makeshift locks on the outside were still in place. If she had gone back to feed on those three, we would have found her in there today."

Hope took root on the teams' faces as Ladso began his final remarks. "We know Sharon was a hybrid. It seems possible that she was feeding on them to maintain or build her strength. Perhaps, even to complete her transition to a full vampire." Now he shook his head. "We may never know for certain, but those bodies were all that was left. There was no exit used or usable to escape. I am convinced they were all destroyed, including Sharon."

After several moments of silence, Frank said, "We'll have to watch for any suspicious reports over the next several months. Those things were very clever, but if any did survive, they'll eventually give themselves away. I, for one, will be super-vigilant in watching for clues."

Ladso nodded in approval. "But until such evidence reveals itself, our attention and support must remain with Britt."

It was only days later that Britt awoke. Long weeks of rehabilitation, first in the hospital then in a rehab facility, were dedicated to recovering from his wounds and learning to function without his left arm. The team rotated hospital visits, assuring that unless he awoke in the middle of the night, someone would be there. As he grew stronger the constant visitation eased, but he was never given the opportunity to believe he'd been forgotten.

Finally, Britt was allowed to return home with the knowledge that therapy and healing would continue. The gift by his teammates of Murray, a Weimaraner puppy, was intended to ease the hard times that lay ahead. As Britt hugged the puppy during the ride home, it seemed new healing had already begun.

Everyone settled into a routine. Nikki, Ladso and Pi continued to live in Britt's home, and Frank visited at least once or twice a week, assuring everyone that it wasn't just for Ladso's cooking.

After a month, Britt was adapting, and learning to overcome challenges. Nikki helped however she could, but Britt was determined to do as much one-handed as possible. With a grin he did occasionally acknowledge that there were times when two hands were required. In return, he was teaching her dog training, a valuable skill and one she'd come to realize she loved.

One morning, Pi surprised Nikki with her decision to move to Chicago to join Ladso on his life's work of dealing with dark creatures.

Murray had named Ladso his heir, which was no surprise since he had treated Ladso like a son for decades. Ladso was now the owner of the lavishly-sized home in Chicago, which included Murray's many souvenirs from decades of travels, and his astonishing library. The volumes spanned not decades, but centuries, including anything and everything about mythology, religion, demons, other creatures. There were things that needed Ladso's attention, and it was time to return to his home. He was happy for several reasons that Pi was coming with him, including her support. His many memories of life with Murray in Chicago would be difficult to deal with alone.

Worried over her safety in her Order's cavern, Sharon had abandoned it before the authorities had detonated and brought down the hazardous remains of the Vagrants' Cavern. The first few nights she spent in a hole she'd dug for herself. Allowing the dirt to fill in behind her, she'd curled up with the worms and rested through the day. "Disgusting," she hissed the next night as she exhumed herself and then washed in the icy water of the Mississippi. The cold didn't bother her but the indignity of burying herself by day and then drying slowly over the night was only lessened after she'd killed and fed. The nightly feedings were more than her body could handle, but she had no desire to be discovered because of some fool with a bite wound that would not heal. Her only option was to kill them, which she did in a variety of unpleasant ways. Thrown from one of the flood walls between the Arch and the river, shoved in front of a moving truck, drowned in the river...

While she lived homeless and survived day to day, her time was not wasted. She practiced her more powerful mind control, and had nearly dematerialized. It was an ability she'd seen her vampire Sisters do but had never been able to accomplish in her hybrid state. Now she had the power but did not know how to use it.

Picturing the blood chattel who had killed her Sisters and nearly killed her, she was determined to master all her new abilities. Then she would use them to wreak her revenge, both slowly and painfully.

The night before Ladso and Pi would be leaving, the team gathered for another meal together. Frank started with a dark joke about a "Last Supper," but after the deaths, injuries, and the upcoming separation, no one found this humorous. He quickly shifted gears, hoisted his glass, gesturing for the others to do the same. "To absent friends, gone but never forgotten."

"To Murray." Ladso's voice cracked as he spoke.

"We'll miss you so much" Nikki's eyes were bright with unshed tears.

"Murray." Pi lifted her glass with the others.

Britt intoned the English translation from the Latin. "Eternal rest grant unto him, Oh Lord, and let perpetual light shine upon him. May he rest in peace."

They drank and were quiet for several minutes, each remembering Murray, and other lost friends. Finally, Ladso broke the silence. "Let us see if the reputation of this restaurant is deserved. I admit, it is nice not to cook."

Nikki grinned at him. "I worried you'd be back in the kitchen telling the chef his business!"

Ladso laughed aloud, something he hadn't done in a long time. "I would not dare. No chef worthy of his toque would tolerate anyone entering his kitchen without his express permission."

The restaurant specialized in tapas, but with eclectic fusions, resulting in outrageous but delicious plates of morsels to share.

As always, eating and talking relaxed everyone. A little wine eased tensions further.

Frank set down his wine, wishing it was a Cop-achino. "So, back to Chicago."

Ladso nodded in confirmation. "Not to worry, Frank, we will return for visits, but yes, it is time to return home, and eventually, to work." He looked over at Pi. "*We* need to get home and back to work."

Frank nodded, not surprised the two had paired off. *I may be a cynical bastard, but I'm not usually wrong,* he thought, a fleeting grin flashing across his lips. It vanished quickly as he rearranged his expression into its usual scowl.

Britt said, "You know you always have a place to stay here, any time you come to visit, which I hope you do. And frequently!"

Nikki pouted. "I'm going to miss you terribly. Are you sure you have to leave already? Couldn't you stay just a few more weeks?" She knew the answer before Pi spoke.

"We're rolling out in the morning, Nikki. I hope you come up to visit us as often as we come to see you. And I meant what I said, about checking out the music scene in Chicago. You might just find you like it better up there than here in St. Louis. You must keep singing, sister."

The waiter brought the bill, and the ensuing arguments were hilarious if predictable. Ladso won, on the basis that, as Murray's heir, he could best afford it.

Frank raised his hands in surrender. "On a detective's salary, I'm happy to bow to your math." The rest conceded as well, and Ladso tucked a number of crisp bills into the folder left by the waiter.

Once outside, Frank shook hands all around and left as the rest piled into Ladso's SUV for the drive back to Britt's home.

Ladso parked and everyone got out of the vehicle, puzzling as to why the dogs were barking out back. "Let's go through the house,"

Britt looked at the others. "You stay inside, Nikki and I will check on them."

Britt unlocked the deadbolts, swung the front door open, and stepped inside to disarm the security system. He then turned on the lights and stepped back, bumping into Nikki.

"What's up?" Instead of answering, he stepped aside, so everyone could see.

The living room had been ransacked. Cushions were shredded into pieces on the floor, books and papers were scattered as if a whirlwind had churned through the room. Broken shards of wine glasses made the floor hazardous and Britt's antique Duncan Phyfe dining table had gouges all across its top.

Britt became all business. "Ladso, you and Pi check the upper floor. I'll check this level with Nikki, then we'll see about the dogs."

Near the front door, the umbrella stand had been tipped over. Among its contents on the floor were several of the stakes they'd used during their hunting. Ladso grabbed one. Pi checked her pockets, pulling out her can of Mace and a lighter. "Do not burn down the house." Ladso glanced at Pi as they walked up the stairs.

"Shut up," she hissed back.

They checked each room on the second floor, which wasn't as trashed as downstairs, but books, papers, and clothes were strewn around the rooms. They didn't find anyone, so they went back down to join Britt and Nikki who were just finishing their search. Agitated, Britt said, "The house is a mess, but there's no one down here."

Britt looked down the basement stairs to see the door was still bolted. "It's not much more than a cellar, but no one could be down there with the door bolted on this side," he said, forgetting that the doors to the house had also been secured before they came in. "There's not much to damage down there. Even the furnace and hot water tank are up here. Let's check on Murray and Trooper."

They turned to head into the yard to check on the dogs. As Nikki unlocked the deadbolts on the back door, Britt wondered, *How did whoever did this get in?* The dogs were still barking as they hurried to the small stable that functioned as their quarters.

Both dogs were agitated, fur standing up on necks and backs. Britt called to them and they quit barking. Their fur stayed upright, but neither were hurt. Britt led the dogs inside for the night, knowing people and dogs would all feel better being together. As they walked, an eerie wind keening high up in the trees kept everyone's nerves on edge.

Trooper was well-trained and would stay put if told, but Britt put Murray on a leash, not wanting him to cut his paw pads on broken glass.

Britt, Nikki and dogs entered the house. Britt re-armed the security system and locked the deadbolts, but he looked worried as he did so. He turned to Ladso, "I had to disarm the alarm system and unlock both the front and back doors. None of the windows are unlocked or broken..."

Ladso nodded.

"Then how did they get in, whoever *they* are?"

Everyone was mystified. Britt offered an idea. "I can pull up the security camera feeds, see what they caught, but my laptop has been smashed." He sighed, pulling out his cell phone. "Network's down." He scowled.

"Both modem and router are smashed as thoroughly as the laptop. I hope that at least some of the data got uploaded to the cloud before everything got smashed. Maybe there's something. Give me a few minutes, I've got an app I can use to access the feed."

He stared at his phone. After several minutes, he looked up, face ashen. "We need to call Frank. Now!"

Frank had driven all the way home before changing his mind and deciding to head to his office and a backlog of paperwork. He wouldn't admit to anybody, even himself, that it was lonesome at home despite having a cat, whose name was Cat. He'd redirected again to pick up a bag of day-old doughnuts at his beloved shop. Now, as he drove to the department, he bit off most of a glazed doughnut in one bite while musing over the group. "I hate..." He chuckled. "Well, I'm surprised to admit it, but I'm going to miss that bunch." He shook his head. "I'm still knocked on my substantial butt that we fought and killed vampires!" He stuffed the rest of his doughy treat into his mouth as he thought, *No one will ever believe me and I couldn't blame them.*

His cell phone rang, startling him. He looked at the caller ID, then quickly answered. "Britt, what's up?"

"Frank, have you gotten home yet?"

"No, I'm heading in to do some paperwork, still in the car. What's up?"

"Can you come to my house? Now!" Britt sounded distressed.

Suddenly worried, Frank answered, "Of course, I'm on my way." He hung up the phone, pulled a u-turn, and floored it. He wanted to know what had happened but wasn't going to delay his arrival with questions that would be answered once he got there.

He parked quickly at the curb and rushed to Britt's front door which swung open as he approached, only increasing his concern.

"What's wrong?" Frank stepped over the threshold. Rather than answering, Britt stepped aside, giving Frank a clear view. His eyes widened at the destruction. "Holy shit! What happened, a break-in? How's the rest of the house?"

Britt answered, "Same condition. No one was here when we arrived. The dogs were in their kennel."

Frank frowned. "Your security system. Didn't your alarms go off?"

Britt shook his head. "No alarms were triggered, and everything was completely locked up when we got here, just like I left it. Deadbolts all secured."

"Cameras?"

"My electronics were all destroyed. Laptop, modem, router, NAS, everything, but my system is set to upload live video feeds immediately to the cloud. We've got a record of what happened. That's why I called you — your home may not be safe, either."

Frank's brows rose in surprise. "What happened?"

Britt passed his cell phone to Frank who watched the small screen. "Oh, shit."

♪

Standing in the foyer with the front door shut, Frank replayed the video with Ladso at his side. Frank didn't want to believe his eyes, although he didn't really know what he was seeing. The camera was focused on the front stoop of the house. The light above the door suddenly dimmed and something appeared, swirling like a dust-devil, turning in upon itself. Then it slowly diminished, the last of it seeping into a crack between the door and the frame.

Everyone stood in silence until Ladso spoke. "Just for an instant, someone..." He shook his head. "Something stood there, before becoming vapor again."

Britt nodded. "Whatever it is, it's bad news." Looking at Frank, he said, "Ladso has never seen this ability to transform into a mist before."

Frank scowled. "Bela Lugosi did it. Crap! I thought we'd killed all of... How did it get away, and is there more than one?"

"We do not know," Ladso answered.

"Do we know it's one of them?" Frank asked, with no clue as to what else it could be.

Almost simultaneously, Nikki asked, "What else could it be, though?" as if echoing Frank's thoughts.

When no answer came, Britt waved everyone toward the back of the house. As they walked, Frank asked, "Are there other videos?"

Britt answered, "It's tough navigating this app by phone. Tomorrow I'll buy a new laptop and we'll see what else we've got."

Frank looked around, "The rest of the place as bad as this?" He winced at Britt's nod. "So what are you lot going to do for tonight? Hotel room?"

"Not sure," Britt answered as he looked at Frank. "Your home may not be safe, either. It seems though that we didn't kill all the vampires, and now, we're the ones being hunted."

Frank thought for a moment, and scowled. "Yes, you're right. Damn!"

Nikki and Pi walked in silently, holding hands but with bold expressions. Pi spoke up. "You are the master of understatement,

Frank. Yeah, we need to get away from here until we've got some sunlight to prevent this…" She waved at the destruction around her. "…From happening to us!"

Ladso nodded. "Yes, in the morning we can get new computers, and begin to plan." He paused in thought. "I think we select a hotel near the airport, far from here."

Frank said, "I've got nothing of real value in my place but my cat. I hate to think of one of those things getting her, but I won't risk any of you to get her, and you bunch better not be willing to let me go there alone."

Pi teared up at the thought. "You're damned straight you aren't going there alone." Stepping over, she hugged him.

Hugging back, Frank said, "Thank you, dear lady. Let's get to a hotel. Tomorrow's going to be a hard one."

Britt looked displeased as he took another look at his damaged home, but he had no intention of arguing the group's decision. On his phone, he found a studio suite hotel that allowed pets. He booked two joined rooms, and a suite with two more bedrooms and a sleeper couch for the dogs.

No one, including Trooper and Murray, slept very well that night, but the emotional fatigue kept them in bed until almost seven. By eight, everyone was dressed again in yesterday's clothes and ready to move. Breakfast at a Courtesy Diner did not equal Ladso's usual cuisine, but it was tasty, filling, and the coffee was surprisingly good. It was also strong which they all needed. Bacon and egg sandwiches were taken out to the SUV for Trooper and Murray.

The decision had been made to stop for laptops at an electronics store with early hours. It happened to be on their way back to Britt's house, so that was a little break. Frank joined them inside after calling the department to say he wouldn't be in that day. Catching up, he was surprised to see the boxes already in the cart. They were purchasing a high-end laptop, and all the gear necessary to reestablish internet in the house. The internet wouldn't be back online until later however, so they almost stopped again to use some restaurant's internet, but Britt would need to update the laptop and load several programs before he could even start. They didn't want to waste that much sunlight and Britt said he could use his phone as a hotspot for now, so they headed directly to the house.

Coming back into the wreckage was upsetting again. The coffee pot which had been swept into the sink but was unbroken was the first order of business. Soon a bracing cup of Pi's darkest brewed coffee sharpened minds, but also calmed them. While they enjoyed the brew, they discussed the best way to clean up the trashed house. Britt suggested, "Let's divide into two groups and focus on the first floor. Primarily the kitchen and dining room. That way we'll have clean areas to cook and work."

Ladso immediately volunteered to work on the kitchen. "It leaves me feeling — violated — to have the kitchen in such a condition."

Britt replied, "That's how I feel about my entire home. It's my domain. Knowing that something can penetrate my defenses so easily, come into my space, destroy my things… I can better relate to robbery victims now."

Pi offered to help Ladso in the kitchen. Nikki looked at Pi then turned to Frank. "Frank, can you help me in the dining room?" She smiled at Pi who returned the expression. Nikki continued, "Britt needs to get the new laptop up and running so we can see the rest of those videos."

Britt nodded, realizing his injury prompted Nikki's comments more than an eagerness to see videos, despite their importance. With a smile, he pointed out that there was no place for him to work until some cleaning was done. Making a face, Nikki quickly shifted back to a smile. Running into the living room, she uprighted a chair and grabbed an unbroken tv table. As Britt entered with Frank carrying the box with the laptop, Britt smiled again and took the offered seat.

Nikki and Frank then left to grab supplies from where they'd been scattered. Ladso and Pi were already hard at work on the kitchen.

The kitchen was a particular mess. Glassware smashed, jars of various foods thrown against the stove and refrigerator, which were also dented. Pi frowned at several smears which looked like blood.

Ladso considered taking samples, but sniffing allowed him to identify each.

"At least the appliances are all standing upright," Ladso said. "Let us get the stove cleaned up first. I want to bake the apple torte I prepared yesterday. Pink Lady apples will give it a lovely tart flavor. Fresh ground cinnamon, nutmeg, sugar and spice, and everything nice. Once done, we will be in need of a treat."

Pi shook her head at him. "At a time like this, you not only think of food, you prepare and schedule it in advance, just so it'll be ready when we need it. You are amazing, you know that?"

Ladso blushed and laughed. His work in the kitchen was how he cleared his head and made his plans. It had given him a reputation that he had earned, but not because he'd put an effort toward that goal. It was merely a bonus effect of his method which allowed him to accomplish more important work.

Without comment, Ladso handed her a pair of gloves and a scrub rag. Wrinkling her nose, Pi said, "You're a romantic, too!" They both laughed, then started cleaning.

Finally, the stove was spotless. Ladso turned the oven on to preheat while they continued cleaning. When the timer gave a soft ding, he removed the torte from the refrigerator, and set it on the center shelf in the oven. Setting the timer on his phone, he returned to cleaning.

In the dining room, Nikki spent ten minutes sweeping. She finished with a huge pile of broken glass and other debris. "Now we can walk through here without damaging the floor or our shoes."

Frank was collecting strewn papers in the library. Most were shredded, but others were simply scattered. Fewer of the books were damaged, but those that were had been torn to bits. Frank had no idea what went where, so decided to just collect and organize. Soon, he had a big pile of papers, and several stacks of books. The ruined books he'd put in a pile. He sighed remembering that Ladso had already shipped Murray's books back to Chicago. He sighed, wishing Murray was there and safe as well. *A good man.* Next, he began to right overturned furniture, and collect cushions. Several were undamaged, and those he returned to their place. The torn ones he set aside for repairs.

Returning to the dining room, he looked at the antique table, at the deep gouges in its formerly pristine surface. "Those don't look like they were made with a knife. They almost look like — claw marks made by a powerful animal."

Nikki shuddered. "I agree!"

Frank set up the chairs and cleaned the table of debris, including wood shavings before putting on a white linen tablecloth to hide the gouges.

Soon, they noticed a sweet and spicy aroma coming from the kitchen. An hour later, Ladso and Pi entered, Ladso wheeling his dining cart. The huge difference in the dining room was apparent immediately, and both Pi and Ladso looked a little stunned at the transformation.

After a bow to Nikki and Frank, Ladso announced, "I am happy to have a light repast to strengthen us after such valiant efforts. The kitchen has also been restored. We have a carafe of coffee, and a freshly baked apple torte."

Frank spoke up, "Yum! I sure don't mind working for wages like these!"

Nikki went over to Ladso, gave him a big hug, thanked him, then gave Pi a bigger hug, and a conspiratorial grin as she whispered, "Is that all you two cooked up in there?" Pi tried but failed to look shocked before they both laughed. Calling Britt, Ladso waved his cohorts to the table.

A moment later, Britt entered. His laptop balanced in his one hand. "The laptop is ready and I've loaded all the videos into a folder. The videos can be watched whenever you want."

"Have you watched them yet?" Ladso's smile had dissolved.

Britt shook his head. "I haven't. I've only loaded yesterday's files since the house was intact before we left for dinner."

Ladso's brow furrowed. "Would everyone be willing to watch what Britt has before we eat?"

No one objected so Britt set the device on the table. With some difficulty, he used the touch pad and keyboard to reopen the program and bring up the first file. He wished the indoor video system had been running, but he had turned it off as a way of being polite while he had live-in guests. He hadn't thought they'd need it and hadn't bothered to ask if it would make anyone uncomfortable to leave it on. He wished now that he had.

The first file turned out to be the kitchen entrance. Scanning to fifteen minutes before the light effects they'd seen on his phone, everyone watched and eventually saw the light quickly diminishing as it had by the front door, but it then returned to normal and there was nothing else out of the ordinary.

"This one will contain the scene we saw on my phone," Britt said as he clicked on another file. Scanning to the proper time, everyone leaned in as the video showed the now-familiar darkening, but then, on the larger screen, they could see something different. The darkness began swirling like a small dust devil. Flickering with wind and something more, it coalesced into something almost human shaped, then madly it spun into nothingness."

"That looked like someone was there for a moment," Nikki gasped.

"Could it have been a vampire?" Pi asked.

Britt didn't answer as he backed up the scene and played it stop-motion, one image at a time. Watching him typing laboriously with his right hand, Ladso asked if Britt wanted to rest. With a sigh, Britt looked over and nodded. As he stood, Pi grabbed a chair and brought it over to sit beside the one Ladso now occupied.

Turning to the computer, Ladso took stills when the darkness looked most solid, most like a figure. "Software enhancements and a little tinkering should show more," he said as he clicked the mouse several more times.

While Pi and Frank brought cups and coffee, Ladso ran the stills through graphic imaging software, doing everything possible to refine and enhance each image. On the third still, he sat back as the program ran. Watching the image depixelate, he lifted his cup but froze before it reached his mouth. He and the team gasped as the image filled the screen.

"That is not possible!" Ladso exclaimed.

"Shit," Pi said as the full team began to talk at once.

"We saw her in the cavern," Nikki cried.

"The gun in her hand ignited the propane!" Said Pi.

Can it even be possible?" Frank asked as he walked over to grab a chair for himself.

Ladso stood. "I need to think. I will be in the kitchen. Please help yourselves to the torte but also please do not follow me. I have got to think this out."

2

"She had to have died in the explosion, they all did!" Speaking as she paced, Pi looked at the kitchen door again but continued pacing beside the table.

"She was not a 'full vampire' and did not have any of their evil tricks, other than the mind control." Britt wiped at his face with his hand and then used it again to pick up his glass and take a gulp of the wine that had been opened.

In her seat, Nikki asked, "How can this have happened?"

After several moments, Pi asked, "Britt, can you show me how to run the videos? There might be something showing when she left. Whatever there is I'd like to see it."

"Of course, and I can do it." Sitting again in front of the laptop, he scanned the videos, freezing the frame whenever someone asked. Finding nothing new, they returned to the still of Sharon. They studied her, trying to identify anything new or different about it. Her skin looked an ashy gray, but that could be the darkness, or the swirling of her gaseous change. Her eyes were still that murky, swamp-green color. Finally, they turned it off, knowing only one thing for certain. With her transmutation into gaseous form, there was no doubt that she was no longer human.

After sitting through several more moments of silence, Frank jumped.

"What?" Pi asked.

Taking a breath, Frank said, "According to the time on the video, you may have missed her by mere minutes."

Wide-eyed, Pi said, "Yes, and if we'd walked in, unprepared, and Sharon, now a full vampire, was hiding, waiting to launch at us."

"Oh God, stop!" Nikki gasped.

It was half an hour later before Ladso returned to the dining room. He noticed the torte sat undisturbed and the bottle of wine sat empty. Surprised by neither, he said, "While we still have daylight, we must decide on our plans for the night."

Britt said, "Staying here is not an option. And Frank, we don't know if anything's happened at your home, but you can't stay there either." Frank nodded in silence. Britt continued, "Let's quickly grab what we need for another night at the hotel and then follow Frank to his place so he can do the same. We'll also see if our intruder has visited his home as well."

The rooms upstairs had been tossed, but there was little damage so Nikki was able to quickly fill her overnight bag and then went to help Britt while Pi grabbed toiletries for them both. By mid-afternoon, all were ready to leave for Frank's.

Despite rush hour, it didn't take long to reach Frank's home. Everyone wondered what they would find as they turned into a south city neighborhood of small homes with smaller front yards. They parked in front of his house and followed him as he climbed the front steps and unlocked his door. He had no security system to disarm.

Frank pushed the front door open and was immediately greeted by an unearthly howl. Everyone, including Frank, jumped until they saw the large cat weaving around Frank's ankles and crying at him. He scooped up the cat which quieted the noise, except for an occasional soft mewling.

Frank explained, "Cat came with the house. She's never acted this way before." His eyes tracked over the front room. "Something's set her off."

Stepping inside, everything looked orderly, but Cat's regular mewing kept everyone on edge. As they progressed through the house, Nikki opened blinds and pulled aside curtains, letting afternoon sunlight pour in.

At first all appeared as neat and clean as Frank had left it. In the kitchen, Frank looked at Ladso who pointed to a door and asked, "Is that the basement?" The question reminded Ladso that they'd yet to check Britt's basement. He dismissed the thought however thinking, *It would trap the vampire during daylight, leaving it with no escape if found.* While fast and powerful, he did not believe their prey would put itself into such a position. Every confrontation with the people on the team had gone poorly for the vampires. He still resolved to check it during daylight the next day. Regarding Frank's basement, he said, "They will not come out in daylight, let us check the rest of the house first."

Continuing through the house, all appeared normal until they reached the spare bedroom, which served as his study. Cat grew agitated again. Frank set her down and she hurried off toward the front of the house.

Reacting to Cat's behavior, Frank studied the room like a crime scene. He looked and listened as Ladso crowded beside him and did the same. His books and papers were scattered as Britt's had been. His service revolver in hand, Frank stepped in.

His file cabinets, while dented, were locked, so the only papers scattered around were personal ones of little interest to Frank, let alone the creature that had run roughshod through the room. Invitations to seminars, catalogs of police equipment, offers for better cable or internet, bills. Turning to his books, all were scattered but intact except for his book on St. Louis caves. It had been pulled apart.

Britt frowned. "The books that were damaged at my house were the ones on vampires. Also, the copies of cave maps you'd made had been destroyed."

"Probably thinks she will lessen our ability to work against her." Ladso paused. "Possibly she has gone back into the caves."

Finding no other signs in the house or basement, Frank gathered toiletries and fresh clothes. Cat sat before the front door, prompting Frank to say, "Cat would not appreciate the company of your dogs, and I'm not going to leave her here. I'll take her over to my neighbor's."

As he climbed into the car after leaving Cat with the woman next door, Pi smiled. "She looked like she might be interested in more than Cat. You got any other arrangements with your neighbor, Frank?"

After telling her to shut up, Frank laughed. "Life is complicated enough with vampires. I don't need that kind of trouble too."

The next morning, breakfast involved a return to the Courtesy Diner, but as they waited for their food, Ladso was looking for an available Airbnb rental. "I need a kitchen so I can think," he muttered.

While the others went to Britt's for the day, Frank had to go to work. He walked through the door into the detectives' section, typically ignoring the other detectives except to wave to his friend, Mike Gently, who waved back. Frank continued to his office, opened the door and slammed it behind him.

"Hey Mike, I see your buddy is feeling even sweeter than usual this morning," called one of the detectives. "What happened? You two break up?"

Mike retorted, "He's still got the Captain on his tail. We all know what that's like."

Another detective muttered something and was answered with snickers, but Mike ignored them. Frank Bolden was his friend, even though the burden of that friendship was sometimes heavy. He didn't feel like having it out with the other detectives. Peace-maker was not a job Frank made easy but Mike got as much out of the friendship as

24

he put into it. Sometimes. With a single chuckle, Gently decided to check on Frank at lunch.

Frank compartmentalized his thoughts flawlessly. He put aside what was happening away from the office and spent the morning working through his case files. His Captain was a big enough pain in the butt without giving him late paperwork to complain about. Frank grunted, thinking, *I'll soon be taking time off to moonlight as a vampire hunter again.*

By noon, he was done. Still planning for the time off he'd soon need, he looked at the two new case files on his desk but was distracted by a soft tapping on his door. A moment later, the door opened and Mike Gently's head poked through. "Safe to come in?"

"Yeah, come on, Mike, Was just thinking of grabbing a sandwich," he lied. "Wanna join me?"

Mike's brows raised. Frank hadn't suggested lunch in months. Mike asked often and was just as regularly turned down. He squinted at his friend and asked, "Frank? Looks like you but…"

Frank chuckled, another rarity. "I'm guessing that's a yes. I just caught up on my paperwork and need to get out of this chair."

"You jerk! I've been working the whole morning, and I'll be at it all afternoon, just to get last week's paperwork done. What, do you just stuff it in the can?"

"Yeah right. Our beloved Captain and me are such good buddies that he waives half of my paperwork and doesn't read the rest. I usually just turn in copies of the comic section. That keeps him happy." Frank shrugged. "So lunch, or is your paperwork piled too high? Far be it from me to get between a man and his paperwork."

They were standing in line at the deli when Frank got a text. He pulled his phone, read, closed his eyes, and exhaled. When he opened his eyes, he read the message again as if it might have somehow changed. His scowl was back.

Mike noticed, but only asked Frank for his sandwich order. They both got sloppy Reuben sandwiches with a dill pickle on the side. Mike asked, "Want to take this back to the office?"

Frank replied, "Nah, let's eat here. Ten minutes away from that place will do us both good." They moved to an open table and began doing serious damage to their sandwiches as Mike steered the conversation in a safe direction. "So, what have they got you working on?"

"I don't know, haven't opened the files yet. I spent the morning on the Captain's crap, remember?"

The rest of the meal was spent on Mike leaning on Frank's expertise of many things job related. As he spoke Frank struggled to focus, knowing that he needed a friend at the department. He wished he could share his problems, but even if he could get Mike to believe, he didn't want to burden him with such horrors. He had confidence in his other hunters and hoped Mike would never need to learn what a Saturday night horror show he really lived in.

The two men finished, left the deli, and walked back to the precinct. Mike went back to his computer. Frank returned to his office but only long enough to shut down his computer. Glad I got my paperwork done, he thought.

The other detectives ignored Frank as he left. Mike was on the phone. He waved, made a face and pointed his finger like a gun to his head. Frank grinned with understanding. Minutes later, seated in his sedan, Frank texted Pi that he was on his way, and prepared to step back into the horror show he knew was real.

# 3

No longer willing to spend her days in self-dug graves, Sharon returned to the rubble of the cavern that allowed access to her order's last home. She knew there was another entrance but she would not use that space. The evil ones knew of that entrance as well and they might return. *I must understand and be able to fully use my abilities before I face them again.*

Searching the ruins of the vagrants' cavern, she had crawled through the debris and found a newly opened cave. Much smaller, it was also positioned high on the old cavern's back wall. Difficult and dangerous to reach, it would keep her safe from the living and was deep enough to suit her needs for her daytime sleep.

Her time residing adjacent to the vagrants' cavern, had taught her the benefits of relying on the unnoticed poor for sustenance. She'd found that by completely draining her victims, she only needed to feed once a week, but avoiding detection, she primarily fed on rats and other small mammals along the river. Her only focus those first weeks was maintaining her strength and learning what and how the ancients' blood had changed her.

It had taken her weeks to master the transformation into a heavy but gaseous smoke. She'd seen her Sisters do it many times but unable to do it herself, she'd never been taught its secrets. Fortunately, the descriptions she'd heard gave her clues to solving the puzzle. Transforming simplified her reaching her new dwelling and left her ready to begin her hunt for her enemies. She more easily caught their scent when in solid form, but she now had no need to acquire another vehicle. The transformation was not tiring and allowed her to cover large distances easily.

Hands folded neatly across her chest, ankles close together, she realized she had no need for sleep. In a near-somnambulant state, her eyes often remained open, even when dust mites landed on them. She spent those still hours focused on revenge. *I will find and kill them all!*

Before angrily destroying their papers, Sharon had read many of them. She even looked at some of the wounded one's books. *They know much about us, about me! But not all.*

For a moment, she reconsidered her discarded option for a residence in Britt's cellar. *It would undoubtably be more comfortable than this small, cold and often damp cavern, but it would not compare to my quarters at SERA.* Looking with her supernatural sight, she studied the walls of her lair and remembered the book about caves she'd found in the policeman's home. How she'd wished she had a book like that when looking for a place for her Sisters. Shaking that useless thought away she instead thought, *Luck has been on their side, but no longer. They are nearly defenseless. It will be simple and a joy to avenge my Order when I harvest them. But not just death. They must suffer first, and they must know that I caused their end.* Her eyes flashed a petulant green. *I will turn one of their members and use that slave to execute my plan.*

Frank finally pulled up in front of Britt's house, walked up to the front door and entered using his key. Britt greeted him in the dining room. "Thanks for coming so fast. We didn't expect you till late afternoon."

"I'd finished what I had to, so left early."

Nikki stepped through the door from the kitchen. She returned his wave and stepped out again.

Frank turned back to Britt. "What's happened?"

"New information on Sharon, but let me finish this first. Nikki has something for you too, but I expect she'll bring it to you." Frank nodded and settled onto a chair.

A minute later, Nikki entered again and came toward Frank with a cup.

Britt smiled at Nikki's approach and gathered the papers spread before him on the table. "I'm almost ready."

Frank was also smiling at Nikki. "My mouth is about to be distracted, but the rest of me is all ears."

"Pi left this for you." Nikki handed over the steaming cup. "The circling in the microwave and my carrying seems to have demolished your little piggy. Sorry."

"I doubt my tongue will notice." Frank smiled and sipped.

"I've got chores. I'll leave you to catch our good detective up on the latest creepiness we've uncovered." Frank's brow furrowed at her words. His eyes shifted to Britt as he raised his cup.

Britt took a seat beside Frank. "The news is nothing of immediate concern, but we found further evidence of Sharon in my cellar."

Frank lowered the cup from his lips. "Your cellar!"

Britt nodded. "She had turned over empty shelves, broken several wooden crates, and torn or thrown a bunch of cardboard boxes around. Oddly, she then seemed to have begun digging a grave."

Frank's eyes widened, and he set his cup on the table.

"That was the wrong word. We believe she'd considered using my cellar as a daytime resting place."

Rubbing at his face, Frank thought for a moment. "She'd have left herself vulnerable right beneath us?"

Britt shrugged. "That's how it appears, but she clearly thought better of it. The hole was only six inches deep at its lowest point. Ladso takes it as further proof of her intelligence that she realized it was a bad idea."

Frank snorted and looked at his cup. "Damn, if only she was as stupid as her Sisters were ugly."

Now Britt snorted, but his was a laugh. "Well put, my friend." He sobered. "We have some learning to do about Sharon. She didn't have the abilities of the other vampires before. She was still human, or mainly so. She did have the mind control, but she was definitely still alive, and evil. She's dead, now, or rather, Undead."

"How did that happen?" Frank shook his head, sad eyes on his cup.

"We don't know. Research might help. Another reason to miss our dear Murray." Britt sighed, wondering what wisdom his old professor would have offered. "We need access to Murray's library. I foresee a visit to Chicago." He sighed and looked at Frank. "Please stay for dinner. Ladso's in the kitchen, cooking and thinking. I need to join Nikki with the dogs. You can join us or sit in the kitchen with those wonderful smells. Pi has run to the store for some secret supply our chef requires.

Thinking of the blustery weather outside, Frank walked toward the kitchen. "I'll stay and visit with Ladso, and leave the dog-wrangling to you two." Britt grinned and nodded as he went to grab his coat.

"Don't really blame you. Make yourself at home." Britt barely struggled as he one-armed his coat over his shoulders. Frank gave him a thumbs up, and they both smiled.

Little Murray was growing and mastering the basics. He knew 'sit' and 'down,' but not 'stay.' He was also struggling with 'heel' and did anything other than walk calmly at his trainer's side.

Britt showed Nikki a new technique for enforcing 'stay.' He fastened a very long rope to the pup's collar and commanded Murray to 'sit,' and then 'down.' He walked ten feet away to a tree and circled the tree while still holding the rope. Walking back to Murray, he stopped, praised him, then reinforced his commands again, following with 'stay.' He walked to where Nikki was standing.

After a minute Murray tried to run to them, but the rope held him where he was. Britt called again, "Murray, stay." This time, the puppy stood calmly. Britt waited for another minute, walked back, let Murray off the lead and praised him lavishly.

Britt explained his training method. "If you want a rough estimate, take the dog's age in months, and that's how many minutes he can pay attention to a task. You'll notice when Murray did as I wanted, I made a point. I was the one to release him after only a short time. He's learning, but we'll repeat it daily. Within the week, we won't need the rope."

Nikki paid rapt attention, memorizing his words and loving to learn.

♪

Frank walked into the kitchen, finding Ladso wrist-deep in flour. The chef looked over and smiled.

"Hey, it is good to see you. Take a seat and get comfortable. Pi knew you would appreciate your Cop-achino."

Dropping onto a chair, Frank nodded and sniffed. "Smells fabulous, but are you going to be done in time for us to eat before nightfall?"

"Considered that before I started. Yes, there will be time."

"Excellent!" Again, Frank sniffed. "Smells like good food, but I have no idea what kind."

"These are uszka — Polish little ears dumplings. Simple to make, but both filling and delicious. It is an old recipe, one I learned from my Nonna, my grandmother." His fingers flashed and folded, never stopping their movements, even while he talked. "I stuff the little dumplings with savories, meats, mushrooms and such, then boil them in broth."

"They commonly serve them in beet barszcz — a beet soup, on Christmas Eve, at the vigil dinner. I serve these little lovelies in a simple beef bone broth, instead. That is one of my little flourishes."

He continued working in a companionable silence, making a mountain of little dumplings. He set the tray to one side and cleaned up the prep area before retrieving an enormous stock pot from the refrigerator which he put on the stove.

Ladso noticed Frank's surprised expression and laughed out loud. "My friend, we are traveling the globe with this meal. The dumplings are Polish, the side dishes are Bulgarian and Czechoslovakian, the beef bone broth is Asian, and the dessert is American. Such a tour and all in one sitting."

Pi entered with a grocery bag. "I love to travel."

Frank thanked Pi for his drink and toasted Ladso. "Anchors away!"

Everyone sat around the dining room table. The tablecloth concealed the gouges, but no one was unaware they were underneath. Pi caught herself uneasily tracing the shapes and concentrated to make herself stop.

Ladso's soup was fantastic, with all those tiny stuffed dumplings floating in it. The tomato salad was Bulgarian, the braised cabbage, Czechoslovakian. He finished with strawberry shortcake topped with mounds of whipped cream for his "All-American" dessert.

He apologized for the quality of the tomatoes available during the winter. "Hot house tomatoes have no flavor. These dishes are much better in the summer." Other than that, there was little conversation, just lots of hungry appetites being sated.

During dessert, Nikki smiled. "I don't remember the last time I had strawberry shortcake. My mom always fixed it, and my brother always snuck slices ahead of dinner. He got into trouble over it, too. I'd just sneak the whipped cream, never got caught." Pi grinned at Nikki's story, while Britt nodded in agreement at her critique of the dessert. Frank wondered where Ladso bought the shortcakes. Ladso, pretending offense, explained that he had baked them fresh that afternoon. Frank bowed in apology as everyone laughed.

While Nikki and Pi cleared the dishes, Ladso returned with cups and coffee. He poured, then sat at the table and started the conversation. "Everyone has seen the videos, the stills. Sharon is clearly now a vampire. We do not know how she managed it but she is now more dangerous and we cannot keep her out so protecting ourselves is a problem. I believe we need to go to Chicago, search Murray's library for clues to what her new powers might be. This ability to take gaseous form is new to me, but there may be some mention in the Chicago library."

Britt nodded. "It appears she can flow through the cracks around doors, so locks and security systems are no protection. She does, however, show up on camera. I have indoor security cameras, which are currently disarmed. I will re-arm them." Everyone agreed he should. "Good, before we leave for the night they'll be on. If she comes again, we'll see what she does."

Ladso continued. "I have cancelled our Airbnb and renewed our hotel rooms pending our leaving for Chicago. As far as we know, Sharon is unaware of that residence. We would be safer and better able to prepare."

Nikki looked at Britt. Both nodded. Turning to Ladso, she said, "The dogs too."

"Of course," Ladso nodded with vigor.

Frank spoke up. "I'm going to bring my car in case I need to come back for work." He paused for a moment, thinking. "Cat is all I need to care for at home. I'll put her in a pet hotel."

Pi looked up at Frank. "What kind of cat is she?"

Frank shrugged his shoulders. "Brownish grey."

Chuckling over Frank's answer, Ladso stood. "We will rest in the hotel tonight, gather clothes in the morning and leave." All nodded — none wanted to face Sharon — yet. "Excellent. I will put the remaining dishes in the washer. Everyone grab whatever you need from your things. Nikki, if you can prepare the dogs, we can be on our way to the hotel well before sunset."

Ladso finished in the kitchen and hurried upstairs to grab some clean clothes. On the way back, he passed Murray's old room. His mentor and friend's possessions had already been shipped home with his books. Ladso stood inside the door sobbing softly. After several moments, he turned and found Pi standing in the doorway. Stepping close, she put her arms around him and hugged. A moment later, when they stepped apart, she grinned at him. He grinned back. "That gamine expression on your face — I love to see it."

"Gamine? You mean like gaming? I don't get it."

"It is French. A "gamine" is a young girl on the cusp of the first stages of puberty." Pi's brows rose. "She is cute, assertive, mischievous, and sometimes on the verge of being rude." Now she giggled. "They compare grown women to them, but the women are not gamine themselves."

Pi was still smiling. "I know I can be honest, to the point of being rude. I thought that was just a me thing." She grew serious. "Look, I know we're moving into a new phase. I want you to know that it's okay for you to take every step just as slowly as you need to."

He looked at her, astonished that she somehow understood his position. He drew her into his arms, hugging her tightly. "Pi, you will never know how amazing you really are."

"Come on, big boy, let's get moving." Pi's voice was gruff with emotion. Her expression, however, showed the warmth she felt toward him.

Closing the door to Murray's room, the two went to join the others.

The next morning, Pi and Ladso looked over several items. Weapons might be a better word: Ash stakes and mallets, machetes, lighters and cans of mace, even bags of jelly beans. They were tempted to bring them to the hotel, but expected they wouldn't need them until their return. Placing them in Murray's room she watched Ladso's face as he shut the door. He smiled weakly but nodded that he was fine.

Nikki and Pi collected the dogs, their food, beds, and a few toys. Trooper, as always, followed closely at Nikki's heel, while Murray, the quickly growing Weimaraner, still needed a leash. Both went to the bathroom in the yard before going inside. It was a long drive to Chicago, and while Trooper was safe, little dogs had little bladders.

While still outside, Pi looked at Nikki and gestured toward the puppy. "You know, we all thought it was a good idea, naming him after Murray, but every time I hear his name, I think of our Murray. The little guy needs a nickname. What do you think about Ray?"

Nikki nodded. "It gets to me too. I like Ray, but we'd better check with Britt. Murray is his dog." Pi nodded as they watched the puppy sniffing at the grass. "I bet Britt will agree. The frequent reminders are hard for everyone." She smiled and petted Murray as he stepped close. "Hard, despite our love for the increasingly less small puppy."

A mound of luggage sat beside the front door. Ladso, and Frank were already loading the luggage carrier on top of the SUV. Britt looked on wishing he could help.

When they'd finished, Nikki frowned at Frank as he walked up from the curb. "Are you sure you don't want company? It's a long ride by yourself."

Frank shook his head. "Normally I'd appreciate the company but I've got to pick up things at my place and get Cat to the Boarder. Don't worry, I have some podcasts to listen to during the ride. You stay with the others. I'll be fine."

Nikki's frown held. "If you're sure, just know the offer is sincere."

Her smile almost made him re-think his refusal but he shook his head. "You're a good kid." He patted her arm. She rolled her eyes but grinned.

Pi overheard him. "Yeah, you're alright too, for a pig."

Frank's dour expression cracked into something resembling a smile as he considered the cappuccinos Pi regularly made for him. Each sported a little pig made of froth. He chuckled remembering the bright, pink pig's head ornament with a police cap. She'd picked it out to decorate the team's Christmas tree. It now hung from a stand on his desk at work. It brightened his day every time he looked at it.

By noon, they were ready. Frank loaded Ladso's address to his phone, then said he'd see everyone in Chi-town.

The others piled into Ladso's SUV. The puppy, Murray was a novice passenger, with only a few car rides under his collar, but he was a fan. Trooper was also a fan. He hopped in like the veteran he was.

As they pulled off, Nikki asked Britt about Murray's name change to Ray. Britt almost looked relieved as he replied that it was a great idea. Ladso smiled sadly as well.

Before pulling off, Ladso looked at Britt. "The cameras are on, inside and out?" Britt nodded. "Excellent. If she returns, we will want to know."

"The cameras are motion-triggered. Every time a new video file gets recorded, it's loaded to the cloud. We'll see all that's goes on, if anything does."

They drove off with the sun high above them. Pi wondered about their arrival time. Nikki looked at the puppy between them. "Ray can't make it that far without a potty break." She grinned. "I'm not sure I can either. We'll need at least one rest stop." Britt nodded in agreement, as he looked at the covered cup of coffee in his hand.

# 4

Traffic was light, and Ladso's foot was heavy. The miles flew by, even allowing for two potty breaks for the puppy and company.

The SUV pulled up in front of Murray's home. Ladso parked, then put his face in his hands quietly crying. Pi, who was now in the front seat, leaned over and wrapped her arms around him. No one said anything, offering quiet support.

Ladso regained control, and wiped his eyes with a handkerchief. Sitting up, he apologized. "It just hit me. I will never come home to Murray again."

"You have nothing to be sorry for." Britt insisted that he take as much time as needed. Pi didn't speak, just left her left arm draped over his shoulders.

Ladso ran a hand over his bald head and sighed. "OK, grab your bags, and we will get inside."

Pi kissed his cheek softly and climbed out of the car. Nikki followed with the dogs. Pi took Ray's leash and the women walked the dogs over to some convenient grass while complimenting Ray over no accidents on the drive.

Britt's suitcase came with free-spinning wheels and a handle, easy to manage one-armed. He grabbed it and carried it up the steps, waiting for Ladso and the key. He looked around, saw nothing out of the ordinary but quivered, remembering, *my house looked normal from the outside, too.*

Ladso came up, disarmed the alarm, and unlocked the door. As the sun had set, he turned on the porch lights and the ones in the foyer.

Everything looked in order as Ladso set his bag inside. As the others entered, he went to the study to start a fire. He stopped on the way to raise the thermostat. The big house was dauntingly chilly. A roaring fire would help, in more ways than one.

Everyone left their bags in the foyer, making their ways to the bathroom or kitchen. Nikki led the way as Pi followed with a cloth bag and marveled at the size and splendor of the house. Stopping, Nikki turned, remembering her wonder on that cold late night she'd first arrived.

Later in the kitchen, Pi had set up her cappuccino machine but not before starting the elaborate coffee maker. As Ladso entered she both praised its quality and wondered why it didn't make cappuccinos. As he began to explain she talked over him. "Don't bother, all's good and I brought my machine from the Lou so I'll be ready with a Cop-achino for Frank's arrival." She then handed him a cup and began marveling over the kitchen and house.

"Wait until you see the study," Nikki used her fingers to stretch her eyes wide. "I could hardly believe it!"

"The kindling is building up a grand blaze and I have called Food Doc to make a delivery of a variety of Thai dishes. It should arrive soon." All were pleased with the announcement. Cups, glasses, coffee and wine were gathered for the move into the study.

"Prepare yourself," Nikki warned.

Flames were crackling merrily on the hearth with larger logs stacked to one side, ready to add when the fire was more established.

Ladso opened a bottle of red and one of Pi's favorite whites as she stood in the center of the massive room with her mouth hanging open. Chuckling, Ladso suggested she sit close to the fire as he presented her with a filled glass.

Ladso poured glasses for all but Britt who opted for coffee as he strolled the room commenting on how wonderful it felt to straighten his knees after the long drive. Ray started playing with Trooper, climbing over him, nipping gently while Trooper played back with good nature. Nikki giggled when she looked over moments later to see Ray fast asleep. Trooper, unfamiliar with the house, sat on guard.

Britt set his cup aside, checked his watch, and wondered aloud. "I wonder when Frank will get here? It's near seven. Surely, he's on his way." The team nodded together. "Getting his things and delivering his cat to its kennel could have taken a few hours. With the drive, it's bound to be late when he arrives unless his foot holds much more lead than Ladso's."

Nikki shrugged. "Why don't you text him?"

"I expect he's driving. Maybe I'll call to see if he has an estimate for his arrival." As he dialed, he shook his head. "I doubt his car has hands free calling."

Pi laughed. "He's a cop. Probably drives while on his phone all the time."

Britt put his phone to his ear and waited for it to ring. With a suddenly worried expression, Britt looked around the room. "We may have a problem."

Frank had driven toward his home. He squinted into the early afternoon sun, appreciating it more than usual now that his fellow vampire hunters had left the city. "Sleep on you ugly hag. We'll be coming face to face with you soon enough, but until then…" He growled, angry that his city remained in peril, but also to boost his courage a bit.

Stopped at a street light, he speculated over what they might find in Murray's library. A book titled *Vampires, their Skills, and How To*

*Destroy Them* was not likely to be on the shelves, but he supposed Britt would find something. He hoped so, anyway.

Sharon's ability to vaporize, undeterred by doors and locks, was disturbing. The thought of her just showing up in his room, he had to admit, freaked him out. *It's good we'll be out of Sharon's reach until we can figure things out.*

Chicago made him speculate on Ladso's and Pi's budding relationship. *I'd put my money on that holding together.* Despite their superficial differences, they are two of a kind: fierce and single minded. He was happy they'd met, although he would have wished for better circumstances. He guessed if they really were continuing Murray's odd business, they were their own first customers.

His phone rang. With a snort, Frank pulled the annoying instrument from his pocket and then sighed when he saw Gently's name on the caller ID. He opened the connection. "Sorry Mike, I'm not going to help with your paperwork." His grin dissolved as he listened. "On my way."

There was a shooting of a child, and a fellow officer, a friend, needed his help. Frank arrived, studied the scene, listened to witnesses, made suggestions, even spoke to the press. By the time he was done, the sun had set. Night had returned. Gently thanked him as he left.

Frank parked two doors down from his house and shut off the car's motor. It was night, but it was early. *Why would she be here? She'd torn up a book and left. She won't be here.* He checked his watch again. *The Boarder place is still open. I just need some clothes and Cat, then I'll be gone. If I drive straight through, I should be there shortly after midnight.*

Having convinced himself, Frank headed to his sidewalk and up the steps to the door. Police training had him alert as he slid his key into the lock. He opened it, sure of what he'd find: his bachelor's home, sparse, tidy, and untouched.

He was correct as far as the living room was concerned, but after a quick scratch on Cat's head, he checked every room, leaving lights on as he went. He ignored the basement so his last stop was the kitchen where he saw Cat's food bowl empty. Relaxed now, he filled the bowl. The sound acted like a feline magnet. Cat was instantly there, twining around Frank's ankles, meowing like she'd feared dying from starvation. Frank left Cat to enjoy one last meal before heading to the Boarder.

Frank walked to his bedroom to quickly pack. Finished, he put the suitcase next to the door, then returned to the kitchen.

Cat's bowl was empty and clean. She lay on the floor digesting as Frank rinsed the food and water bowls while thinking, *Stupid cat probably won't even notice I'm gone as long as she gets fed.* Turning, he looked at his roommate. "Okay ya little pig, let's get you to your home away from home." As Frank crossed the room, Cat suddenly hissed. Startled, Frank watched as the cat arched its back high, hair standing on end. It spat like a cobra toward something behind Frank, then yowling, bolted for the front of the house.

"What in hell?" Frank began to turn to look behind him, his hand reaching for his pistol.

"What is wrong?" Ladso looked anxiously at Britt.

"Frank's phone went straight to voice mail, like his phone's turned off… or broken. Damn it, we shouldn't have separated."

Nikki frowned. "He still had plenty of sunlight. He easily should have gotten out of town before sunset. Sharon couldn't slow him down during the day. Maybe…" She stopped, running out of words.

Pi stood up. "What do we do? Do we go back?"

Britt shook his head. "We stay together. We don't know what Sharon can do. That's part of why we're here. Murray's library may provide those answers, but regarding Frank…"

Ladso interrupted. "We do not yet know there is anything wrong. I suggest we call the precinct. Frank has a friend there. Mike somebody."

"I think it's Gentle." Pi frowned. "Or something close."

Ladso nodded. "We shall tell him that Frank was expected and we cannot reach him. Ask that someone go to his house to check."

Britt smiled at the suggestion. "Excellent! Let's make that call now. Once we have more information, we'll be in a better position to choose our next move." A quick query provided the main line for the police district. Britt dialed and waited. An officer answered. "Hello, Desk Sergeant Murchison, how may I help you?"

"I need to speak with a detective. His first name is Mike. I believe his last name is Gentle or something similar. He's a friend of Detective Frank Bolden. I know it's late, but this is vitally important."

"It's Mike Gently, sir, and you are in luck because he's still in the building. May I put you on hold?"

Britt answered yes and a moment passed before a friendly voice spoke on the line. "Detective Mike Gently. Can I help you?"

"Britt Blasengane is my name, detective. I'm the friend of a friend of yours, Frank Bolden."

"Yes, I know Frank. What can I do for you?"

"This is difficult to explain, but, well, I'm worried that Frank may be having some kind of trouble. He was expected in Chicago this evening and we are unable to reach him."

"Yes, he told me he was headed there to meet some friends. He helped me with a case this afternoon which probably ran him late."

"I see, but he hasn't gotten in touch and we can't reach him." The others looked on concerned, as Britt frowned. "What time did you last see him?"

"It was shortly after five when he left the scene."

"About dusk." The team reacted and Britt held up his hand. "Did he say where he was going?"

"Home for his cat and to quickly pack and get on the road."

Britt kept his agitation from his voice. "I'm not in St. Louis, so I can't drive by to check in on him. Could you do a wellness check on him; it's important."

Mike's response was immediate. "I wouldn't worry. Frank is very capable…"

"That is certainly true but…"

"I understand." Gently lifted his jacket from the back of his chair. "Fortunately, I am ready to leave for the day. Frank's home is about 10 minutes from here. Let me have your number. I'll call you when I get there, although I really don't think you need to worry."

"I'm sorry Detective, but I fear you may be mistaken. " Hoping to give the detective some protection if the worse was true, Britt upped the ante. "The situation is difficult to explain but…" Britt licked his lips, struggling for a way to state his concern without convincing the detective that this was a prank call. "Frank has been investigating a matter, an individual, who I believe is very dangerous. I can't explain further, but it is possible Frank may be in danger. This probably sounds ridiculous, but can you go and have backup officers with you?"

Mike lifted a brow. "Do you have a friend who's an exceptional chef?"

Surprised, Britt realized the detective was doing what he could to verify the call. "Yes, his name is Ladso."

Gently nodded. "Alright, give me your full name and number." He wrote on a slip of paper and shoved it in his pocket. "Frank is a friend and I believe his friends would not make such a request without cause. I'll call you with an update from his home." Gently hung up and hurried out the door.

Britt repeated both sides of the conversation to the team and they all waited quietly for Gently's call. Worry was etched on all their faces.

Gently left the precinct without even considering a back-up. *Whatever this is, if anything. I'm confident that Frank is fine.*

*I've only been to Frank's home a few times despite our years together on the force. Few would argue against Frank being a crusty old S.O.B. He also likes his alone time.* Pulling off the lot, Gently had a moment of sudden worry but shook it off. Frank knew how to take care of himself.

Mike drove through the city traffic with autopilot reflexes, thinking about the odd phone call. The scenario seemed unlikely, but he remembered the mention of a Britt and a man with a foreign name. He thought it might have started with an L. Frank had used the word chef to describe his cooking. On the way to his car, Gently's own call attempt had also gone straight to voice mail, but Gently still assumed he'd find Frank reading and dressed in his pajamas with his phone turned off. He won't appreciate being bothered. At least, that's what Mike hoped.

He pulled up in front of Frank's home, noticing that all the lights inside were on, which seemed odd. He unfastened his holster grip, just in case, and approached the front door. Mike rang the bell, waited, rang a second time.

The far corner of the porch held a flower pot with a dead plant in it. Mike picked it up and sifted through the dirt. In moments his fingers found a key wrapped in plastic.

He remembered Frank's words — when they come for the body, the keys are in a pot on the front porch! Mike approached the door, key in hand as he loudly announced himself. Hearing nothing from inside, he proceeded.

He unlocked the front door and entered. "Hey Frank, it's Mike, checking up on you. You OK?" Despite Gently's calls, the house remained silent, until a cat lifted his head and meowed from Frank's recliner.

The living room seemed undisturbed, as were the bedroom, bathroom and study.

The kitchen was as clean and orderly as the rest of the house, then he saw Frank sprawled on the floor.

He dropped to his knees, saying, "Frank! Frank! Can you hear me?" He checked and found a thready pulse. He immediately grabbed his phone and called for an ambulance.

Mike checked Frank carefully, finding nothing wrong, other than him being unconscious on the floor. He looked closer and found two small puncture wounds on his neck. Both were puckered and raw. He grabbed a kitchen towel and gently blotted them.

Did someone overpower him and inject him with something? Mike worried. He straightened Frank out on the floor, went and grabbed the bed cover. Bringing it to the kitchen, he covered him to keep him warm.

Soon he heard sirens and went to the front door. One of the EMTs said they were taking Frank to the ICU at Barnes Hospital. Mike said he'd follow in his car.

Mike locked up the house, holding onto the spare key. In the car, he pulled out his phone and the paper with Britt's number. This Britt had known something was wrong. After things settled, Gently was going to get more information on why the man thought something was wrong. For tonight, he needed to let them know their friend was injured and on his way to the hospital. He dug out his cell phone and dialed the number.

In her small cave, Sharon laughed over the mayhem she'd soon cause. The officer had been easy to overpower! She could just as easily have killed him, but she had a more diabolical plan. Now that she'd drunk from him, they were connected. A connection that would allow her to sense him, listen to his thoughts, even to control him. She would have him turn on her tormenters, and destroy them one at a time.

Sharon chuckled evilly, pleased to use one of their own to take them down. They had killed her Sisters, ruined her plans. Left her alone and without a home. She would see them all destroyed. Not Undead, they did not deserve eternal life. No, they would die, knowing how and why. The officer, too, would die after he'd completed his task.

She grinned, imagining him waking up on his floor tomorrow morning, confused, oblivious to his bites, until he saw or felt them. She awaited the next night and the mental connection to him. One he would be unaware of... until she wanted it otherwise.

The call from Gently had greatly disturbed Britt and the team, particularly his telling of puncture wounds on Frank's neck. "What is the hospital likely to identify from Frank's condition?"

They all looked toward Ladso. "They will diagnose anemia because of the blood loss. Typically, the victim appears dead. In days of old, everyone believed they were. With modern equipment, they would now identify it as coma. Fortunately, Frank was fed on lightly as he is clearly breathing and has a pulse."

Pi took Nikki's hand. "So he's going to be okay?"

"Many who are not killed do recover, but we need a better description of his condition before I can hazard a guess."

Britt immediately looked up the hospital's main phone number and called. He explained he was trying to get information on a friend, a police officer recently taken to the hospital, who was in the ICU. He listened, looked crestfallen, nodded. "Yes, I understand, thank you for your help." He hung up the phone.

"There is no way to talk to him, and no way to get an update, unless we're a blood relation. The person I spoke to suggested calling in the morning, said he should be in a regular room by then. Once he has access to a phone, we can talk to him."

Ladso stood. "There is nothing we can do for Frank now, other than to do what we came here to do. He will be safe in the hospital. We need to find all references to supernatural powers of the vampire."

"Right now, I am not sure I could even focus on words, much less make sense of them. As much as I would love to dive into Murray's library, we are all tired. I propose we all get some sleep so we can be fresh to get to work in the morning. I will just clean up the mess from the catering first."

Volunteering to keep the dogs in her room, Nikki stood. "Which rooms do we use?

"I phoned and had Murray's staff prepare the rooms. Both you and Britt will use the same rooms you did on your last visit."

Pi smirked. "I haven't been here before."

Ladso smiled and reddened a bit. "I have a couple of options for you."

Nikki and Britt started toward the front hall as Ladso began collecting cups. When Nikki looked back, Pi gave her a wave and a wink. Giggling, Nikki turned away again and called to the dogs who followed.

# 5

Up early, Ladso was cooking a simple breakfast of toast, scrambled eggs, bacon and the always present coffee. Sounds from upstairs were shortly followed by Nikki and the dogs who headed for the yard.

Nikki returned with the dogs in tow. Pi had now come down as well and was talking seriously with Ladso. Embarrassed about intruding, Nikki loitered at the doorway until Pi saw and called her in. As they entered, Ladso waved the dogs toward their bowls and handed Nikki a cup of hot coffee. "I'd like one of those too, if you don't mind," Britt said from the door.

With everyone at the table, Britt took a sip of coffee and spoke. "I called the hospital on the way down. They gave me a number for Frank's room. I thought waiting until we were together was the thing to do, as I know we're all anxious to hear from him."

Pi nodded but set down her cup. "Are we going to return to St. Louis?" When no one answered immediately she continued. "We have access to information here that we don't have in St. Louis. Also, if we go back, we'll have to be on guard against Sharon since she's clearly decided to start wreaking revenge. That said, we can't leave Frank on his own. What are we going to do? We have…"

Ladso interrupted, as he took her hand. "I suggest, once Frank is able to leave the hospital, that I charter a private ambulance to transfer him here. Then he can stay here in the house. I'll arrange any medical care he needs. It removes him from danger, and keeps us out of Sharon's reach while he recovers."

Britt looked at him. "If you can really afford that, it would be our best option. I'll start with the library after we talk to Frank. I'm assuming the research will be a group effort."

Everyone agreed with Ladso's offer and Britt's words. Having a plan, suddenly the notion of breakfast was more appealing. Sniffing the bacon, Pi looked to Britt. "How late do we have to wait before calling Frank?"

"He's in a room and the nurse did say he's responsive. The nurse suggested, though, that we wait until after 10:00AM. Give him time to eat, get cleaned up and into a fresh gown."

Pi grinned tentatively. "If he's feeling up to it, I'm sure Frank is loving all the attention."

Everyone laughed as Ladso began bringing over platters. Pi jumped up to grab the coffee and everyone settled in to eat.

When everyone finished it was only nine. Ladso did the washing while Pi dried the dishes. Britt went to Murray's library to get started while Nikki left to walk the dogs. At 10:00AM, they gathered in the kitchen again as Britt pulled his cell and called Frank's room number. From his wide grin, it was obvious Frank had answered. Britt quickly put the detective on speaker so everyone could hear.

"Can't a guy get some shut-eye?" Frank's cantankerous voice made them all smile.

"Hey Frank, are you wishing for a Cop-achino?" Pi called.

"I'd settle for anybody's cup of Joe instead of the dark yuck they have here. Some of your cooking too, Ladso. I don't know about the care, but they get you to go home by giving you this crap three times a day. If it doesn't kill you, they let you go home thinking nothing else will!"

Everyone laughed and called out friendly greetings.

"How are you feeling, better?" Britt's smile had withered.

"I'm fine. They think I've got some kind of — ammenia?"

"Anemia." Again, the nurse's voice came through the phone.

"Whatever," Frank spoke again. "Never had it before. Can't believe I passed out in my own kitchen. I'm working on them to let me out this afternoon."

"Maybe," the nurse interjected again.

Frank chuckled. "Yeah, maybe. They gave me some blood transfusions, and I feel fine if a little tired, but they're adamant I have someone to watch over me for a few days. I live alone, so my choices are here or Shady Acres Rest Home. This sounds minimally better than that so…"

"Well, Frank, I may have a proposal to suit you." Ladso leaned in to be sure he was heard. "What if I hired an ambulance to drive you here? We can keep an eye on you, and you can help us with our — well, you know, our project. I think it is wise for us to stay together. We should not have separated yesterday, and you paid the price."

"An ambulance ride all the way to Chicago? Are you nuts? I'll make them let me out of here and I'll drive myself. I'll…"

Again, the nurse spoke. "You can forget about that Mr. Detective. They aren't letting you go home. You think they're going to let you drive? Forget about it hot shot!"

Frank grunted. "I keep looking at this nurse. She doesn't look anything like Pi, but she's sure got her mouth!"

"Pie?" The nurse laughed. "Pies don't have mouths, Sheriff. You behave yourself. I've got other patients. My sympathies to your friends. They must be saints."

"Thank you Madam Nightingale," Frank called to the departing nurse who he was clearly enjoying. "If they let her be my nurse all the time I'd stay here happily. Sure Ladso, if you can arrange it before her shift ends, you'll make me a happy man. I'm looking forward to getting to work on our ugly phlebotomist. That's what they call the ones that come for your blood in here."

Britt corrected him. "You'll be resting and recuperating like your doctors say. No working. But we'll happily have your input as we gather information."

Ladso added. "Since you are agreeable, I will contact the ambulance service, and they will arrange the rest. Hopefully, you will be here in time for supper."

Frank said, "Now you're talking. Don't tell me what you're making. I want to be surprised. I'll have my friend that you sent after me put my cat into the Boarder place. He can grab my packed bag from the house too. I got nothing else to do. Put out a plate for me and cook enough for seconds." He sobered, his tone serious now. "Thanks for sending Mike and for getting me out of this place."

Ladso said, "You are welcome," and hung up. He then went to Murray's... his office, to look up the number for and then call the private ambulance company.

When Ladso returned he was beaming. "They expect he will be here tonight. No more sleeping under different roofs."

Britt went up the stairs to Murray's library. He didn't ask, but the team's impression was that he wanted a little time alone there. They all understood, so they chatted for several minutes before following him.

When they left, the dogs stayed in the kitchen. Trooper lay down immediately. Ray, not as well-behaved, got up to explore. Sniffing industriously all over the kitchen, he found, in the pantry, a pair of leather moccasins. He looked over at Trooper who was already asleep. Delighted over a new toy, Ray carried one of them to his bed, and settled in for some chewing.

Britt worked his way around Murray's library. Murray didn't sort under the Dewey Decimal system. Browsing, though, Britt quickly noticed a pattern. One section of shelves to one topic, regardless of the languages or ages of the books. Nothing was labeled, but with some guidance from Ladso, he was confident he'd fully understand Murray's methods. "It was an intriguing system — or was it an insane system?" he chuckled.

Their task would be daunting, Britt hoped he was up to it. With a notepad and pen, he made a rudimentary map of the shelves' contents. *We'll need to identify characteristics, strengths, and weaknesses. Much of that is in Murray's notes and Ladso's head, but both men had mentioned myths and legends that were never disproven. Taking on gaseous form was one that had never been documented. That ability surprised us. We can't afford such surprises. They could easily get us killed.*

Ladso and the ladies arrived, and Ladso gave a brief tour, explaining Murray's filing system. It was an arcane way of collating similar things. He also showed them where Murray stored his extensive collection of leather-bound journals. In chronological order, many were stained with water, grime, or blood, but all were labeled in Murray's neat hand. "There are things other than vampires in these volumes." Ladso intoned his words like a chant. "The world is darker than most would like to believe."

Britt gave the final instructions. "Write down any, everything, you find, noting the book and page." He pointed to an empty table. "Place the books in which you find something there. The others, apply a post-it note and return them to their proper places."

Turning to begin his search, Britt wondered how Sharon, any of them, managed her conversion. Hoping to find something relevant, he filed that question with the others in his mind and prepared to read.

He started in the section of the library dealing with myths and mythic creatures. Some titles he recognized; about most he was totally ignorant. He pulled out a heavy volume, struggling until he had it braced between his arm and chest. Carrying it to the table where he intended to work, he thought, *next time someone goes out for supplies, I need a shoulder bag to carry things in.*

It was hours later that Britt realized Ladso was calling him to break for lunch. Britt stood stiffly and stretched, thinking, *A break will be good and give us all an opportunity to share anything we've found. I'd also like to take the dogs out.*

Frank's arrival that evening would give the detective a chance to settle in. Britt was happy they'd no longer be separated. He was uncomfortable not knowing how Sharon found their homes, though.

He put those disturbing thoughts aside as he went downstairs in the mood to gather up the dogs. Fresh air and working with his dogs were how Britt practiced mindful meditation. *Doggie Zen,* he thought with a grin. Arriving on the first floor he found Ladso already serving lunch, which postponed his Zen.

Britt walked into the kitchen where Ladso met him with a curious grin. With one hand behind his back, Britt wondered what he was hiding. Ladso laughed and brought his hand around, displaying the soggy, thoroughly chewed moccasin. "Just like Mikka, your little Ray is determined to wriggle his way into my heart, even by following his same errors!"

Mikka, another of Britt's dogs, had died protecting Frank from one of the vampires several months before. For years earlier, Ladso and Murray had occasionally dog-sat for Britt. As a puppy, Mikka had chewed up Ladso's favorite pair of leather Moroccan slippers.

Britt apologized profusely, but Ladso waved away his words. "It is no one's fault except my own, for leaving them where they would be a temptation to a bored young puppy. Please, do not worry yourself about it."

The team enjoyed grilled cheese sandwiches and tomato soup, a far cry from Ladso's usual masterpieces. "I must go to the store this afternoon. We need many things for the kitchen. Please let me know what you would like for my list. I will also get chew toys for our puppy." He looked across the table and winked toward Ray.

Talking over coffee, the team extended their break before going back up to Murray's books.

Pi looked into her cup. "It's nastier for us, now that she's Undead. What do they remember as vampires? If she remembers everything, then we are really in the hot seat. We ruined her plans at the school. Then we hunted down and killed the ones who'd survived. Now she's alone — we hope! She sure has a bone to pick with us."

Ladso spoke up. "I would like to know how she knew where to find us. I would feel more, well less uncomfortable, knowing she is unlikely to show up here."

Britt made an unpleasant guess. "It's possible that, bringing Frank to us, may also invite Sharon here. Or at least provide her with a map. She may read Frank's mind, or sense where he is. We just don't know." He set down his cup, then picked it up again and refilled it. "I need to get back to the library. Back to work."

"We need to learn what other powers she might have. That might tell us how she found us."

Ladso spoke up. "Britt, look in Murray's bound journals. While they have many pages, there are fewer than in the other books. They contain details that Murray felt were important even if unproven."

"I will join you again after I restock our larder. The kitchen is nearly empty despite the items I had the staff purchase before our arrival. Even the mice are complaining." He smiled despite trying not to. "Pi is going to come with me. Nikki wants to be your library research assistant. You will have a helper. Is there anything else I can provide to assist you?"

Britt described how awkward it was to carry things one-armed. Ladso's eyes lit up. "Oh, we have carts in the library for just that purpose. I stocked them a few years back when I noticed Murray was having some difficulties. Let me show you where they are before I leave."

Ladso accompanied Britt to the library and retrieved the carts for him. Britt beamed, as they were just what he needed. He placed volumes for Nikki on one. He would stick her on the characteristics, strengths and weaknesses of the Undead in volumes focused solely on their particular monsters.

He then rolled a cart to Murray's leather-bound journals. Volume after volume lined three shelves. They were truly a lifetime's work. He looked backward chronologically until he found the journals from 20 years ago, before, when he was a young, naive student. Ladso was slightly younger, just a peasant, but was less naive because he'd been raised with the tales of family and others who believed and had experienced the Undead. Britt shook his head. *We were both just a couple of dumb kids... but since Ladso grew up on vampire folklore, known to Murray and now to us as fact, I guess he was less dumb than I.*

Suddenly, he stood up and headed back toward the kitchen. Once there, he called for Nikki. He'd promised himself some doggie-Zen before the afternoon grind, and he was going to deliver on that promise. He was certain Nikki would join him. She loved working the dogs as much as he did. They could both use a few smiles before the afternoon's grim work. Nikki entered the kitchen with leashes in hand, a treat bag round her waist, and a smile on her face. Seeing her, Britt grinned as well.

♪

Britt carefully observed Nikki as she put Ray through his paces. He decreed both puppy and trainer graduated from 'basic' to 'intermediate' level of training. "You see, Nikki, during this next phase, Ray will learn how to follow commands, despite distractions like other locations, other people, even other animals. Right now, he thinks all these commands mean 'Do this action in this place when only you tell me.' Now he must learn to do them regardless of the surroundings." He broke into a big smile. "You are doing an amazing job. I hope you know that."

Playtime came after the workout. Ray was getting the hang of catching a tennis ball, but the frisbee was still beyond him, despite Trooper's example. Ray liked to chew on them, but he just couldn't catch one. Returning it or the ball was not something he understood either. Once he got hold of it, the game was over.

Britt and Nikki came back in laughing, cheeks red from the cold, and in high spirits from watching the two dogs play. The big shepherd, Trooper, would pretend to be startled by a clumsy Ray attempting to stalk him. It was a comical farce as then he would pounce, and the two would chase each other around and around the yard.

"All that exercise has worn Ray out." Nikki petted the puppy whose eyes were already closing. "He's ready for a nap."

Proving her right, the puppy padded straight to his bed and flopped down, tongue hanging out, and panting. Trooper walked over to his own bed and lay down, more dignified, but just as happy, grinning a wide doggy grin.

They left the dogs to nap and returned to the library. Britt showed Nikki the cart he had stacked for her and explained what he wanted her to look for. "We need to understand what these creatures are capable of: what they can and can't do. I'm going through Murray's journals, reviewing the excursion where I met Ladso and first ran into the Undead, as well as his other encounters with vampires before and after. Fortunately, he included a contents list in the front of each volume."

Nikki looked at the enormous stack of books and heaved an equally oversized sigh. She rolled the cart to a nearby table and pulled the book on the top of her stack. She opened her notebook first, then she sat down, opening the book, and frowned at the page as she began skimming for some mention of the vampires' abilities.

Britt sat at his table with the other cart holding the journals. The first journal he opened was dated the months he'd first met Murray. The writing instantly transported him back into that world. Living in London where it seemed to always be raining. When it wasn't drizzling or foggy, they'd get a peek of the sun before it retreated behind a cloud again. Britt remembered Murray's lectures. How they fascinated him and made him want to know if there was any truth behind the legends. The students often went to the pub afterward, and Murray regularly joined them. Those were amazing conversations, he recalled.

Now he had the volume that covered his only excursion with Murray. It surprised him to find that Murray gave him the job of historian in order to let him gain experience. Seeing promise in him, Murray was keeping him safe, while expecting Britt would be joining their group and possibly taking on the role Ladso ended up filling. Murray first wanted Britt's eyes opened. He suspected the young student's disbelief and hoped writing about what he experienced would help him realize its truth.

Britt was ashamed now as he remembered how he'd insisted that Murray and his group were insane. Hunting down a man who was obviously mentally ill. He cringed at his own naivete. The man was not mentally ill. He was Undead and killing villagers.

Britt continued reading Murray's notes. The story engrossed him despite remembering almost every detail. The small villages, the ridiculous bus he had slept in multiple nights when there were no beds for him in the small inns available. He remembered the young and eager Ladso's offer to help as an oft needed translator.

He made notes when he read Murray's plan to kill the creature, before he had the chance to become more powerful. It was believed that the more times he fed on his victims' blood, the stronger he would become. Britt wondered how many victims Sharon had killed, and was still killing. Even Frank's blood had probably strengthened her further.

Murray warned extensively about the dangers of trying to hunt the Undead at night. The only reason he chose that night to attack was because this newly created vampire, was only going to grow stronger. Britt shuddered as he remembered its strength that night.

Murray had assured them that the best method of killing a vampire was to find its lair, where it hid from the sun during the day. That's when it would be weakest, possibly helpless. Murray stated that preparing for our attack, and waiting for the vampire to find us was the best method when its hiding place couldn't be determined.

Britt paused. Just sit and wait? He continued reading, hoping for methods to lure such a creature.

Murray listed their weapons which included a wooden stake and a mallet to drive it through the vampire's heart. Cutting off the head was another sure method of killing the vampire. They ended up doing both to the creature terrorizing Ladso's village, before burning the corpse, making absolutely sure it would not rise again. A gruesome tactic with which Britt wholeheartedly agreed.

Later, he included the gruesome details of Yasminka's burial. She had been Ladso's fiancee. First, she was fed upon like Frank, but left alive until the monster returned and killed her.

Nikki came over, drawing Britt out of the narrative. "Hey, the others are back. I can hear them. I'm going to take a break and help them unload." Britt waved her off and turned back to Murray's journal.

Nikki helped Ladso and Pi carry in armloads of groceries. She headed outside with Pi to grab more as Ladso began putting things away.

Ladso moved through the room, placing items into the refrigerator, cabinets, the pantry and the freezer that was in the pantry. Ray kept getting underfoot, so Ladso opened the back door, shooing him out. Trooper was happy to go out as well. Without Ray underfoot, Ladso caught up with the women in getting everything already inside put away. He made the last trip to the car with them carrying three of the final bags. With all the food inside, he shooed the ladies this time. "I need to cook and think. Besides, when Frank gets here, I need a meal that will live up to his expectations." As he began pulling out some of the items he'd just put away, assembling his menu on the fly, he grabbed a bag of dried peas.

Nikki wrinkled her nose. "Ew, dried peas? Are you going to make us eat peas?"

Ladso shook his head. "They work like jelly beans. I also purchased a box of baggies. We'll make our own counting-bombs before our return to St. Louis."

"And what's with all the boxes of salt?"

Pi pointed out, "That's for sprinkling around the outside of the house. Another unproven item in our armory, as my man puts it, but the Undead can't cross over a line of salt without counting every grain. That, with motion alarms, buys us time."

"You are learning, my dear." Ladso threw Pi a smile when suddenly, his phone rang. "Yes, this is he. Excellent, you have the house number? What is your ETA? Good, I will expect your call when you arrive."

Ladso clapped his hands. "That was the ambulance service. They are only twenty minutes away and dinner is still unprepared." Ladso looked at the ladies. "Please double check the suite Frank is going to use." He nodded toward Pi. "I showed you the door last night." Pi nodded back. "I know it is cleaned and there are fresh linens on the bed, but please check for towels, washcloths and anything else he might need. I have got to get to dinner."

When they came back, they reported that all looked perfect. "There're no bouquets of flowers like my first night here, but somehow I doubt he'll notice — or care."

Pi stayed out of his way, grinding coffee beans and putting on a pot of coffee while Ladso performed his magic. She'd rarely been allowed in the kitchen while he worked, but his focus was clear as he pulled pre-made cinnamon rolls out of the fridge, set them on the counter, and started the preheating. It wouldn't be his own cooking, but he thought a hot snack and some coffee would do everyone some good after a long day, and hopefully hold Frank until dinner was ready.

With no discernible pause, Ladso turned to the fridge and before Pi could tell what he was doing, he was on to the next item on his menu.

Ladso was surprised. He hadn't realized how much he cared about the detective. Losing Murray was a hard blow, but it wasn't just that. It was more that Frank had somehow gotten under his skin, and become a loyal friend, someone he cared for. His sage advice, and his straightforward, cynical view of things, helped on multiple occasions.

Dicing onions, he wondered, how badly Sharon had injured Frank? She bit him, based on the reports from Detective Gently and what he'd pulled from the nurses. Ladso could not help but remember his dear Yasminka, and the same injuries. He shook his head, feeling vaguely guilty about his new relationship with Pi. He glanced quickly at her, but watching his hands and the quickly diced onions he was producing, she didn't notice.

Yasminka was frail, but valiant in spirit. He hadn't seen the actual bites. Murray had taken care of those. He wished he hadn't been so squeamish then, but the past was unchangeable. He'd seen other bites and would be seeing Frank's in short order. He could compare Frank's bite to Britt's shoulder wound, which fortunately was no more, despite the arm it had cost his friend.

Ladso made a mental note to ask Britt for Murray's journals covering that time. He wanted to re-read them, to see if Murray described Yasminka's wounds, and anything else that may have happened to her. He knew his village's final precautions had been brutal. There was no need for him to read that portion as he'd seen it performed other times. He was happy he'd been spared it at the time, and had no desire to lock the description into his memory as he knew Murray's description would be detailed. Minka remained the sweet, loving, innocent girl he once loved so much… in his memory.

His cell phone rang again, signaling the ambulance's arrival. With Pi in tow, Ladso hurried toward the front door, leaving his memories behind him for the moment. He disarmed the alarm, unlocked the door, and swung it open. Below, he heard Frank arguing with the drivers, and grinned. He headed down the stairs to see what the problem was.

"Ladso! Just the guy I needed to see. These mokes are refusing to let me off this contraption." The attendants had attempted to tighten the straps holding him on his gurney as they prepared to take him up the stairs. Ladso grinned and signed the invoice for the driver, slipping in a couple of $50 bills for him and his companion. The driver grinned back, thanked Ladso, tore off his copy of the invoice, and they stood on either side of the gurney.

"Frank, it is cold out here, and these guys are just doing their job. You have experienced folks unhappy with you when doing your job. Do not be one of them. Let them…"

"Look at your steps." Ladso stopped, confused by Frank's request. "Now look at me and then look at them." While both attendants were fit, neither looked up to the job before them. "I'm not fit as a fiddle, but I'm ready to play and I'm not going to let these young men put all three of us in the hospital."

Ladso and the attendants laughed. "May we stand on either side of you and give support if you need it on the climb?"

Frank looked at the man and nodded. "Now, that's reasonable. Undo these damn straps."

Frank took in the house as he slowly climbed the stairs. "Hell of a place you got here, Ladso. I've seen apartment complexes that were smaller." Frank cast a glance back to see how his words landed. Ladso laughed.

From the top of the stairs, Pi called. "Come on, Grandpa Frank, only a few more steps to go. It's cold out here."

Predictably, Frank snarled saying he was in fine shape and no grandpa. "We may be a little out of my jurisdiction but I can still give you a world of trouble. Those tasty Cop-achinos don't give you leave to not think about what comes out of your mouth!"

They reached the door and entered. Ladso thanked the attendants, said goodbye and shut the door. "Welcome to my humble abode."

Frank puffed and looked around. "Humble?" Taking a deep breath, he looked at Ladso. "Where's the nearest chair?"

Ladso stepped aside and pointed toward a couch in the next room. He set Frank's luggage in the foyer and walked over to sit with the detective while he caught his breath. Pi had already sat beside Frank and all was forgiven as she hugged him and gave him a peck on the cheek. "Now that's more like it," Frank looked at her and smiled.

After a few moments, Nikki and Britt arrived, both saying hello and how happy they were to see him. Ladso pulled Britt aside and surreptitiously handed him the shoulder bag he had procured. Britt's face broke into a grateful smile and he clapped Ladso's shoulder.

Eventually, Ladso invited Frank to accompany everyone into the kitchen. As they approached, the fragrance of cinnamon wafted over them, and Ladso knew the rolls were ready to pull from the oven. He couldn't help allowing a small grin at his own impeccable timing.

# 6

The kitchen was in chaos-mode. The dogs were underfoot with even Trooper falling victim to the overall elation. The team continued greeting Frank, citing their concern, and asking how he felt. Through it all, Ladso navigated Frank to his seat. Britt called the dogs to order and was pleased when Ray joined Trooper in moving to his rug. Everyone settled down still grinning but also bubbling with curiosity.

Ladso pulled the cinnamon rolls out of the oven, then poured everyone a fresh cup of coffee. Frank picked up his cup, inhaled deeply, and cracked a smile. "Pi, you have been an excellent influence on our friend Ladso. The quality of his coffee is improving."

Pi grinned while patting Ladso on the back. "I'm afraid I made the coffee but yes, he is learning."

Frank shrugged and sipped the hot brew again. "It may be just the contrast between that brown mud-water the hospital dared to call 'coffee', but your abilities have not suffered while dealing with our ugly vampires." He gulped half the cup in two long swallows before putting the cup down, a beatific expression on his face.

"Pi, in fact, **insisted** on brewing the coffee," Nikki explained with a smile. "She said nothing else was good enough for you." Ladso grinned and blew a kiss to their brew mistress.

Conversation temporarily ceased as Ladso set saucers before them and everyone took one of the hot, gooey, sticky-sweet, & spicy rolls.

Still chewing, Frank spoke around the sweetness nestled on his tongue. "Ladso, I'm impressed but also confused. How did you break me out of that joint?"

"It was quite easy. You said they would have released you to home, except for the fact you lived alone. I spoke to your doctor, and offered to have you here in my home, where you will have people around you 24/7. He immediately agreed."

"We all want you here, with us." Britt took a seat beside their recovering member. Setting down his cup, he patted the detective on his shoulder.

Pi shone with joy. "He's put you in your own suite. What you've seen of the house so far is nothing. Wait till you see your room and ride up in the elevator to reach it!"

Ladso was serious as he met Frank's eyes. "Pursuant to your doctor's orders, you will rest and relax. You will **not** work until your doctor here says you may. You must agree to that provision." Ladso held Frank's gaze as the detective turned slitted eyes toward him. "Frank, that was the price of your release."

Frank's eyes slitted tighter until he heaved an enormous sigh and picked up his cup. "It's gonna cost you in Cop-achinos."

Ladso's expression relaxed. "I have stocked our shelves with enough of the required supplies to drown you in your favorite beverage. You need only to rest and get better. That is your only job for now. There will be a visiting nurse checking on you every other day as well."

Frank's eyes rolled.

"They will also see to those bandages on your neck."

Frank's face pulled into an uneasy frown as he put his hand to the bandage. Ladso noticed but didn't comment.

Britt looked up from his cup. "Frank, do you feel up to telling us what happened?" The team perked up expectantly. Even Ray's ears rose in attention.

Frank groaned. "You won't like it." Everyone waited. Frank shrugged. "I warned you. I remember almost nothing. I got home, fed Cat…" He frowned. "I guess I went to change. When I got back to the kitchen the damn cat went nuts. I don't remember why, but I thought something was behind me. As I prepared to turn…" He frowned again. "That's all I can remember. I woke up to beeping machinery, an IV in my arm, and wondering what the hell happened."

Frank took a sip of his coffee, set the cup back on the table, and frowned. "They ran all kinds of tests. I didn't have a stroke, heart attack, seizure, or anything that could have caused me to black out. Whatever's on my throat... I said I had no idea, maybe the cat. They didn't suggest anything else and neither did I. They said I was anemic, that I should start taking iron pills, eat plenty of fruits and vegetables, and rest. Hah! This old body doesn't know how to rest."

Ladso spoke sternly. "Learn, Frank. We need you at your best when we go back to St. Louis." Frank scowled but didn't argue. "Now, I am cooking you a special 'welcome home' dinner, but not if I do not get back to it."

Nikki stood. "Frank, why don't you come with me while I take the dogs out? Watching them play is fun and the fresh air will do you good too. There are chairs on the porch."

Pi jumped up. "You like movies Frank? I'll make a list of what looks good on cable. Might as well enjoy your resting."

Frank flinched as Britt gave him a sympathetic look. "The time will pass quickly. We'll tell you what we're doing. Listening isn't the same as working."

Ladso, still stinging from Murray's passing was clearly worried for Frank. He pursed his lips, but nodded.

"Then give me a quick summary. What's going on?" Frank held his cup but looked from face to face eager for someone to speak.

Ladso sat at the table, his eyes on the detective. "Frank, I will not sugar-coat this." Frank's eyes widened. "You were attacked, and bitten, by a vampire."

Frank eyes widened further. "You're sure?"

"I am afraid so. The punctures on your neck are bite marks. I have seen pictures and verified them. Fortunately, it fed lightly on you, which almost certainly means it planned to return. You will continue to feel weak, sometimes confused — especially in the evenings. The vampire typically would try to feed on you again, but I hope we have confounded that by bringing you nearly 300 miles away."

The news was clearly not what Frank had expected to hear. He'd not even considered it. He sat up straight. "Wait, something happened at Britt's house too!" The worried expressions on the team darkened as they began realizing how little Frank was remembering. Not noticing their worry, Frank looked at his hands and then at Britt. "You got some video from your home security. Were you able to clear it up? Did it show what's attacking us? Attacked me?"

Britt nodded. "Yes. The vampire is definitely Sharon. You were with us when we saw it. I will show it to you again. We decided to retreat to Chicago together. To research, and for safety." Britt's face was a mask of worry. "It appears the attack has affected your short-term memory."

Frank frowned, looking nervous for the first time. "Yes. I don't remember any of that." He looked more morose than usual.

Ladso interrupted. "OK, grilling session is over. Join Nikki out back while I get your welcoming meal prepared. Watch the dogs, take in some sun and air. It will do you good. Tomorrow, Pi will hunt you down and force you to sit still and watch movies with her. Look at this as the holiday you would never plan."

Frank raised an eyebrow, but refrained from comment as Nikki stood. "I'll get your coat, Frank. You can get comfortable on the porch and watch the dogs." With that she hurried to the front of the house and back again. Helping Frank on with his coat she noticed his expression of concern was gone. "Good boy Frank. Focus on getting better and don't worry about a thing."

His eyes raised and Frank smiled. "What? Me worry? Alfred P. Newman was one of my direct ancestors." Both were chuckling as they stepped out the door. Before closing it, Nikki looked back and shrugged, lacking familiarity with the name.

Pi moved over to take Ladso's hand. "Is this memory loss thing normal?"

"I am afraid it is something new to research. I do not remember it with Yasminka."

She pursed her lips. "Well, I hope it isn't permanent. Frank acts like someone on drugs. He's sure not his sharp self."

Ladso lifted his cup. "This is not common. Usually, the vampire kills their victims the first time. Murray once told me that he had read of a surviving victim having memory issues. There may be some component in the vampire's saliva that causes amnesia. Getting a sample to test is of course difficult. When it has been managed it degrades so quickly that few observations could be made. Frank will be slow thinking for some time, but for how long I could only guess. Since we have gotten him away, he should recover. Until then, everyone pay close attention." He turned to Pi. "Thank you for the movie distraction. That will keep him occupied and still."

Britt looked sadly toward Ladso. "My reading of Murray's journal mentions Yasminka, being confused. She was placed in a room with the maids regularly checking on her. I know you did as well." He nodded to Ladso who nodded back without making eye contact. "She had not remembered being attacked. She improved over several days, although her wounds would not heal."

Ladso nodded at the memory as Pi laid an arm across his shoulders. "All that is true but it was a matter of days. We do not know what might have followed." He reached up and squeezed Pi's hand. "I have to get to work on dinner, and to think." Giving him a peck on the cheek, Pi left, heading for the sitting room and its large screen TV while Britt went back to the library. Ladso moved to the counter thinking of ghosts from his past.

Taking a deep breath, Ladso's eyes cleared as he turned to his favorite distraction. Moments later he'd prepared two already smoked briskets. One pork, one beef. He imagined how both would crumble at his touch when he slid them out of the oven, warmed again.

Frank watched the two dogs with a troubled smile. He hadn't gotten to know Mikka, but the dog had died saving his life. He hoped these dogs would be safe and live well into their old age. He stretched his arms wide, enjoying the warmth of late afternoon sunshine as he thought. *Now that those damned creatures are destroyed, these pups should be fine.*

As Frank watched, Trooper took off at a run, with Ray struggling to keep up. Trooper slowed down, and the younger dog nipped at his tail. Trooper dashed off again, leaving little Ray to try and catch up. Frank chuckled and inhaled deeply of the late winter air and decided he could learn to appreciate this concept of "time off."

Nikki called the dogs and prepared to go back inside after what seemed a very short amount of time. Frank shrugged and followed. Once inside, he realized he was chilled and directed his steps toward the coffee machine.

Ladso was busy working with pots heating up and meat and bread in the oven. He nodded to Frank, but with an apology, continued mixing some kind of sauce. Frank sniffed and studied Ladso with interest. "What's for supper?"

Ladso grinned. "You will find out soon if you let me continue. I will tell you, however, that it is home-style cooking, which should prevent your missing St. Louis."

Nikki escorted Frank to the sitting room, made sure he was comfortable and left him to watch the evening news. Two lamps fought against the evening's darkness. Warm and comfortable, Frank was asleep before the sports segment started. Pi came in and smiled at the big lout. Reducing the volume, she left to see if she could, or if Ladso would allow her, to help with dinner.

As she left, Frank's brow furrowed. His lips moved but he didn't make any noise.

Three hours later, Frank was awake and surprised by Ladso's St. Louis-style barbecue buffet. The smoked brisket, pork and beef, were so tender they fell to pieces on the plate. There were different styles of barbecue sauce as well as potato salad, cole slaw, baked beans, deviled eggs, macaroni and cheese, and slices of toasted cheese garlic bread.

Frank smacked his lips. "I'm drooling here. This smells better than Super Smokers, and I always thought that was the best around." He loaded his plate and headed for the table. Ladso had that special grin on his face reserved for people enjoying his cooking.

Conversation was limited to lavish compliments, which made Ladso's ears turn a delicate shade of pink. Frank and Britt went back for seconds, but finally, everyone finished eating. Ladso cleared the dishes and returned bearing a fresh-baked apple pie, with a quart of French Vanilla ice cream tucked under his arm. No one could resist hot apple pie à La mode, and in short order they were eating silently again.

By prior agreement, no one asked for coffee or mentioned it and Frank didn't seem to notice its absence. His first enormous yawn took him completely unaware. He grimaced. "Apparently it's been a long day." Another gaping yawn muffled his words. "I think I best head for bed."

Ladso stood. "Let me show you to your suite. Your luggage is already there."

"Suite?" Frank looked baffled, echoing Nikki's surprise from so long ago. "Sweet! I've been booked into the Ladso Luxury Inn!"

Ladso grinned. "I just may borrow that name." He directed Frank toward a door. "The elevator is this way. You are on the fourth floor and should be very comfortable."

Frank still put on his tough facade. "What, you don't think I can climb stairs?" He followed Ladso quickly enough, despite his grumbling, and entered the elevator with no further complaint. The machine ran silent and smooth. At the fourth floor, Ladso held the door and waved Frank forward. "To your left." He guided Frank. "This is your door."

Frank opened the door and looked around with wonder. "Now this is how a man ought to live! You said my stuff was here. I'd like to unpack, so I can take a shower before bed."

Ladso gestured toward a large closet where Frank's suitcase was stacked on a folding support table. "Would you like some help?"

Frank assured Ladso he knew how to unpack, and was well enough to shower unassisted. Ladso grinned. Reassured by Frank's snark, he quickly showed him the intercom button by the bedside, and left.

Frank opened the suitcase, grabbed a pair of pajamas, and headed for the bathroom which was like a hotel, already equipped with all kinds of required toiletries, including soaps and shampoo. There was also a stack of fluffy towels on open shelves. Frank stripped, stepped into the shower, and turned on the water which poured out immediately hot. He stood there for long moments letting the water beat down on his head and chest. Finally, he got to work scrubbing up, enjoying the novel fragrances.

Finished, he stepped out onto a fluffy floor mat, and grabbed a towel. He put on his pajamas and used some of the provided supplies to brush his teeth and shave.

In the bedroom, he remembered the bandage around his neck. It was dry. They must have waterproofed it. He nodded remembering that showers would be fine, but not baths.

Nothing in his long, eventful life ever looked so inviting as that bed. He turned back the covers, climbed in, turned off the nightstand light, and was asleep almost before the room got dark.

Back downstairs, Ladso discovered Pi had already brewed a pot of coffee. Ladso took a cup and joined Nikki, Britt and Pi at the table.

Britt pointed up with his thumb. "He's settled for the night?"

Ladso nodded. "He looked dead on his feet. I bet he is in the shower, maybe even in bed." He looked embarrassed. Standing, he walked over and pulled out a device from a high shelf. "I installed a baby monitor in his room. I thought we should observe him."

He increased the volume until they could hear the pounding of the shower from the bathroom. The video showed an empty bed.

Pi looked at Ladso admiringly. "I guess it's spying, but it's also genius."

Britt agreed. "I'm glad you thought of it. We don't know what Sharon's bite is doing to him. He seems like Frank." Britt groaned. "Is it possible he's becoming one of the Undead? We know the change involves blood but really nothing else. Sharon ingested blood at least twice while still human. We need to be careful with him."

Nikki frowned. "Should we set up a watch for the monitor?"

Ladso shook his head. "I will keep it by me while I sleep, with the volume turned up. It has motion sensors activated. I will wake if Frank so much as uses the bathroom during the night."

Pi nodded. "I guess I'll wake up too, but I don't mind. The old grouch has grown on me."

Nikki looked troubled. "Frank seemed so happy outside watching the dogs. To be honest, that's what's bugging me. He was happy and cheerful, very un-Frank. He'd always have a complaint about the weather, or aching knees… something! That's just not like him."

Ladso set down his cup. "We will have to study Murray's notes but this is not a regular occurrence so I do not think we will find much. Hopefully since he is away from Sharon and will not be bitten again, he will become more 'himself' over the next several days, gaining strength and regaining his original personality. Britt is correct. We have to be very careful. We should not tell specifics about our research with him. Are we all agreed on that?"

Everyone nodded.

"Britt, you and I will continue with research. Pi, Nikki, if you could team up as babysitters, keeping Frank occupied and away from the library. Britt and I will shift our attention to the once-bitten."

Nikki yawned. "I'm going to follow in Frank's footsteps and get an early night's sleep. Tomorrow could be a long day."

The others agreed. Britt and Nikki headed upstairs with the dogs trailing them. Ladso looked over the kitchen and surprised Pi in deciding to be a heretic and leave the coffee cups until morning. She smiled and supported his decision. Ladso grabbed the monitor and they headed upstairs.

On the steps, Britt looked at Nikki. "I'm going back to the library for a bit. There's a book I was reading earlier. Something's tickling the back of my brain. I know I've read something important. I'll bring it to my room and see what I find." He wished Nikki a good night. Ray looked at Trooper with a tiny bark and followed Britt.

Walking to her room, Nikki worried. It hadn't occurred to her that Frank might be dangerous. He was so sweet earlier. She'd been happy to see him in such a good mood but had to admit it was odd.

How does a vampire infect somebody anyway? Is their foreign blood like a virus, or a parasite? That thought gave her a chill. Can it be fought off like the flu? Reaching her door, she paused. *Don't let Sharon win, Frank.*

Feeling anxious now, she was happy Ladso had set up that baby monitor. Later, in bed, Trooper snuggled up with her, making her feel protected and she quickly drifted off to sleep.

Ladso and Pi were sitting up in bed, talking seriously. "What if Frank is somehow a lure for Sharon? Leading her to us."

Ladso believed the distance involved would be a hindrance.

"But we don't know what her capabilities are. She might be searching for him."

He gave her a queer look. "You are a cheerful one, right before bedtime. Did you teach the Brothers Grimm all their stories?" Then he pulled her to him. "You are right however. The inside and outside motion sensors are armed. There is a ring of salt poured around the house and I have scattered the dried peas as well. They blend with the grass well and animals will eat them. I will get some bright beads tomorrow. Honestly, I do not know what more we can do at this point."

She nodded then grinned at him, an entirely different expression on her face. "I can think of something."

Ladso awoke, but didn't know why until he heard the sound again, the motion sensor chiming on the baby monitor. He grabbed it off the nightstand to better see the video. The volume was up, but Frank was silent. He was also not in his bed.

Ladso squinted and saw that Frank was standing at the windows in his room. He tried to open the lock. Failing, he looked troubled as he placed his palms on the glass as though wishing to touch something, or someone, outside.

Pi sat up beside Ladso. "Hey, what's up?"

"Look at this!"

She rubbed her eyes, and looked at the small screen. "How long has he been standing like that?"

"I just noticed, but unless I slept through more than the first signal from the monitor, several seconds."

Sounding sad, Pi kept watching. "He looks troubled that he can't open the windows. What's he looking at?"

The windows in their room and Frank's windows all faced the front of the house. Ladso got to his feet and hurried to a window. "Nothing but empty street. Is he still looking?"

Pi nodded but just then, Frank turned from the window, walked back to his bed, climbed into it, rolled onto his side. Almost immediately he looked asleep.

Pi looked over at Ladso. "He just got back in bed." She shook her head. "That wasn't sleepwalking. Do you think he was looking for Sharon?"

Ladso nodded. "It is possible. She may be summoning him. We will continue to watch our friend." Ladso sat on the edge of the bed. "It is frustrating that we can do little more than sit and watch. Britt and I will intensify our search. I only know of one occurrence in which something like this happened. It did not last long but the victim behaved oddly before his death."

"His death!?" Pi reacted.

"Like my Yasminka, he had not been separated from the vampire, although his second attack did not happen as soon as hers." Noticing Pi shiver, he reassured her. "I believe Frank is safe, but if Sharon is still in St. Louis, her range is greater than I had imagined." Agitated, Ladso stood. "We must get more information. This inaction is maddening."

Pi nodded. "Yes, I want action too, and to know that Frank is safe. This needs to be figured out!"

"We will do our…" Just then, the baby monitor chimed again. This time, Frank was just going to the bathroom. They'd both looked away when he closed the door. Five minutes passed making them both anxious. Ladso quickly kissed Pi. "I am going up to check on him." Pi nodded as he left, her eyes back on the small screen.

Ladso ignored the elevator in favor of the stairs, jogging up to the fourth floor. He entered Frank's suite, rushed across the sitting room to the bedroom door which was closed. He knocked, calling Frank's name. There was no answer so he opened the door, saw the bed was still empty, and turned on the overhead lights.

He walked to the bathroom door, again knocked and called. Still, no one answered. With no other option, he turned the handle and pushed. The door swung partway and stopped, blocked by something.

Frank was lying on the floor, eyes open, a hand to the wound on his neck. Ladso squeezed through the partial opening and knelt beside Frank who was muttering something Ladso couldn't make out. He gently shook Frank by the shoulder, calling his name, but Frank's muttering grew louder, more agitated. Suddenly he shrieked. A moment later he blinked, focused his eyes, and looked puzzled. "Ladso, why are you in my bathroom? Wait. Better question, why am I on the floor?"

"You must have been sleep-walking, Frank. Do you remember getting out of bed? Had you been dreaming?"

Frank sat up, wobbling, and thinking hard. "I remember that amazingly comfortable bed. Yeah, I had all kinds of crazy dreams. Someone was calling my name." His frown deepened. "It was someone I wanted to see, but couldn't find. I think they were far away." Frank rubbed at his face. "So vivid. I usually can't remember my dreams. Anyway, I tried to call, but they couldn't hear me."

Frank's eyes suddenly widened. He sucked in a deep breath and grabbed Ladso's arm. "My attack! I remember what happened! That's when I screamed and woke up to see you looking down at me." He took another breath. "I'm glad it was you!"

Ladso offered to help Frank to his feet just as Pi came to the door. Frank looked over. "What's going on? Is everyone here?"

Pi knelt by Frank. "No, there's just Ladso and me." She looked at Ladso. "The doctor recommended that we check on you during the night, so Ladso came up."

Sounding annoyed, Frank began, "Well that seems…" He grunted a sigh. "Well, I guess it's a good idea with me stumbling around in my sleep and falling."

"Let us get you up," Ladso took one arm while Pi took the other.

"Don't cripple yourselves now," Frank strained to do his share. "We don't want nurse maids for all of us."

Back on his feet then back in bed, Ladso peered intently at Frank. "You remember what happened when Sharon attacked you?" Pi's eyes widened but she only sat beside Frank and listened.

Frank nodded. "Yeah. I was at home, thinking about getting out of town and the drive to Chicago. I was in the kitchen, Cat started howling. Having a fit!"

His eyes grew wide as his memory brought clarity "Under the bright ceiling light in my kitchen there was smoke, turning in on itself. It was whirling faster and faster, getting darker as it pulled into a human shape, then Sharon was standing there. She must have gotten into my house the way she'd gotten into Britt's. In a flash she was on me, holding my arms and biting into my throat. I couldn't fight her. Then I must have passed out."

Frank drank from the glass on his bedside table. "I woke up in the hospital, but didn't remember what had happened. Had no idea why I was there."

Ladso explained as he took a seat on the other side of Frank. "We were wondering when you might get here. When Britt could not reach you, he called Detective Gently and asked that he go by your place. He found you on the kitchen floor and called the ambulance."

Frank shuddered. "I had the weirdest feeling. A dream, I thought. Sharon was trying to find me, and I wanted her to." He looked at his friends. "I don't want that now!"

Ladso shook his head. "I am no expert. That was Murray, and gods, do I miss him and his knowledge. I know a vampire bite contaminates the victim. Human mouths are full of bacteria. I doubt vampires floss regularly." Pi and Frank cringed at the oddly timed joke. Ladso smiled and shrugged. "It seems their blood can do more than kill or corrupt its victim. It may create some kind of connection."

"Connection is suddenly an ugly word." Frank's face wrinkled in concern. "What are you saying?"

"Again, Frank, I am not an expert. I am only guessing, but I have heard of an incident. Britt and I will find it tomorrow. My only true experience was…" Realizing what he was about to say, Pi reached over Frank to take Ladso's hand. He nodded to her in thanks. "Long ago my fiancée was bitten. She also did not remember her attack. The creature came back and finished the job some days later." Frank reacted and Ladso spoke quickly. "We believe that getting you far away from St. Louis has provided a buffer, making it too hard for Sharon to find you."

Frank said, "Sharon finding me. There's a phrase to bring bad dreams." He cleared his throat, glanced toward the clock. "I know it's very early. Pi, would you mind brewing me a Cop-achino? Somehow, I don't find myself interested in sleeping."

Pi nodded. Ladso said, "I suspect all of us are done with sleep for the night." He grabbed Frank's arm and helped get him to his feet. The three headed for the elevator, then the kitchen.

In her dark cave, Sharon seethed. Her eyes glowed green as she rocked back and forth. She'd been reaching out with her mind, trying to connect with her policeman and failing. What she knew of this blood gift was that she should be able to sense him, find him instantly. Instead, all she got was a faint, indistinct sensation. One that told her nothing except that he was — somewhere.

She snarled, glaring at the rock wall before her. *This should not happen! He is alive. I can feel him. How is he hiding? She shook her head. How are **they** hiding him from me?*

Her eyes suddenly glowed an uglier green. They have taken him away. There is no other way they could do this. But where? She felt no geographic tug, no direction. Picking up a stone she threw it out of her cave's only opening.

She'd revisited the wounded one's home. The policemen's home as well. Both were empty, stale. They had left. Gone somewhere further than her blood sense could reach. *They don't know about my power. They've simply run away. Afraid. As well they should be.*

She chuckled, a dry sound, humorless as rattling bones. She would leave this dank opening. *They are gone. Their houses are at my disposal.* She knew Britt had a cellar. Unlike the policeman's basement, it had no windows. Her daytime rest would be in darkness and safety. There would be more opportunities to hunt there as well.

She moved that evening. Deciding to combine chores, she flagged down a taxi and grinned in anticipation of controlling the driver's mind. Making him obey her. She laughed. The driver's reward will be a dinner invitation.

She realized there was some risk in staying in the wounded one's house, but she was not afraid. She would sense the policeman if, — no, **when** he returned. She would smell the others, and she was far from helpless, even during daylight hours. *Let them come.*

Turning into smoke, she bade her uncomfortable dwelling farewell. Materializing again on the ground she decided, I will reach out to the policeman again tomorrow night. They cannot evade me forever.

She wrapped a purloined shawl tightly around her shoulders and went in search of her ride and dinner.

At an intersection, a cab pulled to the curb. The driver had considered not stopping. There was something about this woman, dressed shabbily, out late, and alone. Then his eyes met hers and he was suddenly compelled.

As he stopped the car, he unlocked the doors and hurried round to open the rear door for her. She cut her eyes at him and pointed instead to the front passenger door. Once she was in, he hurried back to his seat at the wheel.

Sharon easily controlled him. It had been a simple matter to erase his concern and fill him with the desire to do as she ordered. "Soulard," was all she said and he pulled into traffic.

Sharon knew where Britt's house was, but not the address. She didn't want the cab to be sitting near the house anyway, so she directed him to the commercial district.

As he drove, she studied the neighborhood and was delighted. Bars were on nearly every corner: foot traffic makes for easy targets.

Finally, she told the driver to pull off the main drag and then into a dark alley. He left the keys in the cab and got out. Suddenly a horrified squeal pierced the night. Silence followed, broken only by a disgusting, sucking sound.

At 6:00am with dawn still an hour away, Ladso and Frank sat in the kitchen. Pi had visited until the Cop-achino was ready, then, convinced all was well, went back to bed.

Ladso saw that, despite Frank's agitation and his consumption of caffeine, he was exhausted. Today will be a nap day, he thought. Possibly for myself as well.

Frank had said all he was going to say for the time being. Ladso stood, stretched, and started preparing breakfast. After washing the previous evening's coffee cups, he peeled and sliced cantaloupe, rinsed strawberries, blueberries and blackberries, the whole time keeping an eye on Frank who seemed to be thinking of nothing but his drink. His previously furrowed brow was as smooth as he'd ever seen it.

Ladso preheated the oven, collected a sheet of handmade croissants from the refrigerator and set them in to bake. Next, he removed a container of fresh cream which he poured into a mixing bowl and he turned the beaters on; soon the cream had stiffened into peaks and mounds. He returned the bowl to the refrigerator and set two frying pans on the stovetop. One he filled with bacon, the other with sausages patties.

Ladso took a look at Frank, whose eyes were closed over his coffee.

Soon, the room filled with amazing aromas which opened Frank's eyes. He watched quietly as Ladso laid out a European-style buffet breakfast. Everything from sliced creamy Havarti cheese to spicy sausage patties and bacon. Next was the fresh fruit, with whipped cream to top it. All was set next to piping hot croissants, both crusty and buttery. He then placed toppings on the counter — honey, marmalade, jam. Frank, sniffing at the croissants predicted, "They won't need anything smeared on them. Smell almost as good as donuts. By the way, where are the donuts?" Ladso turned at a loss until he saw Frank's grin. Both of them laughed.

Britt and Nikki entered with Pi close behind. Stepping over to the loaded table, Pi grinned down on the detective. "Good morning, Frank!" Looking tired again, he gave a faint wave in return.

Nikki looked at the spread and gasped. "I'm going to weigh two hundred pounds eating like this!" Despite her words, she was quick to take up a plate. Virtuously, she loaded up on fruit… then grabbed some bacon. She joined Frank at the table, noticed his lethargy, and asked if he wanted her to fix him a plate. He lifted his head and nodded. Worried if Frank was all right, she looked toward Ladso who whispered, "We will talk later."

In moments, everyone was at the table with filled plates and cups. With a full plate before him, Frank perked up and was pleased to see everyone as he ate the hearty breakfast.

When everyone finished, Nikki and Pi helped Ladso clear the table and all quickly returned to their seats.

Ladso cleared his throat, getting everyone's attention. "Frank had an adventurous night. Can I tell the team, Frank?" A quick nod and wave from Frank put the attention back on Ladso. "Last night I found him on the floor in his bathroom."

Britt and Nikki, hearing this for the first time, reacted, but Frank waved off their concern. "I'm fine. Go ahead Ladso."

Ladso continued. "He had been dreaming that Sharon was looking for him. Considering he was bitten, her looking seems likely. He also remembered what happened the night Sharon attacked him." After repeating Frank's description, Ladso looked at Frank. "Did I forget anything?"

Frank shook his head. "There isn't that much to tell. Yup, that was everything."

Nikki patted Frank's hand. "How do you feel this morning?"

"Tired. It wasn't a particularly restful night."

Ladso nodded. "Britt and I will be working in Murray's library most of the day. Nikki and Pi are at your service. For you Frank, a nap might be in order."

Frank suddenly gave Ladso a look that would have quailed a fainter heart. "I'm not geriatric. I don't need a nap and I don't need damned babysitters either."

Pi's expression revealed her worry but it had a sharp edge. "We're not babysitters, Frank. Doctor's orders are that you rest. I thought you'd appreciate the company, but if you'd rather sit and sulk on your own, as long as you rest, it can be arranged."

Frank rubbed his face and sighed heavily. "I'm sorry, I'm an ass." Pi shrugged, making a slow smile spread across his face. "You are all being very kind. I guess a bad night's sleep, and the reason for it, have me bent out of shape."

Now, Pi smiled. "That's better."

Frank set down his cup. "Yes, Nikki, I would love to watch you work with the dogs again, and Pi, if you're up for a movie marathon this afternoon, please monitor your grandpa Frank." He made a face but squeezed in a grin as well.

Ladso reminded Frank that the nurse would visit during the day to do a complete physical. He got a scowl in return.

Nikki collected the dogs, and Frank got up and pulled on the coat she'd retrieved for him.

Maybe it was the overcast weather. Maybe it was because Nikki was working on what she called reinforcing the fundamentals of training, but it was pretty boring stuff — sit, lay down, come, stop, drop, no. Frank found himself cold and uncomfortable, as well as bored. He told Nikki he was going inside for a warm drink. She waved and let him know she'd be another half hour.

In the house, Frank discovered Ladso doing prep work in the kitchen. He collected a cup of coffee and sat to watch the show. Ladso was deep in some mysterious food preparations. Frank had no idea what Ladso was cooking — but he always enjoyed eating it.

Pi entered. "Don't you have research to do?"

Ladso replied without looking over. "I have got to get this started or we will starve tonight." Everyone laughed.

"In this house?" Frank shook his head and lifted his cup. "When froth piggies fly." There was more laughter.

"I'm going to make us some popcorn." She looked at Frank. "Movies always go better with popcorn."

Frank agreed.

Before the popcorn began popping, Ladso said, "Let the pots simmer. I will set my phone timer to remind me to check on them. I am going upstairs."

Minutes later, carrying a large bowl of popcorn and directing Frank, Pi walked to the sitting room. There was a ridiculously large screen on the wall above a shelf holding a DVD player. "We also have cable and a streaming device." Pi frowned. "All the DVDs are intellectual documentaries and other brainy stuff so we better find something good on the wires."

After a little searching, Frank chose Bela Lugosi in "Dracula." "Did somebody say cheesy?" Pi giggled and sat with the popcorn between them.

Frank seemed interested, commenting on the characters, admiring the costumes, and laughing at Lugosi's over dramatic delivery of his lines. Everything went well… until the scene when Dracula came in through a window, and hypnotized the woman with his look. Frank fidgeted, muttering under his breath. "It wasn't like that. Not at all."

Pi listened without comment. When the movie ended, she declared herself tired of dark and gloomy. She grinned at Frank. "Have you heard of 'The Princess Bride'?" Frank looked at her blankly, making her laugh. "Oh boy, you have no clue what a treat you're in for!"

The next ninety minutes flew by with laughter, a random popcorn fight, as well as the occasional snore from the sleeping Frank. As the final credits spooled, Frank shook his head. "How did I miss this movie before now? It's amazing!" He didn't seem to notice that he'd missed several parts.

Pi asked if he had any requests for the next movie. Frank shook his head. "I leave it to your excellent taste, madam. I doubt you'll find one better than the last."

She pondered for a few minutes, gave a wicked grin. "I've got it!" A minute later, she turned off cable and switched to the streaming device. "My Cousin Vinny." Her eyes flashed and Frank admitted it was another movie he hadn't seen. They had an uproarious viewing despite Frank's short naps. At the end, he claimed his sides ached from laughing so much. Pi declared the same was true for her.

With the final credits still rolling, Ladso popped his head in the door. "Frank, your nurse is here. Pi, can you get him to his suite? You are going to be examined from head to toe. The doctors are also watching your blood count. He is certain to draw blood, too. I have to sign some paperwork and I will bring him…"

Frank's mood had turned like the shark from Jaws. "Get me to my room? You don't think I can find my own damned room? I'm not brain dead or decrepit!" He stood. "I'll be upstairs." He cut his eyes toward Ladso. "In my room. When you bring him up, don't come in." Frank stomped toward the door but turned before going through. Looking back, he spoke sweetly. "Thanks Pi. That was a hoot!"

After the door closed behind Frank, she looked at Ladso. "He was fine through three movies." She shrugged. "That mood shift could give a girl whiplash. Did you see that grin as he left? What the hell!"

Ladso looked worried. "I hope his mood holds through the nurse's visit."

Pi looked at Ladso. "What do you think?"

Ladso looked at her with sadness darkening his eyes. "It is the vampire blood working on him. His body fights against it. It is more than poor sleep that causes his fatigue. His bouts of sleepwalking do not help either. I believe the mood shifts are his psyche struggling against another's thoughts in his head. Britt and I have found very little so far. Unless something is uncovered, we are riding blind. Watch him closely."

Frank escorted the nurse back to the main floor of the house and steered him toward the kitchen. Ladso and the team were there. The nurse smiled as he lifted his pad. "Good news. Mr. Bolden's numbers are all within the normal range."

Frank was pouring himself a cup of coffee. "Not bad for an old geezer addicted to coffee and donuts."

"Old geezer?" Pi looked at Frank with wide eyes.

"Well, if I'm to let you occasionally refer to me as Grandpa…"

The nurse continued. "We are waiting on the results of the blood tests, of course, but those will not be in until tomorrow." He looked toward Frank. "Someone will call and update you."

Everyone smiled toward Frank and he mirrored their expressions.

Ladso took Frank's hand and shook it. "As soon as you get a clean bill of health, you can rejoin the team with our planning."

Frank resembled a racehorse champing at the bit. He was looking forward to the end of enforced rest and relaxation.

Ladso chased everyone out so he could complete preparations for dinner. He also needed time to reflect on his conversation with Pi. Sharon had found them easily in St. Louis, although how remained a mystery. Their research had yet to reveal anything helpful and Ladso was nervous about the vampire's range. *Did distance reduce Sharon's ability and what distance was enough?*

He felt confident that Chicago put enough distance between Frank and Sharon, but they still had nothing concrete to support that confidence. *Our security system and locks will be as ineffective as Britt's were if she comes to the house in gaseous form. Also, we don't know how she sees in that state. Will the salt surrounding the house affect her in that state? There are so many unknowns. Sharon is certainly a vampire now so she should have arithmomania.* He shook his head. *For the safety of the team, "**should**" is not enough. I will be sleeping with a lighter and mace on my nightstand. Except for Frank, the rest of us must do the same.*

Ladso lifted the stew pot lid, and carelessly dumped diced vegetables and fresh herbs into the stew which would finish simmering an hour from now. Tonight's bread was already kneaded into loaves. He brushed them with egg white before slipping them into the preheated oven. He looked over the kitchen, ensuring that all was well before he took off his apron, and washed his hands. Then he set his timer, and went to join Britt in the library.

Britt was buried deep in a volume. Not one of Murray's journals, but a crumbling tome that looked centuries old. He started when Ladso entered. Britt grinned. "Ladso, come look at this."

Ladso moved to Britt's side. "Does it explain how Sharon found us? That is most on my mind."

Britt looked excited. "I believe it does — if it's correct, of course. All these old legends and folktales are questionable." He flipped to a bookmarked page, pointed at a paragraph, and read aloud. 'Upon becoming a vampire, incredibly enhanced senses result, including the sense of smell.' "It goes on to detail sightings in which this was confirmed." He looked up at Ladso. "It seems Sharon has a better nose on her than Trooper." He shook his head. "Actually, she's more in line with a bloodhound. It's not surprising she found us in a relatively small corner of the city. Bloodhounds have exceptional abilities. Finding Frank's home is a bit more surprising but it better exposes the extent of her powers. As we are 300 miles away, that ability won't help her locate us here." Sitting back in his chair, Britt reached over to hold the stump of his lost arm. "Of course, now we have Frank here. That may change the situation."

Ladso nodded. "We will need to plan before we return to St. Louis on how we will avoid her detection of us while we hunt for her. Bringing Frank with us is likely to make that impossible if she is able to enter his mind." He paced across the room. "We cannot possibly return until we are completely ready to do battle." Britt nodded vigorously.

Ladso was sitting at a table with Murray's journal from the excursion when he and Britt met. As he turned a page, his timer chimed. Carrying the journal, he stood and left for the kitchen. Britt was so focused on what he was reading that he barely looked up.

Dinner that evening was hearty, simple and delicious — "peasant fare," Ladso proclaimed. He dished out the rich beef stew into bowls, passing them around the table. The bread was hot, crusty and delicious, perfect for soaking up the extra stew broth. Nikki poured glasses of a rich red wine, which Ladso had selected saying it was the perfect accompaniment to the dinner. Pi, who preferred white wine, took a sip, followed by a bite of her stew. With a wide-eyed grin, she gave him the "thumbs up" gesture. Ladso looked at Frank. "I checked with your nurse, and wine fits your diet, so enjoy."

Conversation was subdued, but everyone ate and drank heartily. Dessert was tiny tartlets, like miniature cheesecakes topped with fruits, just one bite to each tartlet. They were delicious, and everyone said so.

The ladies insisted on washing up as Britt and Ladso chatted idly with Frank. Soon everyone was off to bed, dogs included.

Before too long, the motion sensor's soft chime on the baby monitor woke Ladso and Pi. They'd been expecting a night like the one before, but tonight was different. Frank, already out of bed, wrapped his robe around himself, and left the suite. *Where the devil is he going?* Ladso wondered as he and Pi also grabbed robes and went to find where Frank was going.

Britt woke to Ray's growling, followed by what was more puppy yip than real bark. Still, there was menace behind the sound. Britt turned on the light, and fumbled for his glasses. The dog was facing the bedroom window, hackles raised and trembling with rage, not fear. Whatever was going on, little Ray wanted a piece. Britt saw nothing out of the ordinary but clearly Ray had sensed something. Turning back to his bedside table, he toggled the intercom to Nikki's room. "Nikki, are you awake?"

There was no reply for a long moment, long enough for Britt to repeat himself. The hair on his neck prickled as he tried a third time. "Are you OK?"

"I forgot about the intercom switch, sorry. I'm fine but something's wrong. Trooper is at the window, and growling. I think every hair on his back is standing at attention but I can't see anything out the window."

Britt toggled the intercom again. "I'll try Ladso." A moment later he was back. "Neither he nor Pi are answering. I didn't disturb Frank but I'm going to see what's wrong."

"I'll meet you in the hall." Nikki was up and at the door seconds later with Trooper at her hip.

They met in the hall just as the house alarm blared. They headed for the stairs.

As Ladso shut the alarm off, the sudden silence was startling. Moments later, he and Pi entered the kitchen, guiding Frank between them. As they sat at the table, Britt, Nikki, and the dogs rushed in.

Looking at the three seated at the table, Nikki asked, "What happened?"

Ladso held up a hand and spoke in a quiet, easy tone. "Frank, what were you doing?"

Frank shook his head mutely, still in a daze despite walking to the first floor and after hearing the alarm.

Ladso looked over at the others. "Frank unlocked the deadbolt on the front door. As you all know, I keep the key in it. He opened the door triggering the alarm. When we found him, he seemed totally unaware of the alarm's blare or where he was." Ladso shook his head. "I think we can guess why he opened the door. He must sense Sharon's call."

Nikki looked solemn as an owl. "She's searching for him, and he's feeling her pull. Does this mean she's found him?"

"I do not know. I am locking Frank's door for the rest of the night. I will sit with him, just in case. The windows are locked, but glass breaks."

Frank was still confused as Ladso linked arms with him and helped him to his feet. "Let us get back to bed my friend." Ladso nodded to the group as he led Frank toward the elevator.

Despite the seclusion of Britt's cellar, the fading sun brought Sharon to full alertness. Although she didn't dream anymore, at times her mind would wander for long periods. She had been reminiscing about the old days at the Academy, when the school was open and full of girls, and it was easy to keep the Old Ones fed.

Now, she decided that tonight, she would hunt children, not adults. It was far more hazardous… but so wickedly delicious! She checked that her clothing looked acceptable, then focused, and manifested outside the front door. It was possible the blood of children might have rejuvenating properties. She had never really tried before, and was looking forward to finding out.

Near the end of the residential area in Soulard, there were several strip malls. One had a Junior Dance Academy, which had evening hours. She walked to it, finding a shadowy spot around the corner. With her preternatural hearing, she knew when each child left the Academy. Eventually, one would leave and walk home; not all those girls had mothers who owned cars.

Vicky left the dance studio wildly excited. There was going to be a pageant, and she had one of the lead roles! She nearly skipped down the sidewalk, paying no attention to anything but her thoughts. She neared the corner where the empty grocery store sat, and as always, angled across the property to cut the corner of that segment of her walk. It was dark and creepy, walking behind the loading docks, all boarded up now, past the big metal storage shed, then up through the dark parking lot until she hit the street again.

As she passed the loading docks, she heard a soft whimpering. It sounded like a puppy. She stood still, listening, straining to hear it again. It was definitely a puppy, and a young one too, from the sounds it made. They came from a dark cavern between two loading docks. Vicky was too worried about the puppy to be afraid.

As best as she could, in the darkling light, she sifted through piles of trash, looking for the puppy. The whimpers and cries were getting louder, as if the puppy recognized someone was searching for it. She moved aside a big pile of old rags, and found the puppy. She was puzzled, because it was tied down, so it couldn't escape. She climbed over the rags to get to the puppy, which was yelping, wriggling, and falling over itself trying to get to her.

She scooted closer, and the puppy climbed up into her lap. Pleased, she worked on the rope knotted around its neck. The knots were stiff and hard to unpick. Suddenly the puppy growled, gave a puppy bark, then climbed underneath Vicky's crossed legs, shivering. She stood up slowly, turning herself around.

A shadowy figure stood between her and the freedom of the parking lot. Vicky was scared, and tried to remember what her dad had taught her. The creature swooped close, and without thought Vicky grabbed the puppy and held it tightly. She raced past the creature, jumping wide in case it grabbed. Then she ran as fast as her feet would go, angling across the parking lot, headed toward the brightly-lit street. *I've made it! I'm safe!* The thoughts flashed through her mind, when she was yanked off her feet. The puppy dropped and raced to safety.

The creature clutched Vicky close to her, glared at her, and suddenly the girl quit struggling. Now that Sharon had control of the child's mind, it was an easy matter to return with her, back to the shadowy darkness of the loading docks.

Sharon gloated at her luck. She caressed the velvety-soft skin, felt the satin hair, smelled the freshness of the girl. A string of drool slid down her chin, unnoticed. She tilted the child's head back, exposing her delicate neck... when suddenly a splash of red and blue lights flooded the back area behind the store, including the loading docks, and the spaces between them.

With a vicious curse, Sharon clutched the child tightly, and dematerialized, reappearing inside the old grocery store. The child was not in her arms. Then she heard her crying outside, a policeman speaking to her, calming her. Sharon manifested again, ending up outside, on the sidewalk on the front street. Luckily, no one saw her sudden appearance. She turned, walked back toward the downtown area of Soulard.

She was seething, deprived of her gluttonous feast. She walked faster and faster, passing people on the street without seeing them, thinking only of her destination. Closing in on the bar area, she slowed down, thinking... *If I can't have a child, I will have a barely-legal adult. Maybe even an underage drinker.*

Sharon began prowling along the sidewalk in front of the bars, looking for those which seemed most raucous, and thus most likely to have younger drinkers as clientele. She found one, Tree-Fiddy, which for some reason had a likeness of the Loch Ness monster on their bar sign. The noise was deafening, even outside. Sharon nodded. This would do perfectly. She went in, was not asked for ID, ignored the bar, and began looking around the packed room. People were dancing, talking, laughing, and drinking. No one was smoking, and Sharon was thankful for small pleasures. The sound of the band, with the roar of voices talking over it, was a physical vibration that Sharon felt in her gut.

Then she perked up. She saw a girl, light chestnut curls and round cheeks, in a small group talking near her. The girl looked maybe 16. Sharon was certain the girl was not 21, so was here with a fake ID. She nodded, pleased. Maybe not as good as the child, but certainly better than stringy old bums. Sharon used her mind control, looking at the girl, willing her to look back at her. Finally, the girl looked up, eyes blank, and turned her head until she saw Sharon. Ignoring her friends' questions, she walked away from them. Passing Sharon, she walked to the main door, and out of the club. Sharon carefully followed at a distance. Culling from the herd like this could be dangerous.

Outside, her girl was standing quietly, near the building, not talking, just waiting. Sharon walked up to her like an old friend. "Hello, my lamb, are you ready for the slaughter? I'm going to walk past you and I want you to follow me when I do."

Sharon walked nonchalantly past the girl, then around the corner and toward the back of the building, to the alley, which was dark, and overlaid with noxious odors. She turned the girl to face her, then slashed her neck open with her fangs, drinking in huge gulps from the jugular. No tidy meal, this was slaking her rage. When she finally finished, the girl was a tiny bag of skin, bones and hair. Sharon picked up the carcass and tossed it into one of the nearby dumpsters.

Feeling somewhat soothed, she decided she could return to Britt's house now.

Ladso yawned, stretched, and tried to ignore a stiffness in his back. The no longer comfortable chair he sat in was better suited for reading than sleeping. Positioned beside the door to Frank's bedroom, it made for lousy sleep. All remained quiet since he got Frank back in his bed.

Frank laid in the same position as he'd been in an hour before and he was snoring, something he hadn't been doing before or Ladso would have heard it over the monitor. Ladso took that as a sign that Sharon was no longer disturbing the detective's sleep.

He quietly left the bedroom, and the suite. The rising dawn gave him confidence that Frank would continue to sleep, because Sharon would be less active during the day.

Barefoot, he padded down the stairs and to his own suite of rooms to shower and change. He'd yet to replace the moccasins Ray had claimed as his. He entered the room silently, wanting to watch Pi sleep. She'd curled up on his side of the bed, he noticed with a pang in his heart.

Ladso grabbed fresh clothes and entered the bathroom to shower and shave. Water poured out the shower head, hot and steaming.

Ladso felt each droplet peppering his body with tiny, lovely bites of heat, turning his skin pink. He reduced the heat and scrubbed down. He shaved in the shower, both his face and scalp. He proceeded by feel alone as it was an exercise on autopilot after many years.

To finish, he turned the water to icy cold, and stood underneath the spray for a long minute. He then shut the water off, and exited wide awake.

Pi was awake as well, sitting up in bed when he reentered the bedroom. She raised an eyebrow, and whistled. "Isn't it illegal in Illinois to look so damn chipper this early? Especially after the night we just went through?" She grinned and reached up for him. He eagerly embraced her, with thoughts of cooking breakfast slipping from his mind. She laughed, a warm, low sound, gave him a peck on the cheek and broke off the hug.

"I'm gross. I need a shower, and nobody is going to kiss this mouth until I thoroughly disinfect it. It tastes like dinosaurs pooped in there last night." She climbed out of bed, collected her own clean clothing, and headed for the bathroom. Shortly afterward, the sound of the shower spray drifted through the room but Ladso was already headed for the kitchen.

He started a pot of coffee, then began peeling potatoes for hash browns. He chopped onions and peppers, then cubed the ham. Next, he whipped the eggs just slightly, but not too much, added salt and pepper, plus a little cayenne, and a few other ingredients before folding everything in.

He started heating the oil for frying for the hash browns. He preheated another heavy skillet, oiled it with butter, and added the egg mixture to it. He put the potatoes into the hot grease, and added salt and pepper while the omelet solidified. The hash browns were ready to flip within minutes, and the omelet was, too. First, he added grated cheddar cheese, and then folded the omelet in on itself.

Pi entered the kitchen as he was finishing with the omelets. She swung by to show off her fresh mouth with a tasty kiss before heading for the coffee pot.

No one else was up, so they enjoyed their breakfast together, not saying much, just savoring the delicious food. Ladso poured them a second cup of coffee after they finished breakfast. Pi smiled in appreciation and he looked at her with a mournful gaze. She tolerated his silent scrutiny as long as she could, which wasn't long. "What?"

"I will bet now I cannot kiss you again because you have coffee breath."

She got up and moved close to him, snuggling underneath his arms. "Let's try it." Her voice was husky. He didn't answer, just bent his head so their lips were barely touching.

"Hey! Keep that stuff for when you're off duty. You'll corrupt my morals." Frank smirked at them as he walked into the kitchen.

Pi rolled her eyes. "Good morning to you, too, Sunshine. You snore, in case you didn't know. Poor Ladso got to spend his night listening to your racket."

Frank was confused. "What would make you do a thing like that?" He stopped, paused, thought hard. "Wait, something happened last night, didn't it?"

Softly, Pi spoke up. "What did happen last night, Frank?"

Frank took a seat at the table and spoke in a soft voice. "Someone was calling for me. They were far away — they couldn't find me. I thought that if I went outside, they'd be able to..." He paused for a moment and frowned. "Sounds weird, but I thought they'd smell me, so I went to go outside. They tried to reach me, but I was too far away. Then I woke up in bed."

Ladso and Pi exchanged glances. Frank was again unaware of things he was doing, as if he was hypnotized. Just then, dawn's sunshine peeked through the kitchen windows. Frank reacted as if someone threw a bucket of cold water on him.

"Ladso? Pi? What? Why am I in the kitchen?"

Pi asked again. "What happened last night, Frank?"

Frank glared. "Why the hell are you asking me that? I went to bed. Now I'm standing in the kitchen and it's evidently morning." He put his face in his hands. "Whatever this is, I don't like it."

Pi cut her eyes to Ladso. Frank suddenly couldn't remember what had happened, though a moment before, he had remembered.

Ladso spoke reassuringly. "Frank, you are still recuperating, and your body is demanding rest. You were probably sleepwalking when

90

you came down for breakfast this morning. I am sorry I startled you." Realizing that the truth would only aggravate Frank, Pi changed the subject. "Would you like some coffee?"

Frank was totally distracted by the thought of coffee, but with his first sip, he grumbled, "You never have donuts."

Ladso just laughed and pulled out a pastry box full of donuts. "Had them delivered by Food Stop this morning. I doubt they will live up to those from your favorite place back home but I thought you might appreciate them." He set the opened box in front of Frank.

Frank grinned. "My buddy Mike Gently would say that you represented all the major donut food groups. I approve." He consumed two cups of coffee and three donuts before standing. "I'm going to go take a shower. I'll come back and talk more with you guys later."

Ladso and Pi looked at each other with troubled expressions. Pi retook her seat. "I think you did right not to go into any detail about last night. Sharon is really messing up Frank's head."

Ladso sadly nodded. "I have pondered about this vampire blood, and its effects on people. It resembles the rabies virus. Enters the body through a bite, and slowly creeps it way toward the brain. We will keep looking through Murray's books and journals, but we will need to detail every observation we can in our notes, so this opportunity to learn is not lost."

He stood. "I've got to prepare breakfast for Britt and Nikki." Together they made quick work and were ready to sit and share their observations of Frank when the rest of their team arrived.

Pi brought over the coffee, and everyone enthusiastically took a cup.

Britt sat at the table while Nikki fed the dogs. "How was Frank the rest of the night?"

Pi dropped onto her chair. "He was fine until this morning."

After hearing their description of the morning, Nikki wondered. "Like he was hypnotized. It sure sounds like what happened to me at the school and the concert." Nikki set down her cup and actually shivered.

Britt agreed. "Also, the 'someone' looking for him." Britt frowned. "Just like his 'dream' the night before."

Pi nodded. "And then he forgot all about it and went up for a shower."

Ladso pointed at the kitchen window. "Yes, and the forgetting happened just as the sun crested the house across the alley and shone into the kitchen."

"Yes." Pi's eyes were troubled. "The forgetting and the anger." She shrugged. "Then he ate three sugar-filled donuts, drank two cups of coffee, and ***then*** went up for a shower."

Nikki wondered aloud. "When the dogs got agitated, Frank was up and trying to help Sharon find him. Do you think they were sensing Sharon in Frank?"

"Maybe." Ladso frowned in thought. "Your description of their agitation certainly sounds like more than just having heard Frank moving around."

Britt pointed out, "At least we know the distance is enough. She can sense him, even reach him but can't find him. Hopefully that continues. My only concern is if it's some kind of, I don't know, echolocation. What bats use when hunting their prey. If each try gives her additional clues to his location."

Ladso shrugged. "Trooper and Ray are very good early alert systems. If they sound off, use the intercom immediately. All we can do is keep a close eye on him. For his safety I will spend my nights in his sitting room. For our safety as well. We do not know the extent of Sharon's control of him. He left his room, travelled down multiple flights of stairs and unlocked the door before opening it. Could she force him to hurt one of us in our sleep as well? We just do not know."

Pi suddenly had a peculiar expression on her face. "Speaking of, isn't it taking him an awfully long time to shower and change? Do you think we should check on him?"

Ladso immediately volunteered, but everyone ended up following him. He quickly jogged up the stairs, then turned down the hall to Frank's suite. He waved the others to hold back, hoping not to anger Frank again. He rapped his knuckles sharply on the door. "Frank, are you OK?"

There was no reply. Ladso opened the suite door, feeling a strong sense of déjà vu. He walked through the sitting room into the bedroom, which, as expected, was empty. The bathroom door was closed. He knocked on it, hard. "Frank! All good?" Again, no response. "Frank, answer me!" Ladso called.

He turned the door knob, and the door opened freely. Frank was standing at the sink, staring into the mirror, lost in whatever he was seeing. He held his toothbrush loosely in one hand, and water was trickling out of the faucet.

Trying not to bring Frank to full consciousness, Ladso took the toothbrush, set it down, and shut off the faucet. Then he gently took Frank by the arm and led him to bed. Frank gently resisted, pointing at the mirror. He softly spoke.

"If I look just at the corners of the room, out of the very corners of my eyes, I can almost see who is calling me. I want to see them. If I see them, maybe I can tell them I'm here."

The blood in Ladso's veins turned to ice.

"Come on, Frank," he murmured. "You need some rest. Then you will see better, I promise." Frank came along, seemingly hearing Ladso's words. Once in bed he fell into a deep sleep within seconds.

Ladso went to the hall and waved the rest of the team in. They stopped in the sitting room where Ladso described what had just happened.

Pi moved closer to Ladso. "Should we be talking in here?"

Ladso pulled Pi close to his side. "He is sound asleep right now, but I agree: we will not discuss anything of importance with Frank. We do not know if this corner of his eyes plan will work, but if he does manage to speak to her, we do not want him to have any information that helps her. It is disturbing that even in daylight she is trying. Britt, can you sit with him for a couple of hours? I have a few things I need to take care of, and I would rather not have him unattended."

Nikki volunteered instead, allowing Britt to return to his research. Ladso reminded her of the intercom. "Call at any sign of trouble." She nodded. Pi left to help Ladso. As their voices faded in volume while moving down the hall, Nikki sat alone, listening to Frank's deep, slow breaths.

♪

In Britt's dark cellar, Sharon's eyes widened. She'd felt Frank in her mind. Unbidden. She smiled and for the first time since her death, closed her eyes.

♪

Pi looked at Ladso, and her face betrayed her worry. "He's getting worse."

"We do not know that for certain, but we need to find answers. I will study while sitting guard in Frank's room tonight. I vaguely remember a case, similar to Frank's. Again, there were ancient rituals performed. To my recollection, Murray reported that they might have worked. If I can locate that entry, it might give us an approach with Frank."

In the kitchen, Ladso began filling the sink. "This is how I think. Please bring all the dirty items from the table, but do not speak." Pi nodded and kissed him on the cheek.

♪

An hour later the kitchen was spotless and Ladso turned to Pi.

"Britt has already altered his research to focus on Frank's problem. He told me about an old tome with practical suggestions. I may take it with me for my overnight watch."

He stopped talking, his eyes on her face. She stiffened. "What's wrong?"

"I will not have you sleeping by my side. I will miss you."

She smiled. "We will have the rest of our lives together. Don't be a worry wart." Ladso was puzzled by the term, making her laugh. "Never mind, what other chores need doing?"

"We need to arrange a caterer to have our meals brought in for a few days. Staying up overnight, I will not have time to cook." He grinned at her, flicked the tip of her nose. "You seem to enjoy eating, my dear."

Pi shrugged. "Don't mind it."

"Also, I want to collect some of Murray's journals, for my night shifts. If you and Nikki can trade off staying with Frank during the day, then Britt can continue his research uninterrupted, and I am the only one who will have an odd sleep schedule. Hopefully, it will just be a few days."

"And lastly, I have paperwork regarding the estate that need my attention. Things I have been putting off which need to be read and signed. That should not take me more than an hour. Please tell Britt I will need Murray's journals for the ten years after the excursion we had together. Then if you could, call the caterers. I will sign papers, do banking, and call brokers."

Ladso went to his personal study, while Pi went to speak to Britt and collect the journals. She hoped to have a few personal minutes with Ladso before he had to sit with Frank.

Pi returned with Britt. "I want to be sure I understand exactly what you're looking for." He put the journals he'd brought with him on a corner of Ladso's desk.

Ladso set his papers aside. "I am looking for something that will allow us to reverse, or break, Frank's connection with Sharon. Murray discussed a case that I believe might be helpful."

Britt frowned. "Some arcane ritual? I know his journals tell how the peasants violated the corpses of dead victims, to keep them from rising. I haven't seen anything like Frank's case, but the book I told you about might have the answer."

"Wherever we can find it." Ladso leaned forward. "I believe there are notes in Murray's journals as well. We will search together. You during the day, and me at night while I watch Frank."

"I certainly haven't gone through all the journals, but the book is fascinating. It contains many notes in Murray's hand. Sadly, it has no table of contents and the organization is — unusual. Although several centuries old, it represents an effort to separate legend from fact regarding the Undead, and other creatures. He included recipes, instructions, descriptions of rituals. Working as a team we should be able to find it, if there is really anything to be found."

Ladso sat back in his seat. "That scene with Frank in the bathroom this morning was absolutely terrifying. He is trying to reach Sharon, despite not being aware."

Britt spoke up, concerned. "Are you sure you want all the night shifts? I don't mind sharing those with you."

Ladso shook his head. "One of us with a disturbed sleep cycle is too many already."

Britt brought up the dogs. "Maybe having one of them with you would give an early warning to Frank's awakening.

Ladso agreed. "I will bring Trooper in with me. Now, for the day."

"Nikki and I will be trading off. Frank has enjoyed watching her train the dogs, so that will take up part of the morning hours. The nurse has given him exercises since his bloodwork has all cleared. We both will exercise with him. Our working alongside him will make it feel less like Frank's being babysat. He does not particularly like that."

Britt chuckled. "And he's made no secret of it."

"You ain't just whistling Dixie there, brother." Pi accompanied her remark with a whistle and the tip of an imaginary cap. "In the afternoons, Frank and I will continue our movie marathons. I'm picking ones that will keep him amused, without setting him off. I think I've got a handle on his taste. Two movies will easily fill an afternoon. He'll be with all of us during dinner and afterwards, as we unwind our days. Then it's off to Ladso's tender mercies at night."

Britt stood. "If there's an answer to be found, we'll find it. We have to." Taking his cup, he left for the library.

Ladso looked to Pi. "Thanks to you both for handling Frank during the day. Watch him closely for signs of Sharon getting in his head. The caterer will typically arrive about 15 minutes before meal time. They will call when on their way. Please give them your cell number. You get to choose from the menu."

Pi laughed. "Swapping roles. Not what I was expecting but this could be fun too!" With that riposte, she left his study whistling an innocent if off-key tune. Ladso shook his head, chuckling. Then he focused on the paperwork at hand.

Things went smoothly that day. The weather was nice again, and once Frank wakened from his morning nap, he returned to enjoying the dog training session. Nikki said they had graduated from basics and were now working on intermediate training with Ray. Trooper, of course, was an old hand. Part of the training involved having Frank give the dogs commands, rather than just Nikki. Ray did very well, despite looking at Nikki after performing each maneuver. They only worked him for short sets, never more than 10 minutes at a time. Then there would be a play break. Puppies have short attention spans, and Nikki was determined not to ruin Ray with over-training. Moving back to his chair on the porch, Frank appreciated the breaks too.

The afternoon movie marathon with Pi was a Kevin Smith double feature, "Clerks" and "Clerks 2." Frank watched, entranced, laughing until tears rolled down his face at the ending.

"Oh please, no more. My sides hurt." He burst into another round of helpless giggles. Pi beamed with pleasure, seeing her quirky choices so well received. Just then, her cell phone rang. The caterers were 15 minutes away. She collected Frank, still hiccuping occasionally, and they went to the kitchen. Pi started a pot of coffee, and then, with some fanfare, used the house intercom.

"Greetings, fellow inmates. I will serve dinner in ten minutes. Please adjourn to the kitchen for coffee and mystery meals, courtesy of our caterers. Ladso, of course, is paying for all this. Anyway, chow's almost here. Get your butts on your chairs. This is Pi, signing out."

Nikki couldn't help but giggle at Pi's Announcer Voice, not to mention her ridiculous statement. Trying to get serious again, she asked Frank about the movie marathon. Once he mentioned "Clerks," she just started laughing. Nikki was well aware of both movies. and was a huge Kevin Smith fan.

Pi poured everyone fresh coffee, then set the pot back on the stove. She sat at the table with Frank and Nikki, waiting for dinner and the rest of the gang.

Britt and Ladso arrived as the caterers pulled up out front. Pi sent them after the caterers and dinner, since she'd slaved over a hot coffee pot part of the afternoon. Ladso and Britt expressed identical put-upon gestures, then turned on their heels.

The meal was Chinese: fried rice, lo mien, General Tso's chicken, spicy pork, egg rolls, wontons, crab Rangoon, even chop suey. Everyone scrambled to fill their plates then filled their faces.

"Oh, man, I haven't had good Chinese food in, I don't know, forever?" Pi grinned at Ladso. "That's one cuisine you've missed so far, in all your gourmet meals."

"You caught me, Pi. I cook little Chinese food of this kind. Sometime I will make you **real** Chinese cooking. You will taste the difference." He winked at her.

No dishes to wash up, and dessert provided for, Ladso declared himself incredibly spoiled. Britt got out the wine, and everyone except Ladso, who drank coffee, and Frank with a Cop-achino, had a glass to go with their cheesecake dessert. No one complained when Britt filled glasses a second time. Pi and Nikki talked over each other, explaining the finer points of Kevin Smith's body of work. Britt was familiar with most of the movies, but Ladso looked blankly at Frank, who grinned smugly in return.

Britt got up first. "I need to get back to work. There's a book in the library I need to finish, and I can get in a few more hours before bed. Good evening, everybody. I'll see you in the morning."

Ladso stood. "Come along Frank. Let us clear the room so the ladies can have a good gossip about us." Frank got up, yawned, and nodded in response. Ladso led him toward the elevator, then up to his suite.

Once inside, Ladso gestured for Frank to get ready for bed. "I will be here in the sitting room, reading. Just call out if you need me for anything."

Frank muttered something uncomplimentary, then shuffled off toward the bathroom.

Ladso moved to sit when suddenly the hallway door opened. It was Nikki with Trooper. "Don't you still want Trooper with you for the night?"

"I had completely forgotten. Yes, I do, and thank you."

Nikki petted Trooper's head. "Stay here boy. I'll see you in the morning." She looked at Ladso. "I hope you all have an easy night." She waved and shut the door.

Ladso heard the toilet flush, then water running. Both he and Trooper got comfortable. They both looked up when Frank came back out of the bathroom in his pajamas. He turned off the light in his room. "Sorry you think this is necessary, I'll try to catch a few winks for you." Ladso called good night as Frank climbed into bed.

Ladso and Trooper settled down. Ladso with one of Murray's journals, Trooper beside his chair. Ladso intended to scan through them chronologically, looking for the incident that could potentially help Frank. Soon he disappeared into the past, remembering his adventures with Murray as much as reading about them.

He realized what an exceptional journalist Murray had been. He had a way of capturing a scene, bringing you in and making you a part of it, rather than reciting dry facts and figures. If life had worked out differently, Murray might have been a brilliant novelist instead of a hunter of things supernatural.

Trooper raised his head, catching Ladso's attention. He lifted his gaze… and saw Frank standing at the bedroom doorway, staring with a purely malevolent expression.

"Frank, what are you doing up?"

Ladso didn't expect a reply. The chilling response he got was at first unintelligible. Then Frank said, "I want to see the faces of those I will kill."

With Trooper growling, Ladso jumped to his feet. He looked at Frank, whose lips still moved but made no more sound. Neither did Frank make any move to come closer. His horrid stare merged with one of pain as Ladso shouted, "Frank! Are you sleepwalking? Wake up!"

Frank started, shifted unsteadily on his feet and shook his head. "Why am I out of bed? Did I go walking again?"

Ladso was relieved by the transformation. Frank didn't look evil any more, just good old Frank. Ladso walked over and put an arm around Frank's shoulders. "Come on, my friend, you should be in bed." Frank followed willingly. Back in bed, he looked at Ladso with a bewildered expression. "What's wrong with me? Why am I doing all of this? Is it because she bit me?"

Ladso looked mournful. "Yes, it is probably because of the attack. Do not worry, Frank. We are going to fix this, I promise you."

Frank closed his eyes, trusting as a child, and was deeply asleep in moments.

Trooper had followed them into the room. Ladso petted the dog and led him back into the sitting room where both retook their seats. Ladso sat only holding the journal for several moments before he pictured the expression on Frank's face again. His jaw set with determination, he opened the book, looking again at Murray's writing.

Sunset came a few minutes later each day, as spring advanced. Sharon made her move once the sun was down, the sky thoroughly dark. She'd touched Frank's mind again. This time she felt herself take hold. "Show me. You are mine! I want to see the faces of those I will kill." She felt Frank recoil from her words. "No! Obey me!"

Her connection lost, Sharon cursed the slight lightening she'd detected in the policeman's mind. A lightening that showed her a figure but nothing more. Angrily she rose to her feet. Taking smoke form, she shoved at the air, knocking over and breaking the few things around her.

She moved up the stairs, through the space between the door and the floor. Pushing forward she found herself in the dining room. Blowing away the table cloth, she materialized over the table. Dropping onto its top, she drove her nails into the wood and carved new gouges into the polished surface.

An hour later, she rummaged through Britt's closets. Jeans, shirt, shoes, a jacket. All loose but a decent fit on her. They made her look less peculiar, while helping her blend in. Still, no one who got a good look at her would mistake her for human.

Wearing Britt's clothes, she looked out the window, ensuring the street was empty. Taking a breath, the air stirred around her. Moments later she was no longer there. Willing herself forward, she pressed herself through the small gap around the front door, then rematerialized on the sidewalk.

Not for the first time, she grieved the loss of Mother Eugenia. She would have taught Sharon all her vampiric skills. Instead, Sharon's only options were guesswork and practice.

Eyes hard, she walked down the sidewalk. Sharon strode unafraid, aware of her ability to fight off any attacker. To the right were more homes. There were few bars, and many nosy residents.

She turned left, and walked toward the rowdier part of the neighborhood, where bars stayed open late, and young drunks stumbled into dark shadows.

Sharon considered taking someone in a car. She had done that before, and it was useful when she needed a vehicle. Tonight, there was no such need. It was a short walk from Britt's house to the central hub of the Soulard area, where she could easily find a meal. A car would need to be stored, and might draw unwanted attention.

On Ninth Street, she stepped into the shadows of an alley and watched for her prey, away from the bright streetlights.

She knew her wait wouldn't be long. Someone would come by: a young couple looking to slake their lust; drug users sharing a score;

prostitutes, male or female, cutting through to the next bar on their nightly route.

A young man approached. "Hey, mama, you looking to score?" At first, she was annoyed at being seen, but then he stepped closer. "I gotcha, I gotcha. Weed? Speed? Blow? Her-ron?"

Sharon's eyes gleamed. "Yes, I am looking to score, and you have just what I want."

"All right, mama. Tell me what can I do you for?"

Sharon reached out and jerked him into the dark. Twisting his neck, she pierced his jugular with a precision that in life she could never have duplicated. Her sharp fangs pulled away, allowing the artery to quickly drain. The young man's jaw worked as though he was trying to speak, but he made no sound. She shoved the withered remains behind a trash dumpster, and wiped her hand across her mouth. Sated, she began a leisurely stroll back to her home.

# 8

The rest of the night was quiet. Ladso looked through many of the journals while Trooper slept. A few entries were similar, but none detailed the rescue he searched for. He sighed; maybe he had not looked at the right year. He turned tired eyes on the other journals. With a groan, he stood, and stretched away his stiffness. Trooper raised his head, lowered it and then raised it again as Ladso quietly walked to Frank's door. He peeked in and listened to a gentler snore than the previous night. It was past dawn, and he was happy Frank was resting peacefully.

Ladso had truly been spooked earlier. He suspected Frank might have heard directly from Sharon and worried over what she saw or learned on her end.

With Sharon on his mind, he jumped at a gentle tap on the hallway door. He walked over and opened it, finding a beaming Pi carrying a breakfast tray. He let her in, closed the door, then walked over and closed Frank's bedroom door.

"You darling!" He kissed her on the nose, then far more lingeringly on the lips. "And you brought coffee. I guess it was no great leap to imagine how exhausted I would be. Thank you!" He kissed her again.

The breakfast was plain but hearty — bagels with cream cheese and lox, orange juice, and two cups plus a travel mug of coffee. Ladso ate two of the bagels, drank juice, and two coffees. Pi had a single bagel, and a single cup of coffee. "I thought you might need a pick-me-up after a long night. How'd Frank do?"

Ladso cocked his head, trying to find the words. "I was reading Murray's journals when Trooper and I noticed Frank standing at his doorway, looking at me. If looks could kill, I would not be telling you this story. I asked him what was wrong, and he said something about looking at those he was going to kill. I called to him and he woke up, not remembering anything. I led him back to bed, and he stayed there for the rest of the night."

Pi shuddered. "You think that was Sharon?"

"I cannot imagine who else."

Now Pi was starting to panic. "Does she know where we are now? Is she coming to…?"

Ladso took her in his arms, shushing her. "Do not wake Frank."

"Do we need to leave? She might be on her way."

Ladso shook his head. "Frank does not know where he is except Chicago, and her connection to him is still tentative. One shout from me and it was broken. I do not think we need to worry yet, but we do need to get some answers, and quickly."

Trying to calm herself, Pi changed topics. "What about the journals? Did you find anything?"

Ladso shook his head. "No. There are so many. I know Murray would not neglect to record that important finding, even if he followed it with disclaimers. This might take longer than I thought, but we have to figure this out. Frank might not be getting worse, but he is not getting better."

He stood up, gave Pi a warm hug. "Can you can stay here, so I can go grab a shower." She nodded. "I will wake Frank when I get back." He looked into her eyes. "Are you sure you are OK?"

"Of course I am, silly." Pi stood on tiptoe to kiss his nose this time. "Scoot. The sooner you're done, the sooner we can gather in the kitchen." Pi called down to let Nikki know she was sending Trooper downstairs. Nikki whistled from somewhere in the house and Trooper happily went to his master.

Ladso left, and Pi absently browsed through a few of the journals left on the table. The printing was beautiful and the stories read like a novel. Then she realized this was her Ladso that Murray was writing about. Nonchalantly cutting the head off a vampire, burying a stake through its heart, and finally, burning it. *He's seen and done so much of this crazy undead crap. Glad we've got him with us!* Her face paled as she read on, but her resolve only strengthened.

Ladso returned, clean, shaved, and smelling of aftershave, which made it hard for Pi not to stare. He smiled, reddened, but managed to wink as he tapped on Frank's door. Hand over her mouth to hold in the laugh, Pi left wobbling as she carried away the breakfast tray.

Pi quickly cleaned the kitchen and started a fresh pot of coffee, an always popular day starter for the team — Starter, ender, *pastime*, she decided was the best description. She stood, listening to the coffee brew, and watching a crow out the window. It was sitting on a telephone wire, and stared back at her. Its stillness was unnerving. Then the sun burst over the horizon and the crow flew off.

Nikki came in with both dogs. "Britt was up working late, so I just kept Ray and Trooper. Pi grinned and climbed down on the floor to play with Ray. He was growing fast, all gangly legs and whippy tail. Thankfully, Britt did not believe in the barbaric practice of docking working dogs' tails.

Nikki helped herself to a cup of coffee and sighed over the first sip. "Thanks for getting the coffee going."

Pi waved off the compliment, making a gesture with her hand, which Ray took as a signal to continue playing. He attacked her hand with his milky puppy teeth. "No, Ray. Don't bite." Pi spoke in a serious, steady tone, taking her hand out of his mouth. When he tried again, she corrected him again. After that, he gave up, and went to go play with Trooper, who didn't object to being chewed on.

Impressed, Nikki said, "Have you been eavesdropping on my training?"

Pi shook her head. "No, but I took some lessons with my family dog when I was a teen."

"Well, if you decide you want to give up ghoul hunting with Ladso you can join me with the dog training."

Pi shook her head. "Don't think so. The fringe benefits are damn good where I am, despite the goose bumps." They both laughed.

Frank and Ladso entered, both in good spirits. Ladso poured coffee, looking curiously at Pi. "You are sitting on the floor for some particular reason?"

"Meditation." She sprung up with a cheeky grin. "See, it works."

Then she turned serious. "Hey, does it mean anything if a crow sits on a phone line and just seems to watch you? Then flies away as soon as the sun comes up?"

Ladso looked somber. "Folklore says that corvids, crows and ravens are birds of ill omen. That is not precisely correct. They are birds of omen, portending something important. It may be for good, or not. Human nature being what it is, people remember the bad." He looked at her. "Why?"

She told him about the crow earlier and how it creeped her out.

"Ah." He thought for a moment and shook his head. "I would not worry about it. I do not believe Sharon's talents include using corvids as spies." Pi looked unconvinced.

Just then she jumped, as her cell phone rang; the caterers were on the way. She and Nikki went to collect breakfast.

At the door, Pi held an armful of catering bags. "A girl could get used to this."

Nikki slanted a sideways glance. "You mean catering or Ladso?"

Pi just grinned smugly. "Let's get this to the kitchen so we can feed the troops."

They returned to the kitchen and found Britt drinking coffee and talking with the other men. They set the catering bags on the table and began opening them. Breakfast was a mini-quiche, in an assortment of savory flavors, and for those with a sweet tooth, pastries, and donuts.

Frank helped himself to both. Everyone else opted for the quiches. Frank bit into a doughnut. "No cop ever grew big and strong on quiche alone."

Britt interjected. "Well, a big cop belly, anyway," and grinned at Frank, who stuck out a sugar coated tongue.

Nikki stood, whistled for the dogs, looked at Frank. "Ready to help today, not just watch? Some tasks on the agenda for today require two people."

"I know nothing about dog training, but then I helped yesterday so, yes, I am."

Ladso looked after her as she left. "Thank you Nikki." He turned to Britt. "I found nothing in the three years of journals I looked through last night. Maybe I got the year wrong."

Britt looked tired, but proud. "I think I've found the answer. It's in that old book I told you about. A scholar like Murray clearly wrote it. Some of it's pretty far out, but there's a ritual that might be what we need."

Ladso looked excited. "Frank's nurse comes today. He spends half an hour with Frank. I suggest we can all meet then. Britt, will you print copies of this ritual?"

Britt yawned. "I will, and I'll grab a nap before we meet. I was up most of the night with that book." Ladso nodded sympathetically. "As was I. I just hope your time will prove itself more productive." His smile faded as he sobered. "I had a little scare last night." He stopped Britt's unspoken question. "We will talk when the nurse is here. Do not let it disturb your rest."

Britt printed copies before napping, while Ladso went straight to bed. As Britt slid beneath his covers, he hoped for the success of his find and tried not to worry about Ladso's scare.

Outside, Nikki explained to Frank what to do, which was basically stand still. Frank grumbled a little. "I didn't realize my job would be so technical."

Nikki responded, "If you had a donut you wouldn't complain." He grunted a laugh. "I just need you to be a target."

"A thing a cop spends a lot of effort trying not to be."

Nikki grinned. "I don't need you to get good at it. Just be visible."

"Don't have much choice with that," Frank rubbed his belly.

"I wouldn't want to take you on." She grinned. Frank grinned back. She pointed to the dogs. "Yesterday afternoon I started working on some new commands with both dogs, working as a pair. They are understanding the individual commands, but I need them to associate them with a person and function as a team."

"So, I'll be your scarecrow dummy for the pooches." He stood there. "Just don't yell, attack!"

Nikki grinned again. "We'll do that one another time." Frank's brows rose as she walked to the waiting dogs.

The shrilling of his cell phone woke Ladso from dark, bewildering dreams. He fumbled for it on the nightstand. "Ladso here." His voice sounded calm, and wide awake. Luckily, the caller couldn't see his tired face.

"Excellent. That time works very well for us. We will see you then." He hung up the phone, yawned, and stretched. He ached for more sleep, but the nurse was only half an hour away. He got up, splashed his face with cold water, then tapped at Britt's door to wake him. Hearing Britt's reply, Ladso took the stairs to the main level.

He swung by the sitting room, checking in on the movie marathoners. Pi waved and grinned, holding her finger up to her lips. Frank had nodded off and was snoring through the current movie. Ladso grinned, waved back, tapped his watch, and whispered, "thirty minutes." Pi nodded and blew a kiss, which Ladso caught with his hand and placed on his lips.

Nikki was in the kitchen, both dogs slumbering comfortably at her feet. She had a pensive look on her face, staring into nothing. "Nikki, what is on your mind?" Nikki looked up, startled. "You look worried."

"Just wondering what's going to happen to Frank. Working with me and the dogs this morning, he did well, but I worry about him."

"We are all worried. Britt thinks he has found something. He should have copies for us. We will have at least half an hour uninterrupted when the nurse arrives."

"What time will the nurse get here?"

"About twenty minutes."

"Perfect. I'm going to grab a quick shower. The dogs should be quiet. I…" She smiled. "We worked them hard."

She left, and Ladso started a fresh pot of coffee, knowing everyone would appreciate it. Filling the reservoir of the brewer, he thought, not cooking removes my opportunity to clear my thoughts and plan. It feels strange to me. He sat, taking advantage of time in the kitchen alone.

His cell phone rang again. The nurse was outside. With a sigh, Ladso left the empty kitchen. It was the same nurse from two days before.

"Frank is watching movies, or perhaps napping? Let us check."

The nurse frowned. "Is he sleeping a lot? He shouldn't be, if he's recovering from his anemia. How's his appetite?"

Ladso described Frank's eating habits, including his addiction to donuts. "He is a policeman." Both laughed. Ladso also explained that Frank had episodes of sleepwalking, describing them without giving details that would be difficult to explain.

Ladso paused in the hall. "Could you do us a favor? We need time to discuss some things without Frank. Could you extend your examination to an hour?"

"Not a problem. I'd like more time to observe him, actually. It will allow a fuller report to his doctor."

Ladso smiled his appreciation, then opened the door to the family room. Frank was awake and watching an old Mel Brooks classic, "Blazing Saddles." He laughed aloud. "They couldn't even make this movie today. It's just wrong in so many ways., Bigoted, ignorant, totally inappropriate…" He looked at Pi, "and funny as hell."

Nodding, Pi noticed Ladso and the nurse standing at the door. She paused the movie, and promised, "After the nurse is done, we're going to finish this bad boy!"

Frank looked over. "Hey, Stephen, wasn't it? You were here the last time."

Stephen smiled. "Yes, hello Frank. Shall we go upstairs?"

"Just follow me." Frank led him out.

♪

As soon as Frank and Stephen left the room, Ladso and Pi headed to the kitchen.

Nikki had roused Britt again on her way to the shower. He had fallen back asleep. The two of them were waiting when Ladso and Pi arrived. Nikki poured cups of coffee while thinking, *I can feel Murray's spirit encouraging us.*

Britt began. "Ladso, that book is intriguing with its details and theories. I would like to have a copy made to continue studying when this is over."

Intrigued, Ladso nodded. "Of course. What have you found?"

"This book represented the author's life's work. He included a great deal about the supernatural, and wrote in an attempt to separate fact from fiction, folklore from functional defenses. His theories are sometimes difficult to accept, but much of it is well thought out and therefore plausible. Unfortunately, most had been untested by him personally."

"In the section on vampires, he lists concoctions, 'receipts' as he calls them, for various maladies or conditions. I read a gruesome story of a victim bitten once and left alive, like Frank. The 'receipt' is titled, 'How To Turn a Victim From the Vampyre'."

The team reacted as Pi asked, "Does that mean..."

"Yes." Britt nodded. "How to return a victim to normal, and break the vampire's hold on him."

Pi nearly shouted. "Britt, that's amazing! What do we need to get, or do? Does it explain, in enough detail, that we can replicate the cure?"

Britt's face turned somber. "Yes, the receipt lists all the ingredients. They must be combined, in a specific order, then brewed into a drink for Frank under the dark of the moon.

Pi and Nikki frowned. Nikki shook her head. "By the dark of the moon sounds more like a time for dark magic and creating curses than a time for creating something good!"

Ladso interrupted. "Those using dark arts have tried to claim the night as theirs because of the power the moon and stars can supply.

They want that power for themselves. Users of white magic are not deceived, however. Their simplest spells include sitting a container of water in the moonlight and using that absorbed energy to do good. The night is the time when the vampire is strongest, but the night's power can be used against them as well as by them."

Britt nodded. "Getting most of the ingredients should not be a problem. Many of the herbs are common in the spice drawers of many kitchens. One ingredient could be a problem to obtain, however."

Ladso asked, "Which?"

"The potion requires three drops of human blood... from a virgin."

There was silence in the room. Nikki looked uncomfortable as she spoke. "Ummm..." Everyone looked at her. Her blush was tomato red with embarrassment.

Pi's eyes widened. "Nikki! You've been saving yourself?"

If possible, Nikki's face reddened further.

Britt spoke in a soft voice. "Nikki, are you saying you're a virgin?"

She nodded. "I've been waiting for the right man. Neither he nor the right time have come together for me."

Ladso stood. "Nikki, you have protected yourself, and may have saved Frank."

She looked over and saw nothing but respect in Ladso's eyes. She felt the gratitude in the room. Her embarrassment faded and her blush subsided.

Britt had an expression of relief. "I have a copy of the receipt for the herbs and other plants needed. The instructions must be followed exactly."

Nikki frowned. "How will we get Frank to drink it?"

Ladso retook his seat. "When Frank is not under Sharon's spell, he recognizes that something is wrong. He wants it fixed. In daylight, when he is thinking for himself, if we tell him it will save him, I believe he will cooperate happily."

Nikki nodded, looking relieved. "How long will it take to work?"

"The book is less precise about that." Britt shrugged. "It suggests the time to recover depends on the severity of the infection. I hope it's sooner rather than later. Sharon is looking for us. And being such a small group, we need Frank on our team."

Nikki looked nervous. "Britt, do you really think we can destroy Sharon? She has skills we know little or nothing about, like turning into a mist, and passing through locked doors. What else might she be able to do?"

Britt looked sadly at his young friend and team member. "What other choice do we have?"

Nikki frowned. "You're right, we don't have a choice. She must be destroyed or she'll destroy us, and others."

Ladso looked at Britt's list. "I will get busy collecting ingredients right away. I will need to take a trip into the city. Does anyone want to come with me?"

Both Pi and Nikki volunteered. Britt offered to stay with Frank."

They wrapped up the meeting. Ladso continued to study the receipt. He had several of the items in his kitchen, but was happy he knew a specialist for the rarer herbs.

A few minutes later, Frank and Stephen returned. Stephen looked concerned. "Frank has given me permission to share his medical information." Frank nodded. "Some of Frank's numbers are troubling. He's still anemic, despite the transfusions at the hospital. His white blood cells are quite high, although there's no sign of infection. Also, the wounds on his neck are no better. While they are no worse either, they remain a concern." He paused and looked at Frank who distractedly nodded again. "I gave him a cognitive awareness test. He is showing signs of early onset dementia." The team members frowned. "There is nothing in his condition that explains it, particularly how quickly it is progressing. I'd suspect drugs, but he assures me he is not using, and there was no sign of any in his blood tests. I will talk to his doctors, but my guess is they'll want to give Frank another unit or two of blood, probably later this afternoon, if that's possible."

"Of course." With his answer, Ladso cast a worried look toward Frank. "Tell us where and what time."

Frank seemed not to listen, looking both serene and unconcerned. "Ladso turned to Stephen. "Can a visiting nurse be scheduled to stay with Frank this afternoon? My friends and I need to run an errand, and Frank should not be alone."

Stephen agreed and pulled his cell to make a phone call. Ladso walked over to Britt. "Upon further consideration I would like you to come with us in case my friend has questions."

Britt frowned. "Should I bring the book?"

Shaking his head, Ladso answered. "I think one of the copies you made for us will be sufficient."

Within a few minutes, Stephen reported that the office was going to have him remain while another nurse gathered supplies for Frank's transfusion. With the procedure, they feel an additional person on hand would be helpful."

"That sounds wise." Ladso glanced at Frank who was drinking coffee and talking distractedly with Pi. "He seemed fine earlier in the day."

"Yes." Stephen was also looking at Frank. "I noticed a shift on our way to his room. It was as if knowing he was going to be examined again took the wind from his sails. Just odd timing, I guess." Ladso nodded with a frown, but made no comment.

Two hours later, the team in Ladso's SUV moved through traffic, which was horrible. Ladso however, drove it with long familiarity. He took them onto an empty lot off a side street in southern Chicago. Leaving the SUV, they walked, quickly finding themselves in a crowd.

It was obvious they were in a Bohemian part of the city. Passing through a maze of shops and booths, they encountered sellers offering a variety of items, many of which appeared to have originated in another country. Patchouli and marijuana fragrances blended with other aromas of the street. There were small book shops, dedicated to specific sub-categories of literature, science, or philosophy. They passed shops with clothes, food, and many others offering services and items which only Ladso seemed to understand. Nikki's eyes widened when they passed a palm reader's stand and the woman in the booth winked at her and called, be careful in St. Louis.

At the end of another row of buildings which held shops of varying size and far-ranging items, there was a brightly lit outdoor market. The booths offered everything from homemade pottery and jewelry to live animals.

Centered amongst the booths was a two-story building. Ladso led them to a door between two display windows. The items behind the glass indicated the shop was both an apothecary and a spice store.

Inside, the proprietor greeted Ladso with a hardy hug, and thumped on his back with a cheery grin. The two babbled rapidly in a foreign language. Speaking quickly and gesticulating wildly, they were clearly old friends. Turning, Ladso waved to his teammates and switched to English. "These are Britt, Nikki, and Pi." He grinned with the final introduction.

"Friends, please meet Cosmin. His name means 'in solidarity with life,' which suits him very well. He is a naturalist, and a truly amazing herbalist. If an herb grows on this planet, Cosmin has it, or knows where to find it."

Cosmin bowed slightly. "Ladso is too kind, too generous, as always. Please tell me, dear friend, how may I be of service?"

Ladso handed over the list of herbs. "I need these, fresh as possible."

Cosmin's eyes moved as he read then widened as he looked up, troubled. "Ladso, what is this? Why are you dealing with such herbs and plants. They are dark magic."

Ladso broke again into their other shared language. Cosmin listened intently, his face darkening with concern. After several moments, he turned to one side and spat on the floor. Then he crossed his right thumb over his forefinger and kissed his thumb.

Cosmin spoke in English again. "I understand, and yes I can help you. These herbs' purpose can be terrible, but are sometimes necessary. You are saving a life." He shook his head slowly. "I wish your friend well. Come, let us collect your herbs."

Ladso turned to Britt. "Please come with us." He turned to the ladies. "This may take some time. Follow if you wish, or you can wander the market, I will call when we've finished."

Hesitantly, the women nodded and watched the men leave the front of the shop. Stepping outside, they barely wandered beyond the shop's threshold as they worried for Frank and hoped for Ladso and Britt's success.

It was just short of half an hour later when the men and Cosmin stepped out. All looked happy, and Ladso was carrying a burlap bundle, which he held up.

Nikki applauded. "Is that all we need?"

Ladso's smile widened. "Everything and fresher supplies of other items on the list that I have at home. We are ready.

Britt also looked thrilled. "Also, Ladso's wonderful friend Cosmin has promised to be available if we need clarification with our preparation. He's already made several suggestions which should secure our success."

Walking to the street, Ladso turned and waved. "Goodbye, good friend. I will let you know of our success."

Cosmin called back in what they assumed was the language he and Ladso had used earlier. Ladso didn't bother to translate, but he did laugh and wave.

Quickly, they passed again through the maze of turns. Soon they were back in the SUV and entering crowded streets. The team was optimistic as the late afternoon light gilded everything with nature's paintbrush. Smiling, Ladso merged into the frenzied rush of cars, unerringly piloting them toward home.

Sharon was lying on the cardboard she'd spread on the floor in the basement. She could have broken through any of the doors but she wanted her presence to remain secret for the blood chattel's return. The door prevented her bringing anything down to lie on so she'd made do with what was already there. Most of the boxes had been empty and already flattened. It was the best she could do but she didn't like it and looked at her discomfort as another reason to hate the ones she was waiting to kill.

As was her usual custom, she had her eyes open as she rested during the day. Sleep was not something she was capable of, but she did rest in a manner of speaking. Her mind wandered while she lay there.

Today she was reminiscing about her time at the Academy. Back then, they'd only been in the school for four years. The nuns still living taught the students and ran the school during the day. They did not know about their other Sisters in the basement. Sharon saw to it that the door to that dark corridor was locked during the day and that the living nuns did not go down during the evening. She also arranged for her Sisters in the basement to have access to the students. Her eyes glowing green, she would bring the disobedient student down to where she'd gift the Sisters with a small portion of the girl's blood. Afterwards and back upstairs, the student would not remember the incident and blame her symptoms on an unexpected time of the month. Other students, simply in need of tutoring were also brought downstairs. Sometimes they were used during the day, and other times they'd stay after school and receive their — study time — when it was convenient for the nun providing, or receiving the care. Under the green glow of the nun's tutorage, the girls would remember the passages read, or the equations explained. Such successes left the student a little tired for the next week or so, but with better grades. Some continued on to college if their parents' finances allowed.

Sharon remembered one student, Agnes, who was especially troublesome in class. That behavior earned her repeated visits to Mother Eugenia or one of the others in the basement. The lessons attempted during those sessions had little effect on Agnes, however. In fact, after multiple visits she became even more troublesome. To her fellow students, she complained of dreams, in a basement, with women in old habits and green glowing eyes. Such dreams were ignored by everyone except Sharon, who feared that Agnes might begin to remember more, might put her Sisters in danger.

One day, at the end of classes, she called Agnes aside. She had other girls to take to the basement and her abilities, limited as they were then, allowed her to only control one student at a time. Agnes had to wait in Sharon's office, and the door had been locked to insure her obedience. When Sharon finished with the other girls, she sent them home. Then she went to collect Agnes.

For reasons Sharon never understood, Agnes seemed to sense something different. She was anxious and on guard when Sharon arrived. She argued at first and when Sharon focused her green eyes on her, Sharon was rewarded with a blow to her face.

Agnes ran for the door but Sharon had locked it after entering. Agnes ran for a window with Sharon's green gaze having little effect. When Sharon approached her, she was again rewarded with a blow from Agnes' tight fist. The girl backed Sharon to her desk and rushed again. This time Sharon grabbed the letter opener from the desk and thrust it into the girl's neck. When the blood began to flow, Sharon had no choice but to catch it. She often had students, teachers, or living members of the Order in her office. She could not allow her office to be blood-stained. How would she explain it?

Sharon leapt onto the girl, latched on to her throat, and took in the blood. As she drank, Agnes fought. The more Sharon drank, the glow in her eyes grew brighter. Soon Agnes was completely compliant but Sharon did not, could not stop.

Late that night, Sharon took Agnes' body away from the school. She dropped the girl's lifeless corpse into a depression along the railroad tracks.

The next day when the parents arrived, and the police after that, Sharon said, tearfully, that Agnes had been a problem student. That she suspected the girl acted out while away from school, too. "We try," she insisted, "to help Agnes learn to control herself better, but we can do little with her." She told them that Agnes was scheduled for detention the night she was last seen, but that she left against Sharon's commands. When the girl's remains were found, Sharon repeated her story.

That tremendous fount of blood helped to increase Sharon's strength. She no longer had problems controlling her students, or any other chattel she needed to follow her commands. Putting aside her daydreams she — was suddenly aware and on the cardboard boxes on the floor.

She felt Frank's mind pulling away from her control although she did not understand why. This coincided with the start of his transfusion in Chicago

Sharon's eyes glowed bright as she fought to hold her connection with Frank. She writhed with frustration as the connection became no weaker, but grew no stronger. She had not experienced a failure of her power since Agnes. It angered her but frightened her as well.

Ladso parked in his usual spot and carried their package into the house. Stopping inside the front door, the team heard voices from the kitchen. Ladso set his package in the foyer and followed Nikki, Britt, and Pi to the kitchen.

A rousing game of Pinochle was in progress. Frank was playing with the new nurse and Stephen who smiled and waved as the team entered.

"Hello." The nurse nodded as Stephen stood.

Pointing to his patient, Stephen smiled. "Frank has had his transfusion. He is much stronger already. Also, more 'himself.' He'll need another treatment tomorrow. If you're willing to pay for the at home service again…" Ladso nodded. Stephen grinned and looked toward Frank again. "He's been beating the pants off both of us. First it was Gin Rummy, now Pinochle."

Stephen's grin reassured Ladso more than his words. "Excellent! I expect you two are ready to be on your way. Thank you so much."

Stephen and the visiting nurse collected their coats and bags and were ready to depart. Ladso escorted them to the door, thanked them again, then locked the deadbolts and secured the alarm before returning to the kitchen with Cosmin's package. Once in the kitchen, he casually placed the package in the pantry, then joined the team at the table.

Frank was nonchalantly shuffling the deck of cards. "So, we having dinner tonight?" He looked at Ladso, not dropping a card. He'd obviously handled a deck before today.

Ladso laughed. "The caterer is bringing pizza tonight, the very best in Chicago. I also checked with Stephen. You can have an ice-cold beer with your pie. How does that sound?"

Frank almost cracked a grin, but looked gruff again. "One beer?"

"If you push things, it is back to coffee and water." Ladso grinned.

Britt strolled in. "Pizza and cold beer sounds fantastic. No coffee tonight, wine can take a break too." He and Frank laughed together. "I'll be happy with a bottle of IPA. What's your poison, Frank?"

"Cold and without too big a head makes me happy. A dark lager is my favorite, though.

"Hey Frank," Pi stood and looked at the detective. "Want to finish 'Blazing Saddles' after we eat?"

Frank cocked his head. "You're on, cookie. Let's see who blushes more before the ending." He flashed a grin as she laughed.

Pi's phone rang, and she answered. "The caterers are outside." She gave a thumbs up and Ladso left to fetch dinner. Two minutes later he returned with three large cardboard boxes, releasing mouth-watering aromas into the room. Ladso set the boxes on the countertop and opened them before grabbing a slice server. Britt brought over a stack of plates while Nikki and Pi got napkins, and silverware. Ladso pulled packets of powdered red pepper, salt, pepper, and parmesan cheese from the bag. While Pi carried the condiments to the table, Ladso began serving up slices.

Ladso served Frank one icy cold Budweiser, as promised. Frank disdained using a glass, claiming that real beer drinkers drank only from the bottle or can. Ladso laughed and took the offending glass away.

It was a cheerful, rowdy dinner with the teams' thoughts about the day's errand only occasionally interfering with their pleasure. It was after sunset. As far as the team could tell, Frank only mentally drifted away once. Everyone noticed, but the rest of the meal Frank seemed himself, which put everyone in good spirits.

After eating, Pi dragged Frank off to finish their movie. Ladso's eyes fastened on her until she left the room, then he shook his head, bringing his attention back to matters at hand.

He pulled out Britt's receipt, put it on the table, and began reviewing it. Nikki cocked her head. "When do we have to brew this? Outside in the dark? You said in the dark of the moon."

Britt explained. "The dark of the moon is simply the period between the full and the new moon. Approximately14 days. The receipt also warns against brewing during the 'witching hour,' which is from midnight until 12:59, although some believe it can last until twilight. That flexibility suggests that we complete our work before midnight."

Ladso nodded while still browsing the receipt. "Cauldron? We have one. Herbs? We now have them all, thanks to Cosmin! We need a dog's earwax. Our four-legged team members can supply that. It calls for a 'ruby red wine.' Our supply contains a beautiful Cabernet Sauvignon. Last of all, our dear Nikki will provide the most precious ingredient."

Nikki blushed but smiled. Waiting for the right person had always felt right for her. She felt happier than her mom about that decision now.

Britt rubbed his chin. "Now, do we start this witches' brew tonight, or wait until tomorrow? Last night or the night before was the actual full moon, so even though it's bright out, we are technically in the 'dark of the moon.' What do you think, Ladso?"

"I need you to sit up with Frank tonight. I need to rest. While I dislike leaving Frank under Sharon's influences for another day, he will have had a second transfusion tomorrow which should strengthen him further and may weaken Sharon's hold. I propose we brew Frank's remedy tomorrow night."

# 9

Pi and Frank returned to the kitchen, still laughing about the movie. Britt explained he was keeping Frank company that night. Frank had a knowing look on his face as he smirked at Pi, then Ladso, but he refrained from making any rude comments. Pi raised a brow at Frank then kissed his cheek. She then thanked him for a lovely evening. Frank smiled and thanked her as well for not citing any resemblance between him and the variety of horses' asses featured in their cowboy comedy.

Nikki giggled as she took the dogs outside. She planned to keep Ray with her overnight, while Trooper accompanied Britt for the shift with Frank.

Frank and Britt took the elevator to Frank's suite. Britt had his shoulder tote with him which held his reading materials for the night. He wanted to re-read the section about Frank's cure. He intended to take more detailed notes. They could afford no mistakes.

Ladso cocked his elbow for Pi, so she could take his arm, and graciously escorted her out of the kitchen, to **their** room. The thought made him grin with pleasure.

♪

The sitting room chair comfortably held Britt, who had the large volume propped on his lap. A weighted leather bookmark held the pages open. He supposed he was lucky losing his left arm, as he was right-handed, but everything remained clumsy and awkward. To his right was a table holding a small, spiral-bound notebook and a few ink pens. The notebook had a non-skid cover to prevent its shifting as he wrote in it.

He listened for a minute, but all he heard were Frank's snores, sounding even and steady. He hoped that the blood transfusion would make Frank stronger, and end his nighttime activity.

As he lowered his gaze to the pages of the book, the door from the hall opened. Britt turned and saw Nikki letting Trooper into the room. Britt waved at Nikki and Ray as Trooper walked over to sit beside his old master. Nikki waved back and threw a questioning gaze toward Frank's door. After Britt replied that all was quiet, she wished him a good night and shut the door.

Britt patted Trooper's head. "Go ahead and get some rest. You'll hear our friend and wake before I do even if you're sound asleep." As Trooper lay down, Britt focused on the ancient tome in front of him. He started by reading the entire section, ensuring he had a full grasp of the writer's cadence, phrasing, and terminology. Then he turned to the receipt. He read it slowly, line by line, word by word. Pen in hand, he began writing detailed notes.

Over an hour later, Britt stood and stretched. Trooper awoke and raised his head. "Relax boy, I'll be right back." Britt went into the bathroom and splashed cold water over his face to help wake him up. Drying his face, he heard Trooper growl.

He quickly opened the bathroom door. Across the room, Frank stood outside his bedroom. His eyes were wide open but unseeing. Not speaking a word, he swayed lightly back and forth.

"Easy Trooper, down boy." As Britt crossed the room, he spoke in a soft voice. "Frank, are you okay?"

Frank didn't respond, just stood quietly in his trance. Britt took his arm and led him back to his bed. Frank followed along sluggishly.

Once Britt had Frank settled back in his bed, the detective closed his eyes. Frank was snoring as Britt shut the bedroom door.

Britt sighed and shivered. The encounter had been disconcerting despite having no real substance. Frank had barely focused, let alone spoke. Britt looked worried as he walked back to his seat to resume his work. "Tomorrow we'll put this behind you, my friend."

Sharon awoke in Britt's basement. Her lip curled angrily. Until two nights ago, her connection with Frank had been growing stronger. She'd gotten him out of bed and even spoke to the bald one through her slave, as he'd stood outside the policeman's bedroom. Her threat of killing them all had unfortunately spurred the policeman to push her out of his mind. That action had angered her then, but her anger was short lived as she knew he'd continue to weaken.

Her eyes tightened in the darkness as she then remembered the nurse's visit yesterday followed by her almost complete loss of contact.

Last night, after going out to feed, Sharon dropped her victim's dry corpse into a sewer and returned home. When she'd contacted Frank, it had been a weaker connection. She was able to get him out of bed, but could not make him speak. The figure she saw through the policeman's eyes was difficult to make out. Probably male, but she didn't think it was the bald man again. This one looked like he was missing an arm.

Only her confidence that her connection would strengthen again kept her from doing more damage to the house. Standing, she mouthed the word as though it was vile on her tongue. "Transfusion." She moved to a window and glared out. *In times past, humans and their medicine had only strengthened our victims. Allowed them to live and be fed upon longer.* She shook her head. *The true problem is the distance they've put between me and my prey.* With an angry grunt she transformed into smoke and exited the house again. This time it was not hunger she intended to quell, it was her anger.

♪

Early the next morning, Ladso was up and whistling in the kitchen, whipping up breakfast rather than relying on caterers. Pi sat at the table, sipping coffee watching his oddly graceful dance around the room. Ladso turned. "You will be sitting with Frank tonight while we prepare the cure."

Pi's brows went up. "I think you mean, I'll be up there until he falls to sleep. Then I'll come down and keep tabs on him while the three of you are busy outside."

"There is no need for you to come down." Ladso turned, surprised at Pi's objection.

"Listen lover, if you think I'm going to miss all the action while listening to Frank snore upstairs, then you need another shot of hot coffee. Frank will be safe while being monitored from down here and you'll be safe from my frustration for not having missed the whole event."

Ladso moved to speak but Pi shut him down. "You better have a damned good reason for needing me upstairs, buddy."

With a sigh, Ladso raised his hands in surrender. "I do not. You come down as soon as our detective has begun to snore."

Pi nodded, gave him a peck on the cheek and turned as Nikki and the dogs entered the kitchen. "Britt and Frank are awake and will be down soon."

Ladso whistled sharply, catching both dogs' attention before tossing each of them a piece of bacon, which they devoured. Nikki poured herself coffee, then sat down next to Pi, smiling. No words were necessary — Nikki's delight was apparent. Pi basked in Nikki's approval and joy on her friend's behalf.

Britt and Frank walked in. Frank called out, "Bacon! Coffee! You are a gentleman who knows the route to my heart passes through my stomach." He chuckled as he spoke, then noticed the tall stack of pancakes next to the bacon. "My mistake. You're no gentleman, Ladso. You're a bloody genius."

Britt gave Ladso a 'thumbs up' gesture, then went to pour a cup of coffee. He had to wait because Frank, following his usual routine, had gotten there first.

Everyone fixed their plates, buffet-style, and sat around the kitchen table. Catering was nice, but did not compare to Ladso's fresh, home-cooked food. The pancakes and bacon quickly disappeared.

It was routine by now; Nikki and Frank went outside to train the dogs. Pi went to pick out a movie for later, leaving Britt and Ladso in the kitchen. Britt picked up his shoulder tote, opened it, and took out his notebook. The effort was clumsy, but it was obvious he wanted no help. Ladso approved and showed no impatience as he waited.

"Here, Ladso, I want to leave this with you. It is detailed directions for making Frank's cure. Nikki will need a white dress." Ladso looked over with a questioning expression. "The book states that the virgin should be dressed in white."

Ladso shrugged. "If she does not have something I expect she and Pi will be willing to go shopping. I recommend naps so we are wide awake tonight. Was your night with Frank quiet?"

Britt related the unexpected awakening. "I hope this concoction we're going to brew cures him."

"As do I."

Britt went outside to watch the dogs working. Ray was improving by leaps and bounds. Britt wore a broad smile, watching Ray follow Nikki's every command perfectly.

Britt walked over to Nikki asking quietly. "Do you have a white dress?"

She cocked her head. "Why?"

"For tonight's preparation of Frank's cure. It might seem silly but with mysticism we don't really know what's important and what isn't."

Nikki nodded. "I have a white sundress. It's not formal, doesn't even reach my knees."

"I don't believe the style matters, just the color. It must be true white."

She nodded and held a thumb up. Britt complimented her on her improved training skills, as well as Ray's progression.

She beamed. "Show him something once and he's grasped it. I think watching Trooper helps too, but Ray is really just so smart! He's already mastered all the basics plus a few we've been working on to surprise you. He'll even obey Frank."

Britt was clearly pleased but yawned. "I'm going to grab a nap. It was a long shift last night and tonight we'll be preparing Frank's cure." He paused. "The two of you might want a nap too." He looked over at Frank who was dozing in a sunny spot on the porch. "I suppose we'll have to lock Frank in his room while we brew."

Nikki's expression saddened as she too looked at their friendly detective. "Pi and I will keep Frank busy. Since he's alert enough to play cards, I'll challenge him to a poker tournament. You two get your rest."

Britt gave her a 'thumbs up' and returned to the kitchen where he told Ladso that Nikki already had the required white dress. Minutes later, both men were in their beds.

Frank's only friend on the St. Louis Police force, Detective Mike Gently stood beside a wrecked police car. The driver side door was open, the window was smashed. The passenger side window was broken as well. Both were smeared with blood. Large dents covered the doors and roof, but there was no sign that the car had rolled.

The throat of the officer inside was slashed and he had a hole in his chest which looked like it had been torn open. When Gently arrived, he'd been told that several of the officer's organs were missing. In the hour that followed, officers found those organs, in parts, and scattered over an area as long as a city block. The pieces had the appearance of having been thrown although that didn't seem possible because of the distance. While it seemed unlikely that the culprit had run up and down the street throwing the body parts, they could not have been thrown from the car. Not by a human being, at any rate.

Gently had already reported the officer's identity to his Captain. He'd also reported the name of the officer's partner, although there was no sign of her body.

Considering the condition of the officer's body in the car, the lack of blood was puzzling. There was some on the windows. There were also small amounts on the seat, dash, and the interior of both doors, but not the amount that should have been shed as the officer was pulled apart.

Gently wished Frank was there. Frank almost always got assigned these cases, cases which made no sense. There was no obvious motive for the damage that was done here. The officers had a good relationship with the residents of the area they patrolled. There was no other act of crime performed in the vicinity that the officers might have interrupted. Just a senseless killing and a brutal crime.

His phone buzzed. Gently pulled it from his pocket and answered. His eyes closed as he was told of the other officer being found and the conditions at that scene.

Pi joined Nikki and Frank in the yard. Nikki put her friends to work as human distractions, while Nikki gave a series of commands. Ray was doing so well.

The puppy was practicing a compound, 'down, stay' set of commands. Pi and Frank walked by the dog, chattering, but ignoring Ray who held his position. Nikki praised him, then reinforced the 'down, stay' commands.

Frank and Pi walked by again, stopping near where the dog was lying. They talked for several moments. Ray never broke command. Finally, Nikki approached, released Ray from his commands, and fed him a special treat that he only received after performing well.

Then it was play time. Nikki whistled for Trooper while holding two tennis balls. Pi and Frank were employed again with the balls. The dogs happily raced across the yard, chasing balls, bringing them back, chasing them again, panting, happy.

Play was the best reward.

♪

Humans and dogs had come back into the warm kitchen. Trooper and Ray flopped onto their beds, sighing with contentment.

Pi filled cups with coffee while Frank scrounged for donuts. He discovered a couple of glazed, and a lonesome chocolate Long John. Selecting a glazed, he brought it to the table.

Nikki suggested a Poker championship as Frank held his donut. He grinned. "There's still a glazed and a chocolate Long John in the container over there. They can be our jackpot."

"Winner eats all! I like it." Pi held both thumbs up.

Nikki went to get the cards while Pi got dried beans from the pantry to use as chips. Joining Frank at the table, she teased him about the beat-down that was coming.

Frank scoffed. "I was playing poker when you were still in diapers."

"How do you know I wasn't playing poker in my diapers?" She grinned and Frank laughed at the mental image which he described. "Cute little baby Pi smoking a cigar, wearing a fedora, and playing poker with a bunch of pint-sized mobsters."

"Drop the cigar and you're close!" Both laughed as Nikki returned with the cards. "What's funny?"

Frank chuckled. "I bet you didn't know you were going to be playing poker against a Diaper Diva!" He and Pi laughed again while Nikki grinned and removed the cards from their box.

Pi counted beans into a pile. "Ten bucks per bean?" Nikki and Frank agreed with a laugh at the high stakes. Nikki's face glowed as she grinned at these friends before her. "There you go, five hundred bucks each." She handed them their bowls of dried beans. "That will keep them from rolling around the table."

Frank took the cards and shuffled them like a casino pit dealer. He made bridges, spread the cards in a fan, and other fancy moves. Pi rolled her eyes, but Nikki looked impressed.

"OK, ladies, let's get started," Frank glowered at each woman in turn. "Three raise limits, ten-dollar minimum bid. Five-card draw, nothing wild."

He dealt out the hands smoothly and professionally. Then the battle, and almost continuous laughter ensued.

On what turned out to be the last hand, Pi and Frank were well ahead of Nikki who held her own for the draw but acted hesitant. Finally, she slid in all her beans. "It's the last hand, right?"

Pi checked the clock then looked to Frank who shrugged, then nodded. Both slid in all their beans.

Pi took two cards. Nikki shook her head and held firm, getting a raised eyebrow from Frank. She tried to look more nervous and unsure. Frank drew three, scowled at his hand but looked up with a nonchalant expression.

Pi showed her cards first, two pairs, sixes and eights. Frank laughed and showed his three nines. Both were silent as Nikki laid out her cards, the seven through Jack of spades.

Pi's eyes looked like they might pop out of her head. "Nikki, you tricky witch!" Looking over to Frank's equally shocked expression, they both laughed aloud.

Nikki collected the beans, then walked over to collect her winnings. Sitting at the table again, she chose a glazed — then slid the container to the losers. Delighted, everyone ate, the losers splitting the Long John. Licking sticky fingers, they continued to banter over Nikki's sneaky win.

Later that afternoon, Stephen and another nurse arrived to administer Frank's second transfusion. Frank stood and looked at Nikki. "There is a rematch in your future, young lady, but I've got to go deal with these…" When Frank froze in place, the women realized he'd been on the verge of making a vampire reference. Stephen and the nurse stood puzzled at everyone's expressions. Forcing himself to recover, Frank said, "With these fine young men with their needles and…" With difficulty, Frank managed a smile and a silly Lugosi imitation as he said, "bags of blood."

The women reacted while attempting forced laughter. The nurses laughed along, but their faces did not shed their confused expressions.

Frank herded them toward the elevator, with a parting eye roll to the women.

Hearing the elevator doors close, Nikki and Pi looked at one another and began to giggle. That went on for several seconds before Pi stood. "Well, that was an odd fumble but ole Frank pulled through it."

"Could he be recovering?" Nikki looked hopeful. "He seemed his old self today."

Pi shook her head. With somber eyes she explained. "He's had sleep walking episodes both of the last two nights. With Ladso he spoke, but the words weren't Frank's. Ladso believes they were Sharon's. No, Frank is still under that bitch's influence. Ladso thinks yesterday's transfusion benefitted him. Today's will hopefully do so again, but this is Frank's last transfusion. We need whatever Sharon left in his blood to be gone. I think our plans for the evening still need to happen." Nikki didn't object.

Sharon, lay on the flattened boxes she used as her berth on the floor of Britt's cellar. She frowned at the floor boards above her and hissed. As the blood flowed through the needle and into Frank's forearm, Sharon sat up and felt him slip further away. "You won't escape me. My blood will continue to spread. You can push it back but it will not stop."

"She scowled as she rose to her feet. "The blood chattel killed all my Sisters before I could be trained in my new abilities." She cursed in her ancient tongue as she began to pace. "They have ruined so very much. It will soon be time for me to ruin their lives."

Ladso awoke feeling rested. He climbed out of bed, knelt on the floor, and did a hundred push-ups. He followed that with fifty sit-ups and squats. After a quick shower, he got dressed.

He wore a warm, knit, cable sweater and heavy slacks, knowing it would be a bitter night outside.

Entering the kitchen Ladso found Pi, and Nikki, talking with Frank, who had a bandage on his arm covering the site of his latest transfusion. The threesome sat around the table, rehashing their game. When Ladso looked over, Nikki's grin lit up the room. "I beat the pants off both of them!"

Frank grunted with faked annoyance before laughing again. "What's for dinner? I'm dying for a proper meal. Something I can sink my teeth into."

Ladso retorted, "Plastic teeth sink into anything." Frank chuckled and, forming a pistol with his hand, shot Ladso.

After dramatically grabbing his chest, Ladso turned toward the stove and spoke over his shoulder. "Tonight, we are having New York strip steak, baked potato, rolls, and a Caesar salad. Ice cream will cleanse our palate for the after-dinner wine.

"Steak! Now that's what I'm talking about." Frank licked his lips in anticipation.

Britt entered, still yawning, but looking rested. He reacted to all the smiles. "What did I miss?"

Frank said, "Ladso promised steak and potatoes for dinner. That's what!"

Pi's phone rang; it was the caterers. Ladso left and came back laden with bags which he piled onto the counter and started unloading. He quickly filled plates, then set them in front of each diner.

"I ordered all the steaks mid-rare. I will be happy to heat it in my skillet if you want it slightly less pink. You can just eat charcoal from the grill outside if you want it 'well-done.'" He grinned taking the sting out of his words.

All were fine with mid-rare and did the meal full justice.

After dinner, Ladso craved coffee, but he didn't want Frank delaying his bedtime, so he kept silent. Britt looked at Frank. "You'll have a new companion tonight. Pi's going to sit with you. I have a project I'm working on that requires Ladso's help."

Frank shrugged. "Seems a waste of time. Nothing's happened the last two nights." The team diverted their eyes knowing that statement wasn't correct. Despite his comment, Frank made no objections and was soon yawning.

Pi stood up. "Come on, Frank, let's head up for bed." He shrugged as she took his arm, but didn't resist.

After they'd left, Nikki looked at Ladso, concerned. "Are you sure she's going to be OK with him?"

"He had a blood transfusion yesterday and was himself all day and slept all night, except for his one short-lived trance. After a second transfusion today, I think this is as good as he will get until we cure him." He patted Nikki's hand. "Pi is not helpless and once Frank's asleep she'll lock him in and come down. The baby monitor will be on and turned on high while she's there and after."

He turned, went to the pantry and removed a large plastic box. Inside were several sets of small bowls with lids, an expensive and precise kitchen scale, and a Sharpie. There was also a collection of the spices listed on the receipt from Murray's book and the package from Cosmin.

He and Britt set out the equipment and ingredients on the counter along with Britt's detailed instructions. Britt pulled an old medicine bottle which he'd brought in from the kennel yesterday. It was no simple chore to get the minuscule bit of wax from Ray's ears. Trooper had been simpler but barely more productive. Fortunately, according to the receipt, he'd collected enough.

Ladso and Britt, with Nikki's assistance, poured and measured each item. Several seeds required grinding with a mortar and pestle. After measuring, they carefully poured each herb into one of the small bowls, and labeled the lids with the Sharpie. Finally, Ladso got a flask, opened a fresh bottle of Cabernet Sauvignon, and filled the flask with the ruby red wine.

They put all the ingredients into a simple wicker basket. Their other supplies included long wooden spoons, pot holders, cheesecloth for straining, a cooking thermometer, and a small, sharp silver dagger.

Going back to the pantry Ladso returned with a clean, sealed Mason jar. He set the cauldron alongside the basket, and placed a lighter inside it. The lighter had a long nozzle for starting outdoor fires.

Ladso looked at Britt, who was waiting patiently with Nikki. After Britt's nod, Ladso looked at his watch. "It is just past ten. We are on schedule. Now we must start the fire. I have already set the proper wood aside. The receipt was not specific about kindling but to give us even heat, the wood must be burned down, to cherry red coals, by eleven. That is when we will mix and brew Frank's cure."

He turned to Nikki. "Your sundress is very thin. You can wait until we call you to come out. The receipt states that the mixing and heating will take about twenty minutes."

Nikki looked surprised. "I'll change when you guys are outside. Once Pi comes down to watch the monitor, I'll put on my coat and come out. I'll take my coat off when it's time, but Britt will possibly need help assisting you."

"Sadly, she's right." Britt took Nikki's hand. "Thank you. I know this blood draw will be uncomfortable. You know Ladso will be as gentle as he can."

Ladso nodded and smiled. "We will see you shortly. We are lucky that although it is cold, the wind is mild and there is no chance of rain." He looked at Britt. "We should get started."

The men dressed for outside. Ladso helped Britt with his coat and one glove. Britt managed his cap and scarf on his own. He still didn't like that he needed help, but was adjusting.

Outside, Ladso walked to the fire pit, set down the basket and cauldron, and grabbed a fire starter. He added it to the kindling in the pit and, after a nod to Britt, lit the fire. Within minutes the kindling was crackling with a warm glow.

Ladso added more wood and soon they had a raging fire throwing off intense heat. The men turned to ready their labeled containers in the order they'd be needed. The folding table they worked on had been placed there earlier in the day. When they turned back to the fire, there were fewer flames, with cherry embers glowing deep in the logs. Ladso checked the time and was unsurprised that it was nearly eleven.

Finally, Ladso set out a Mason jar. Unscrewing it, he covered the top with cheesecloth, slightly dimpled inside the jar. He screwed the ring around the jar but not the lid, so he could pour his brew through the cheesecloth, and strain it into the jar.

*He's as precise as a surgeon,* thought Britt. Ladso's precision strengthened his confidence in what they were attempting. So much could go wrong. If things went right, they would have Frank again, with no connection to Sharon. He shook his head, remembering the casual banter about their friendly poker game. *We are truly gambling with high stakes!*

Ladso looked at Britt, "The witching hour is nearing. May God guide us to victory."

He swiftly knocked the wood down into a glowing bed of coals, then set a small metal rack over them. As he put the cauldron in place, Nikki came out. Ladso looked toward the door and saw Pi holding the receiver for Frank's monitor. He waved and she crossed her fingers as she smiled back.

The first item into the caldron was a quart of water from a natural spring on a mountain in Tibet. Cosmin said it had been collected on the night of the last summer solstice at 11:34pm. When he heard the water's origin, Britt had pictured some good soul on his knees quickly filling bottle after bottle to be shipped around the world. Cosmin had full faith in his supplier. The water had been filtered by the earth and was purer than water collected anywhere else.

As the water began to boil, Britt read from the receipt. Nikki identified and opened each herb container, and passed it to Ladso who poured the contents into his hand and crushed the herbs gently between his palms. They all thought of Frank as the tiny bits fell into the hot water. The fragrance from the dried herbs grew potent as more were added. The smell was intoxicating and each of them struggled to remain focused on their task. Ladso stirred the mix occasionally with a wooden spoon as he directed Nikki to pour in the required portion of wine.

Britt looked from the receipt to Nikki who shed her coat. In her white sundress, Nikki shivered as Ladso embraced her. Keeping one arm around her shoulders he walked her closer to the fire. From beside the caldron, he picked up the needle-sharp dagger made of silver. It glinted in the moon and firelight as he brought it to her hand.

Nikki's arm jerked at first, but then she stood strong, her hand steady. Britt held up a page and Ladso intoned the Latin incantation imprinted there, Finished, he made a small cut at the tip of Nikki's finger. A droplet of blood fell onto the ground before he moved her finger over the brew. The next drop joined the mix in the cauldron and was followed by two more. He pulled her hand away as Britt handed her a tissue.

Focused again on the contents of the caldron, Ladso gently stirred as Britt held up the page again and Ladso continued to chant, one stir of the spoon on every third syllable. Completing the final chant, he removed the spoon, and set it to the side.

Nikki almost giggled as Ladso used a plain kitchen pot holder to lift the cauldron. It seemed so normal and out of place. While Ladso set the cauldron to one side, Nikki shivered. "Can I put my coat back on now?"

Both Britt and Ladso apologized. "Yes, of course" Helping her on with her coat, Britt added, "Go inside and warm up."

Rather than look at his watch, Ladso peered at the moon. He turned back to the cauldron, and picking up the cooking thermometer asked Britt how much the brew needed to cool before midnight.

Britt checked the receipt. "Anywhere below boiling. After that we can dispense Frank's portion."

Nikki stopped. "Will Frank need to drink all of that?"

Britt smiled. "That might be harder than the rest of this if not impossible, but the receipt says the rescued victims did not complain about the flavor."

"If we gave it to him with a donut, he'd drink it all." Nikki laughed and the men joined her. "So how much does he need to drink?"

"It's determined by his body weight. I don't know what that is yet but we made enough for a four-hundred-pound man. That will cover

Frank with enough to spare." Britt looked at Ladso. "But don't spill any, just in case."

Again, the threesome laughed. All were relieved the job was done and anxious about the brew having the desired effect. Laughter was a release of old tension and a barrier to new fears.

The brew was no longer boiling but Ladso checked the thermometer anyway. "187. Cooling quickly in this weather." He set the mason jar beside the cauldron, and, using the oven mitts picked up the brew and slowly poured it onto and through the cheese cloth. With the cauldron empty and the mason jar almost full, he unscrewed the ring, removed the cheesecloth and dropped it in the cauldron. He then sealed the jar.

Britt and Nikki collected the rest of the gear into the basket while Ladso doused the glowing embers.

Ladso handed the mason jar to Britt who hugged it to his chest with his gloved hand as Ladso and Nikki carried the other gear to the porch. As Pi opened the door, Ladso said, "Let us get our friend back."

Once they were back in the kitchen, Pi returned to Frank's room.

Ladso set the wicker basket of items on the floor, and took the mason jar from Britt. He then removed a measuring cup and a large ceramic mug from a cabinet. Setting both on the counter, he pulled out his phone. "I asked Stephen, Frank's nurse, to get Frank's correct weight. He brought his own scale to do it and texted the result earlier." Ladso verified the number before saying it aloud. "Two hundred thirty-three pounds."

Britt nodded, and looked to the opened app on his phone. He entered several instructions plus Frank's weight. He then checked the receipt and entered more data. After a few seconds, he looked at Ladso. "Twelve ounces."

Ladso nodded and unthreaded the top of the Mason jar. Picking it up, he slowly poured the contents into the measuring cup until the reddish green fluid reached the desired level. He then poured that into the mug which filled just short of the brim, as if the mug was made for this purpose. Ladso grinned. "Perhaps we have someone on our side."

He put the mug on the counter and glanced toward Frank's monitor through which they could barely hear his gentle snores. Another sign that all was well. Ladso turned toward the team. "The receipt says we have a full day to administer our brew, but I can think of no reason to wait. Do we all agree?" The team eagerly agreed.

Moving the mug to a lap tray, Ladso added a few cookies which made the others grin.

Together, the team walked to the elevator and rode up to the fourth floor in silence. The elevator doors slid open silently, and they walked toward Frank's suite of rooms. Britt opened the door; a moment later, the group entered Frank's rooms.

"Still quiet." Pi's whispered voice was barely audible.

As they opened Frank's bedroom door everyone froze. Frank was sitting on the side of the bed quietly murmuring.

Sharon had fed on three victims that night in her rage over the interlopers attempting to foil her plans **again!** The glut of blood had fed her as she tortured and killed several others. A family in Lafayette Square. Parents, two children, and a third child on a sleepover would eventually be found brutally murdered in their home. Blood splattered every wall as she'd flung the bodies through the house. The father, a detective in Frank's squad, had lived the longest. His wife, a doctor, and the children had been fortunate, receiving quick deaths, but their remains were still abused in Sharon's rage.

A vagrant in Benton Park had been pulled from a gangway and thrown across Armory Street. He was found the next day, his throat torn and his body hanging over the limb of a tree.

Again, Sharon had transformed and lifted herself above the rooftops. On Washington Avenue she saw a man on the roof of his apartment complex. It was the next afternoon before an unfortunate tenant came to the roof for some fresh air and found what was left of him. The gory spectacle will haunt that man for years.

Back in Britt's home, Sharon rested on the ruined Duncan Phyfe dining room table and reached for Frank's mind. Nearly engorged and stimulated by her agitation she found him. At first, she couldn't get him up but he shifted under his covers and began verbalizing her commands. Still angry she pulled harder at his mind and grinned an evil canine-revealing smile as he rose to sit on the side of his bed. "Show me your room!" Slowly, Frank turned, gazing into the dark space. When she attempted to have him turn on the light, he'd knocked the lamp onto the bed. Her eyes closed now, Sharon struggled to see anything. Finally, she saw light coming in through the window. She screamed into Frank's mind. "Go to the window, look out, identify where you are!"

The team hurried in. Stopping beside the bed, Pi took Frank's hand. "Frank, are you awake?" There was no response except his continuing to stare toward his window.

"Hey, buddy, are you feeling OK?" Britt talked soothingly as he squatted beside the bed. Frank didn't seem to notice until he turned his head slowly in their direction. He then seemed to try to focus. Blinking his eyes rapidly he became agitated.

Ladso set the tray on a dresser, well out of Frank's reach. "We have something for you to drink. It will make you feel better."

Frank jumped as Sharon shouted into his mind. Pi leaned close. "Frank, can you hear us? Ignore that bitch and come back to us!"

Frank turned to Pi as Sharon shouted again, but this time he barely heard it. Again, he was blinking rapidly as Pi leaned in a second time. "Did you hear Ladso? We've got something that will help you!" She was crying now, holding on desperately to Frank's hand.

Frank turned toward Pi. He tried to focus on her face. "Don't fret, buttercup. I'm here. I just need something to stop these damned dreams. To get that screaming bitch out of my head." Again, but from far away, he heard Sharon screech.

Ladso knelt in front of Frank but looked at Pi. "Tell him it will stop the dreams. It will get her out of his head too." Pi repeated Ladso's words as he signaled for Nikki to bring the mug.

Frank stopped blinking, his unfocused gaze was on Pi. "Are you sure?" He was almost whispering. "I need her to go away."

Pi promised it would as Ladso held the mug out to Frank. Shifting his gaze, Frank wrapped his hands around Ladso's hand and the mug. Together they lifted it to his lips, then paused. Frank looked again at Ladso, who nodded as Frank took a swallow. Frank's eyes seemed to clear. He blinked again but wasn't drinking.

Pi got right up next to his face. "Frank, drink. It will get rid of her!"

In St. Louis, Sharon was enraged again. She stood on the table cursing in the language of her old-world Order. She spat and flailed, the plastic soles of her tennis shoes squeaking against the table. "You can't get rid of me! He is mine. He will do as I..." She stopped speaking. Stopped stomping. Her eyes glowed swamp green but they were so tightly slitted that little light escaped.

Frank's grasp tightened on Ladso's hands and the mug. He began taking long, deep draughts of the solution. After he drained the mug, he continued to hold tight, slurping at the bit of fluid that lined the inside. That continued for several moments as Pi comforted him and Ladso explained that it was done. Finally, Frank released Ladso's hand, went limp and fell backwards onto his bed.

Putting the lamp back on the bedside table, the team worked together to get him fully back onto his bed and under his covers. Frank didn't notice any of the commotion as he was sound asleep.

The team retreated to the sitting room.

"How boring was **that**?" Pi grumbled good-naturedly. "I was expecting, I don't know, something, ferocious, not just Frank drinking up his mug like a good boy and falling asleep."

Ladso laughed. "Well, I am not disappointed. A boring moment in our adventure is welcome."

Everyone agreed with additional laughter until Nikki sobered. "I just hope it worked."

Again, the team was in full agreement. The decision was made to follow Frank's example and go to sleep. Britt set the plan for the next day. "Tomorrow we refocus on Sharon's new powers and how to defeat her."

Ladso nodded. "I am going to stay here, to be sure nothing untoward happens. I got extra rest today, so I am fine." Britt argued that he'd also slept, but a gaping yawn ended his argument.

Holding up the receiver to Frank's monitor, Pi said, "I'll be listening." They all left and went to their beds.

It fascinated Ladso that their found remedy might have cured Frank of his supernatural condition. But then the remedy of virgin's blood and ear wax, prepared under the stars and moon was clearly supernatural as well. His mind wandering, he chuckled. This is truly no odder than penicillin which stops many blood-borne illnesses. It started as moldy bread. The chef in him approved of specifying the order in which the ingredients were introduced. Ingredients were often added in a particular order in cooking for very specific reasons.

Some time later, Frank went to the bathroom and Ladso wondered if their remedy was cleansing his body of Sharon's contamination. He overheard Frank's discomfort which was later verified by a foul odor. He felt sorry for Frank. *Sometimes the body requires help in removing poisons.*

Frank made several trips to the bathroom. Each time he returned to his bed and was quickly asleep.

Ladso wondered if Murray's book might hold other unknown strategies from ancient fights with vampires. He would ensure that Britt didn't abandon the book before all its treasures were discovered.

Finally, dawn arrived, and Ladso felt safe to leave Frank alone. He would stop and get the receiver from Pi on his way to the kitchen and a hot cup of coffee.

He checked on Frank once more before leaving, but needn't have bothered. Frank was on his back, and sleeping as peacefully as a baby. Ladso grinned and shut the door. *Coffee, here I come!*

When Ladso slipped into his bedroom, Pi was sound asleep, the monitor on her nightstand. He took it quietly. In the kitchen, Ladso was blissfully enjoying his first cup of coffee. He listened to Frank through the monitor, as the steam from his coffee wafted the aroma straight to his nose. He quietly laughed at himself, thinking, *I am like a pig with its nose in the trough.* After the nights he'd been through, he thought he deserved this quiet moment with his coffee.

Pi slipped into the kitchen, and his mood brightened further. With no urging, she wrapped herself into his arms, holding him close. He kissed the top of her head, and squeezed her tight. Then she smelled his breath, and said, "Hey, no fair, you have coffee and I don't." He immediately poured her a cup, handing it to her with a boyish grin.

"I would never deprive you in any way." His smile deepened into something far more serious. She tipped her head up to him, and this time, it wasn't her hair that he kissed, but her lips.

They broke apart when they heard someone coming. Nikki entered with Britt right behind.

Nikki asked, "What happened overnight? Anything strange or eerie?"

Britt followed up with, "What effect, if any, did the brew have on Frank?"

Ladso replied, "Well, maybe Frank can answer that for us but he has not gotten up yet." Ladso pointed his thumb at the receiver.

Britt listened with the rest of them for a few seconds. "I'll go up and check on him."

Everyone tensed. Ladso put down his cup. "I will come with you."

Britt shook his head. "No, let me go alone. Just make it a normal day." After a half turn toward the door he looked back. "Keep an ear on the receiver though."

Everyone moved in to listen.

Arriving at Frank's suite, Britt entered the sitting room and moved to the bedroom door which Ladso had left partially open. He paused, listening, but couldn't hear Frank's usual heavy breathing. Stepping in he looked over and saw Frank sitting up in bed and awake. "Morning Britt. You lot ready for me to come down are ya?"

Startled, Britt jumped but quickly recovered with a happy expression. "Good morning, Frank! How are you feeling?"

"Tired." He frowned and shifted in bed. "I was up a bunch doing the 'Toilet Two-Step.' I think the caterers goofed up, or something. Things seem to have settled down now. Woke up feeling pretty good. I guess that last transfusion finally did the trick?" His frown returned. "Got a weird taste in my mouth though. You didn't bring up any coffee, did you?"

Britt apologized and Frank stood. "I'm going to take a shower. You really don't need to wait, I'm…" Frank's face paled. "Crap! That bitch bit me!" He looked at Britt as if to verify his words. Britt's expression gave him the answer. "Shit!" Frank stood. "Am I going to…"

Britt quickly interrupted. "No, you aren't." Frank looked unconvinced. "There are some things we need to explain but we're pretty confident you are safe. That's why we'd been keeping such a close eye on you." Frank sighed, wanting to believe. "Trust me Frank. You're going to be fine."

Britt was in Frank's sitting room when Pi came in with two cups of coffee. Brit turned. "You heard?" She nodded. "He wanted me to stay."

"Yes, we heard that too. I hope you're right about his cure."

With a sigh, Britt looked at Frank's door. "Me too. He was on the verge of panic. I thought it was best to keep him calm, but he sure seems fine. That he remembered the bite and was openly anxious about it is an about-face that seems promising."

Now Pi looked at Frank's door with an expression that suggested she hadn't considered that change and what it implied. Her eyes suddenly filled with hopeful tears. On his feet, Britt comforted her while repeating his belief that their friend was going to be fine.

In the kitchen Ladso grinned as Frank sat at the table with a Cop-achino in his hands. Pi had returned to the kitchen earlier and had it waiting. Britt and the detective had come down a few moments before. Frank looked healthy and well except for the expression on his face as he talked about his night. "Well, you should like this morning's catering if you feel up to it. I specified donuts, all the food groups." Ladso and Frank shared a grin.

The caterers arrived. Nikki went to collect the food while Ladso poured fresh coffee for everyone but Frank who still held his Cop-achino. Nikki came back with two boxes of donuts, all sizes, shapes and colors. Frank hesitated at the choices, but decided to begin with a bite from a glazed. After chewing for several moments, he washed it down. That was all he needed to consider himself whole again. He managed three more, along with two cups of coffee.

After breakfast, Frank grew serious. "I know I was bitten." At that he lifted his hand to the layered bandage on his neck. After applying pressure in several places, he stopped. A look of shock on his face he asked, "What happened to my wound?"

Everyone reacted, fearful that the wound was worse and that it might mean the cure had failed.

Pi hurried up to Frank's bathroom where the nurse had left a collection of basic medical supplies. She brought it down and handed Ladso a pair of scissors. He sat beside Frank and began removing the bandages. There were several layers providing protection from contamination and water from Frank's showers. Finally, there was nothing but a thin layer of gauze which he gently lifted off.

Ladso's forehead, which had been furrowed through the removal of the bandage, suddenly smoothed. As he lowered his brows, he looked hard at Frank's neck and gasped.

Hearing the gasp, Frank turned and saw Ladso's expression. "What?"

143

Ladso turned Frank so the group could see the detective's neck. A hush fell over the team.

"What?" Frank asked again.

"Wha… well," Ladso stuttered.

"Is that even possible?" Nikki shook her head and put a hand to her mouth.

"I don't know how it could be." Pi leaned forward, her mouth hanging open.

"It can only mean one thing." Britt's words sounded ominous considering his stunned expression.

"If someone doesn't tell me what's wrong, I'm gonna…" Frank reached up and put his hand on this neck. He rubbed it as he searched for his wound. "Where is it?" His eyes were now more puzzled than panicked.

Nikki looked Frank in the eyes. "Frank, nothing's wrong. It's gone!"

Frank's expression just looked more puzzled. "Gone? Gone where? What are you talking about."

Ladso put his hand on Frank's shoulder. "Gone as in no longer there, Frank. It has healed without a trace!"

An hour later the team was seated around the table. Pi had new tears in her eyes but Frank was laughing with a wide, happy grin. "So, the damn woman was talking through me! Holy crap, it was like the exorcist or something!" He stuck out his chest. "Well, we kicked her butt again, didn't we!" Lifting his cup, he wagged it and the middle finger of his other hand in the direction he'd chosen to imagine Sharon.

Pi gave him yet another hug and this time Nikki joined her. His eyes wide, Frank said, "I haven't been this popular with the ladies since…" He shrugged and tightened his hold on the women's waists. "Well, let's just let that statement hang there." With everyone laughing the ladies took their seats again.

"So, this bite hadn't healed at all as of yesterday?" Frank rubbed again at his neck which showed no sign of the punctures which had been there the day before and the week before that. He lifted a brow. "Well, that's certainly going to be a mystery for poor Stephen when he comes back to look me over again." Everyone paused, wondering how they were going to explain the miraculous healing. Seeing their expressions, Frank said. "Guys, and gals: That's his problem! We got enough of our own. Let's let him have it." They laughed as their tension continued to dissipate and as the reality of Frank's words set in.

"I will simply cancel further visits." Ladso shrugged. "I will tell them you are going back to St. Louis and will continue your care there."

"That's another way to solve the problem." Frank rubbed his neck again, dropped his hand and smiled. After another relieved sigh, his expression grew serious. "Alright, speaking of problems, where are we, everyone? And what's our plan?"

The team exchanged glances. "Frank," asked Britt, "what do you remember, about what happened at your house?"

"Well," Frank frowned again before answering. "I was feeding my cat, then I was waking up in the hospital. I've been having weird dreams. **Lots** of them. Last night I dreamt about that dark spinning mist that we saw on your porch." He pointed at Britt. "Like in the video, it vanished, and that Sharon creature was there. We all thought that was crazy. That she shouldn't have been there because she died in the explosion, but sure as God's little green apples, there she was." He frowned again. "She didn't die in the explosion." His frown held as the team shook their heads. "She stared at me with those ugly green eyes of hers and then I heard my Pi." He turned to her. "I saw you by my bed. All of you were there. That wasn't a dream." He looked at Pi who nodded. "I asked for help, but everything got… weird. Suddenly, Sharon wasn't there anymore. All you lot were still with me but I was suddenly, well, I guess I fell asleep. At least until I had to jump up and hit the can."

"This morning, not any of the times I got up for the toilet, but when I was in bed, I remembered Sharon in my kitchen, biting me, drinking my blood! I remember … it's shameful to admit it, but…"

He hesitated but decided to go ahead and say it. "I had a boner. I was excited. Then she stopped, and just dropped me on the floor. I felt myself fall, but it was like I fell for miles, and as I fell, I forgot. Next time I woke up I didn't remember anything at all about how I had come to be there. I didn't remember any of it when I was at the hospital. Sometimes I had a flash of... something. I mean, some of the time I knew something was wrong, but most of the time I didn't remember any of it."

Nodding, Britt looked toward Ladso then back to Frank. "What do you remember, since you've been here?"

Frank thought for several moments. "Not much. Doing something with Pi. Something..." He frowned. "Something fun, I think. I kinda remember laughing. I remember all of you..." he shrugged. "Again, just sort of. The dogs in the back yard. Nikki was there with me." His eyes widened. "I remember that nurse, Stephen, and the transfusions! Clear as day I remember that, but..."

Frank sat back in his chair. "I guess that bite messed with my memory." He looked blankly across the room, blinked, then looked at his friends. "It feels like I had Alzheimers, or something. My time here felt, I don't know, fuzzy, distorted. Like I was drugged. The closest thing I can remember feeling like that was after my appendix ruptured. The doctors gave me morphine. I couldn't think straight. Time was long and short at the same time. It kept bending like, like soft putty. I was never sure what was real and what was a dream." He closed his eyes for a moment. When he opened them again, he looked at his team. "Maybe not a dream, but a nightmare."

Pi took Frank's hand again and they gave him a few moments to collect his wits, to recover from the memories that still felt very real. Because they were.

When Frank looked at them again, he was shaken but sat up straight. "I'm fine."

Britt nodded. "Do you remember anything else?"

After taking several deep breaths, Frank met Britt's gaze. "Nothing." He wiped at his face. "No, nothing else."

Frank lifted his cup, took a drink, then set it down again. Ladso leaned forward. "Frank, what do you remember about your dreams?"

Frank shook his head. "They were vivid, real, like they were really happening. And every night it was the same. Someone was reaching out to me, calling me. But I was too far away. They couldn't find me..." He hesitated then added with a frown. "I wanted them to find me. I kept trying to reach back. To tell them where I was, but was never able to. That's it. That's all I remember dreaming about. Just over and over again."

"And what about last night? Did you have the dream last night?" Britt looked sorry to ask but was clearly eager to hear the answer.

Frank thought for a minute. Frowned, and then answered with relief. "No. Not even once. I hope I never have that dream again." He took a moment, frowning in thought. "Everything before I came to Chicago is clear in my head now. Whatever it was that happened, whatever she did to me, I really think it's over."

Nodding, Ladso smiled. "I think the disappearance of your wounds cements the deal, Frank. You are healed and back on the team." He looked at all the team members. "We've got to kill that damn thing, Sharon, before she hurts too many more. She's loose in St. Louis." He lifted his cup. "It's time for us to get to work, but maybe a short period of additional rest for you Frank?"

Frank's peaceful expression suddenly cracked. Looking at Ladso, he scowled. "Rest! More rest? Your idea of rest didn't even include the luxury of reading the sports page. Why don't you get the paper delivered... Actually no, the hell with that. I've **been** resting. Just like my neck, I'm healed. I'll sit in an easy chair if it makes you feel better somehow, but I'm part of this team. That bitch is killing my city. Like you said, it's time for us to get to work. **All** of us!"

Everyone was shocked at Frank's outburst, even thought it was a happy feeling to have Frank back. This was the Frank they'd known.

Looking at the faces of Ladso and the team, Frank sighed and spoke in a softer tone. "Listen, I know I've been through the mill. You folks are more aware of that than I am. I'll take it easy, but we don't have the luxury of taking our time. I'm fine, but she took our Murray, Nikki's friends, and your dog too. We've got some revenging to do. Let's get to it!"

# 10

Sharon was irate. She'd lost all contact with Frank. "This has never happened before. He was mine! How do they keep fouling my plans?"

Pacing around the dining room table she cursed in her ancient tongue. "They have left the city, but they will return. I can't sense my slave anymore but I will smell them when they come back. The next one I bite will die." She smashed her fist onto the table, putting another crack in its damaged surface. Her lips pulled apart exposing her teeth. "These blood chattel have hurt us when others only hid in fear." Crossing the room, she glared out into the night. "When they return, I will teach them to fear."

After insisting he needed to get busy with the team, Frank was brought up to speed on the research they had been doing. He was agitated when he learned their attention had been diverted in looking for a cure for him. It upset him because he was not the only one in danger from Sharon. "She's probably killing people every night. I don't know much about this supernatural crap, but I know how to hunt bad guys and I can read. You were all looking through Murray's books before you had to start babysitting me. Get those books out.

Give me some to look through, some paper to make notes and a spot in the sun. I really want to be in the sun." His pause was meaningful as he thought again of the former bite marks on his neck and what they could have meant, would have meant if not for his friends and their effort.

Britt put his hand on Frank's shoulder. "We're focusing on how to fight, and defeat a vampire. We know fire and wood are effective. The other old-world tactics of beheading and removing limbs are effective but we would have to catch her sleeping to pull those off, and we know that's not easy to do. Besides, Sharon knows that we'll be hunting her. She'll be waiting, and she'll be looking for us too."

"In your reading, check for mentions of wards." Ladso nodded at his own words. "For ways to either keep her away, or at least warn us when she's coming."

Britt nodded. "I'll add it to my list." With that, he headed toward the library.

Frank watched Britt leave then turned to Pi. "I want to park my butt in a chair and do some research of my own. It's time for me to start earning my keep…" He looked at Ladso. "…even if I have to start in low gear."

"Let me show you the study." Pi's eyes widened. "Prepare to be impressed. There're plenty of chairs and windows in there. I'll get my cart of books and share with you." Frank smiled, pleased at the notion of participating again. He wanted his city safe and didn't flinch at the thought of a little revenge either.

Nikki went out to work the dogs before going for her own cart. A discussion with Britt had given her several new ideas of how to proceed with their training, although she wasn't going to employ much of it today. There were more important things to be done. She almost giggled in anticipation. It felt good to be back on track, focusing on eliminating Sharon, and being a whole team again.

She looked at Trooper and Ray on their mats. Both had their heads and ears up in the hopes of going outside. "Come on boys," she called. Both dogs were immediately on their feet with tails wagging. "Sorry fellas. It's going to be quick today. We need to get out and back in again. Mama's got important work to do."

♪

Two hours later, Pi was watching Frank's head nodding in a bright puddle of sun as he napped. *He'd put up a good fight, but his nights of disturbed sleep, first from Sharon and then from his...* Pi rolled her eyes at Frank's term, *"lower quarters" had worn him out.* Along with his fighting Sharon's blood, it all had taken a lot out of him. She appreciated his wanting to get back in the fray, another of Frank's words, although one that didn't leave her feeling squeamish. She let him nap while she turned back to her tome, yet another rarely used word she'd recently become more familiar with.

Moments later, she frowned. *How did Frank put it? I feel the need to go talk to a man about a horse? Something like that. Whatever, I gotta pee.* She stood and looked at Frank thinking, *He might sleep the rest of the morning. Good, he needs to finish healing.* She left quietly.

The bathroom was just outside the kitchen door. As Pi stepped out, she heard water running in the kitchen. Expecting that Ladso was cleaning instead of resting, she peeked, ready to order him back to bed. Instead, she found Nikki cleaning breakfast dishes.

Happy to extend her time away from her tome which didn't seem to be approaching anything near being helpful, she went in. Crossing the room, she saw Nikki's book cart beside the kitchen table. Two large books were open on the table. Both of the dogs raised their heads and lowered them again, looking as tired as Frank. "Want some help?"

Nikki turned and smiled. Soon the dishes were clean, dry and put away. At the table with coffee, Nikki was describing her part in the previous night's ritual.

Pi frowned and shook her head.

Seeing Pi's frown, Nikki grew concerned. "What?"

Pi shrugged. "All this mysticism. Your blood in that concoction. I hadn't thought about it before, but Sharon's blood linked Frank to her. Could yours have linked you somehow to Frank and, through him, to Sharon?"

Nikki frowned. I don't know. Britt didn't see anything about that in what he read. We just knew that Frank needed three drops of my blood, or the brew wouldn't have worked." She shook her head. "It wouldn't have changed my mind anyway, I like Frank. He's part of the team. He helped us and I'd do anything to help him. Also, I **really** hate Sharon. I'll do anything I can if it helps to destroy her."

Pi nodded in full agreement then grabbed a dish cloth and started wiping at what Nikki considered an already clean counter. With a grin, Nikki commented on Pi's conversion to domesticity. In return, Pi threatened to brain her with the coffee pot. The two of them were laughing as Ladso came walking in with Britt.

Ladso looked around. "Where is Frank?"

Pi rolled her eyes. "Sleeping in your study. He put up a good fight. Worked at one of the books, even took some notes. Then he started doing a buzzsaw impersonation." She grinned. It was obvious she was happy to see Frank doing better.

Ladso smiled at Pi and poured himself and Britt a cup of coffee. Pi gave Ladso a hard look. "Did you get enough sleep?"

"Yes Ma'am," Ladso answered, continuing to smile.

Everyone sat around the kitchen table as Britt started speaking. "At Ladso's suggestion I've been looking for any information on wards." The women looked puzzled. "It means ways to detect the approach of a vampire or keep them away."

Ladso cocked his head. "What did you find?"

"Just that there aren't many other defenses other than the ones we know about." He pointed toward the dogs. "Animals are very reliable alarms. Our dogs, Frank's cat, all became alert just before Sharon manifested. We will have to be attentive to their behavior."

"There are other methods that sound interesting, but I'd hate to field-test them. A ring of cornmeal can supposedly stop the vampire, but it didn't explain how. Cornmeal is coarse so possibly it relates back to Arithmomania. Another is the blood of a virgin, worn in a vial around the neck. It suggests that the vial vibrates whenever the vampire comes near. Nikki, if you're amenable to another donation, we can wear them as a precaution. There was no notation however as to how long the effect is viable. Certainly, in a vial around the neck the blood will die in short order."

Nikki blushed. "I'll help any way I can."

Pi tilted her head. "Are we staying here in Chicago or taking the fight back home to St. Louis?"

Ladso said, "Once we are sure Frank has fully recovered, I vote we move back. Until then we continue looking for information that can help us. Britt, as you search, select any volumes you want to bring with us."

Nikki agreed. "We're safe here, but we can't take Sharon out from 300 miles away."

Britt pushed his glasses up on his nose. "So, it's unanimous?" Everyone agreed.

"Unanimous about what?" Frank had awakened and walked to the kitchen.

"That you are fully mended, my friend." Ladso offered his seat. "How are you feeling? Rested?"

"I'm feeling a lot more like my old grouchy self. I've also got a kink in my neck from sleeping in that chair. You shouldn't have let me sleep so long. No more dreams, and my gut's settled down." He shrugged. "I credit the doughnuts for that. Speaking of food, what's for dinner?"

Pi answered. "Italian: lasagna, ravioli, garlic bread…"

Frank grinned. "Makes me feel just like home on The Hill. Hang on — are the ravs boiled or toasted?"

"Toasted, and sprinkled with parmesan cheese. There's also marinara sauce for dipping."

Frank looked happy, then shifted gears. "Hey, what's a guy got to do to get a cup of coffee in this joint?"

Pi cocked her head. "Hey, you said you're top notch. Get your own!" Unprepared, Ladso choked with laughter.

Frank grinned, pleased again by Pi's sass, and did as he was told. He stood by the coffee pot as he drank his first cup then poured a second. This one he savored, sniffing the aroma and taking a sample sip before moving back to the table, to join the team.

"Man, I can't tell you how good it feels to be me again." Frank shuddered.

The team decided to go back to stage one and only monitor Frank electronically so everyone could sleep. Frank did however ask Ladso to walk with him to his room.

Frank decided to try the steps and got all the way to the second floor before reverting to the elevator. "You've got more recovery to do." Ladso put his hand on Frank's shoulder. "I encourage you to keep pushing yourself but not too much too soon." Still puffing, Frank nodded.

At the door to Frank's suite, he asked Ladso to come in for a moment. Once they were seated, Frank started speaking. "Ladso, I'm sorry to trouble you, but I don't think I can sleep right now." Ladso frowned with concern but Frank waved it off. It's this whole "excursion." It's put me off kilter. I don't know how I can go back to work, to life knowing the Undead exist. How do you live a normal life between these trips into hell? How do you merge two contradicting world views?"

A gentle expression lit Ladso's face. "I grew up with stories of such things being real. Finding they were true was still a shock. Murray, he helped me adjust, helped me through so much. On that first excursion, my world was torn apart. I lost Minka, who I loved. The horror stories of my childhood had come to life. I went with Murray largely out of fear. He knew how to survive supernatural creatures, and how to destroy them. I very much wanted them destroyed. I clung to him. His life was a way to fight back, to survive. He was also one branch of sanity in a maelstrom of madness. Murray, his calm acceptance and opposition of the supernatural, took me under his wing."

"We have seen extremely peculiar sights. I promise, vampires are solitary creatures and are few, thankfully. That is why this case involving SERA, where an entire group of vampires lived and worked together, was so fascinating. This is not normal in a world that is not normal."

Frank shook his head. "You sound so nonchalant, like it's another politician goofing up on the news. I'm still coming to terms with knowing the Undead exist, let alone that one of them wants to kill me. Hell, wants to kill all of us."

Ladso nodded. "You are right, Frank. Britt has been doing research in Murray's library. He has already found some very useful things."

"You and Murray have been doing this for decades. How is Britt finding stuff you two didn't already know?"

Ladso's eyes narrowed. "I do not want to make this more difficult for you."

Frank gave a humorless chuckle. "Too late. Go ahead and say it."

"There is much supernatural in this world. Vampires have actually been involved in only a small percentage of our excursions. Witchcraft, banshees, ghosts, curses, werewolves… They and more exist. They are few however. Once this is over it is unlikely you will ever encounter another supernatural creature. At least, you probably will not realize you have."

Frank tried to be comforted by the unlikeliness of another encounter. "I'm so sorry you lost Murray."

Ladso swallowed, eyes down. "Thank you. I miss him very much."

"We're going back to St. Louis soon, aren't we?"

Ladso nodded, curious what Frank's reaction would be.

"Good. My city is in danger and no one there knows how to defend themselves." Frank's eyes no longer held the uncertainty or fear that they did when they'd sat down only minutes before. "I don't know why, but I feel better. Our conversation hasn't been exactly comforting." He chuckled. "It's like the world was all chocolate or vanilla, and now I find out about strawberry."

Ladso was delighted by Frank's apt description. Frank saw that delight and smiled. "You're OK, Ladso. Thank you. I think I'll be able to sleep now, at least I'm going to try. You have a good evening."

Frank went to bed. Ladso found his way back to his bedroom. Frank stayed on his mind, however. He liked the detective's acceptance of difficult truths. *He is a good man to have on our side.*

Back in his room, Pi was awake and waiting to welcome him back to their bed. Their light was soon off but it was some time before they settled down to go to sleep.

As he lay there, Ladso's thoughts were on their return to St. Louis. How would they keep themselves safe, let alone find and destroy Sharon? Fatigue took him, but his mind kept working.

The next morning, after breakfast, Ladso shared the library with Britt. On the other side of the room, he employed his methodical strategy to plot their way forward.

First, they needed somewhere to stay where Sharon couldn't find them. Both Britt's and Frank's homes were unusable.

Next, they would need the dogs. They would be the team's alarm system. He disliked the thought of bringing Trooper and Ray into danger, but they would increase safety for the team, and without the team, Sharon had no one to fear.

He thought finding Sharon's hiding place was unlikely. They'd only found her and the others before out of luck and clumsiness on Sharon's part. He did not expect her to be as helpful again. The city was large, and they had no clues to follow.

The only thing to do was prepare, and, at a time they chose, let Sharon know where they were. Let her bring the fight to them. *First, we must decide how we will destroy her. When we are ready, we return to Britt's place, and we win!*

After dinner, when everyone was on their evening cup of coffee, Ladso began. "When we return to St. Louis, Sharon will be hunting for us just as strenuously as we will be hunting for her. There are basic precautions we all need to take. Never be alone after dark." He looked at Frank. "We have already experienced the consequences of such a mistake. We must stay together until dawn."

"Our tactics are very limited. Machetes and weapons with which to stab. I have received four of Nikki's wooden knives with the metal edge, but all of those are for when other methods have failed. Sharon will be fast, and strong. Hand to hand is unlikely to work to our benefit. Fire is most effective, but we would need the space to avoid hurting one another."

"I have a resolution to one problem." Everyone looked at Britt. "I own another property on the edge of the Soulard. It's another source of income. Right now, there is a single resident on the first level but he is usually away. He's an architect who only uses it when in town on a project. I checked with him this morning and he says he doesn't expect to be there again for months. If we stayed there, even if Sharon was watching my house and Frank's, she wouldn't know we're back in town. At least, not until we're ready for her to know..."

Nikki shook her head. "But it's so close to your house. Our theory is that she found us by our scent. She found your house looking over a whole city. If she's watching your place, a house in the same neighborhood seems risky."

Britt smiled as if he'd set a trap that worked. "I thought about that. I guess since I was thinking about hunting her, and her hunting us we can use Scent blockers, what hunters use!"

Ladso's eyes widened. "This is why we are a team. Many minds find many answers. That is brilliant!"

"They have sprays and wafers." Encouraged by Ladso's excitement, Britt continued. "We could spray ourselves and use the wafers in the SUV and at the house. The upstairs unit has two bedrooms and good sleeper couches in the living room and den. That's a room for each of us as long as Ladso and Pi are willing to continue sharing space." Everyone looked at the couple and smiled. Pi was unfazed so Nikki blushed for her.

Ladso nodded eagerly. "I like it. Simple, close, and sounds like it should be safe, in conjunction with our four-legged alarm systems. It will allow us time to devise a trap to force Sharon to come to us at a time of our choosing." He looked across the table at Frank. "Do you have more sick leave? We will need you with us until we see this through."

Frank's laugh was only slightly bitter. "I never get sick, and I never use vacation time. I could stay off work from now until I retire if I wanted. No problem. My cat though, is at a boarder which is getting expensive. We've got the dogs. Cat doesn't get on well with them."

Nikki looked shocked. "Don't you miss him?"

"Eh, he's a good enough cat, but he usually makes it obvious that I'm just his meal ticket. It's a business arrangement."

"I will cover Cat's boarding costs." Ladso looked over at Frank, then nodded.

Frank nodded his thanks. "Thinking about it, I'm not going to notify the precinct I'm back. I'm on medical leave, so it's none of their business where I am."

"Keeping a low profile, I like it." Britt added a thumbs up. "We should all stay away from public places. With that precaution and our scent blockers, we should be able to stay undetected."

Ladso summed up. "So, we will gather supplies and then we leave. Frank, you keep working on getting your strength back."

Frank's brows rose as he sucked in his belly and put his fists on his hips. "Whatever do you mean?" Before Ladso could respond, Frank relaxed his belly and leaned on the table. The team laughed.

"Just get back to the fine physique you had before Sharon ruined your workout routine." Pi smirked and Frank stuck his tongue out at her.

"We agree, then." Britt scanned the team. All nodded. "Frank gets back to his old fighting self, and once we have all the supplies we need, we go to St. Louis. Once we arrive, we'll drive-by Frank's and my houses, confirming they still stand, but we will not approach. We shelter in my other property, and stay together while we fine-tune our plans."

"What plans?" Nikki frowned. "I've heard plans for how we're going to get to town, how we're going to hide out, and now we're planning to plan to have a plan?"

Pi agreed. "Yeah, strikes me as a trifle bull-shitty."

Britt sighed. "Yes, that's the part we need to work on. The simplest suggestion is to wait and have Sharon come to us when we're ready. We'll be working on how to make that happen."

"I can work with that." Pi nodded. "Thanks for laying it out plain."

Ladso stood up. "We have a lot of work to do. I must make arrangements for the house to be vacant again. Britt, I have put packing crates for books in the library. Select what we should bring with us. Frank, you're going to need more than doughnuts to strengthen you during training."

"Hey, those are usually part of my training!"

Pi saluted. "Nikki and I will handle Frank's training." Again, Frank stuck out his tongue. Pi returned the gesture before turning to Ladso. "Also, I'll clean up the kitchen so you can get to work."

He beamed at her, then clapped his hands. "OK troops, everyone to your stations!" Nikki startled at the clap, making him chortle. "Sorry." She grinned back at him in response.

Sharon came out of her daytime trance, synchronized to the sun's descent. Fully alert as the sun dropped beyond the horizon, she used her senses to scan her environment. She smelled dust, wood, dirt, mildew and decay, the now-familiar scents of her resting place.

It wasn't a hunting night for her. One fully-drained human would fill her for a week. It was fun feeding on several victims, but it was riskier. Much better to go out once a week, and feast fully then.

She scanned the house above her, extending her senses. No sounds or unusual odors, only the same things she noticed every day — the hum of the refrigerator, the smell of dust, an empty, sterile odor.

She used her mind to touch Frank's. She expected a distant echo but she was still holding a dead wire. A phone where the other party had hung up.

Furious, she got up and stalked back and forth, thinking frantically. *Maybe he's dead or moved further away. They can't have outdone me again!*

She decided Frank couldn't be dead. *I would have felt his passing.* A further distance seemed likely and was the only explanation that made sense to her. She had never heard of a bond between vampire and victim being broken, except by death. *Distance is a new factor, but it must be the explanation.*

*So, they are running further away.* She snarled, but shrugged. *They will return eventually.* They have lives here; homes, property, jobs. *I can wait longer than they are able to hide.*

And she would wait, like a loathsome, evil spider. Hiding and waiting to suck them dry.

# 11

Britt had previously noticed the trailer hitch on Ladso's SUV. He discovered its usefulness when Ladso set a frame behind the vehicle. When they were ready to leave, the platform for carrying crates and luggage would be attached. Five people and two dogs would easily fit inside for the long drive.

Ladso grinned. "We always needed extra cargo space with Murray. If he was not hauling a library with us, he was collecting new books. The luggage will ride outside, and we will sit comfortably inside, dogs and all."

Ladso went back inside. He had several hours of phone calls and paperwork to complete. He sighed and rubbed his eyes. He had always loathed paperwork in all its forms. Murray always saw to that part of things, and he only now fully appreciated the value of Murray's efforts.

Britt went to the library and browsed the collection, pulling books he thought would be relevant. His first impression when Ladso put out so many crates was that he was being sarcastic, but now he reversed that thought. Books are heavy and bulky. The crates, which looked like plastic ammo boxes, carried several books each, otherwise, they'd be too heavy. Britt filled several crates, then went to his room for a hot shower and fresh clothes before taking a nap.

Nikki and Frank were having a raucous game of catch with both dogs, involving several tennis balls, a frisbee, and one of those knotted tug ropes. Frank was puffing as he gathered up a handful of tennis balls. With Ray dancing and yelping in anticipation, he cocked his hand back and threw tennis balls in rapid succession and in six different directions. Ray started running, stopped, turned, turned again, almost tripping over his own legs, confused over which ball to chase.

Frank laughed while apologizing to his furry friend. Nikki also giggled, dropping the frisbee she was supposed to throw. Patiently, Trooper stood and waited until she picked up the frisbee and flung it across the yard. Catching it in mid-air, Trooper trotted back, tail and ears flagging with pride. Still puffing, Frank raised his hands in temporary surrender.

In his office, with his calls finished, and paperwork mostly completed, Ladso walked to the corner of the room near the fireplace and pressed hard on a certain hearthstone. A 'click' and the hearthstone swung away on a hinge. In the compartment behind, a hidden box came into view.

Ladso removed the box. Setting it on his desk, he spun the dial of the combination lock and opened it. From inside he removed a document that he put on his desk, a large portion of cash, a pistol, and several clips of ammunition. He closed the box, spun the combination wheel randomly, and slid it back into its concealed cubbyhole. Swinging the stone cover back into place, he pressed until he heard the click. He slipped the cash and the weapon into a satchel which he also locked. With a sigh, he picked up the document he'd removed from the box and walked around his desk again to complete his paperwork.

Meeting the team in the kitchen, Pi kissed Ladso. "The caterers will be here soon with sandwiches, and Frank has earned a hearty meal."

"Yes I have, little Miss." Frank entered dabbing his forehead with a towel. "I just walked thirty minutes round that furnished gymnasium Ladso refers to as his study." Frank looked at the chairs but, with a sigh, decided to continue standing. "I'm glad there was no fire in there or I'd have collapsed half way through my scheduled torture." He wiggled his brows. "That Sharon is going to be toast because, like Schwarzenegger, 'I'll be bauck.'"

"That was supposed to be the Terminator right?" Nikki looked puzzled. "Not Scooby Doo?"

Everyone laughed but Frank who deadpanned and then threw his towel at her. "Snide comments aside, I think I'm back to my former level of fitness. I've always been more of a Scooby Doo than a Schwarzenegger, but St. Louis needs us. Britt or Ladso, get back to the hunter's pro shop and get our hunter's deodorant. We are the calvary and it's time to go home."

After dinner, everyone grew quiet. Frank looked around suspiciously, prompting Ladso to begin. "Frank, before we go, we need to tell you about the last night before your recovery."

Frank frowned. "What? Did you put a spell on me or something?"

"As a matter of fact, and in a manner of speaking, we did."

Frank attempted a smile. "Well go ahead. The suspense is killing me and I don't want to have done all that exercise for nothing."

"It was a potion rather than a spell." Frank's frown returned, but he didn't comment. "Britt found a cure which involved a collection of herbs..." He shrugged. "...and other ingredients. Prepared under the moon and to certain specifications, it promised to break the effects of a vampire's bite. In effect, it also broke the connection between you and Sharon. You drank it. It is what caused your issues in what

Pi says you call your "lower quarters." Frank's eyes tightened. "It was purging you of whatever Sharon had put into your body. It cleansed you and ended her control over you."

Frank walked slowly across the room and sat on one of the empty chairs. "I don't remember drinking anything." He held up his hands. "I'm not saying I didn't, just that I don't remember." Frank's eyes widened. "Wait! I do remember a promise that something would get rid of the bad dreams."

Ladso nodded. "Yes, I told you that."

Frank cocked his head. "That Undead piece of..." Frank sighed and looked at his team. "I owe all of you so much already. I don't have anything I can give you to repay you for saving me from..." He shivered, remembering the ugly, long dead thing behind the school and the others in the Vagrant's Cavern. "I'll never be able to repay you for all you've done."

Pi walked over and slapped Frank on the top of his head. "You talk about owing us anything again and I'm gonna kick you in those lower quarters of yours!" Before Frank could respond, she wrapped her arms around his head and kissed where she'd just slapped. "We love you and are so, so happy you're all right!"

At a loss for words, Frank just hugged her back.

Minutes later, with filled glasses of wine in every team member's hand, they toasted Frank's restored health and their return to St. Louis.

"Supernatural." Frank looked at Ladso. "Magic, witches, and everything else. Harry Potter, get outta the way." He drained his glass and shook his head. "We sure as hell aren't in Kansas anymore."

Chuckling, Britt looked at Frank. "Do you have any questions about your cure?"

Frank looked Britt in the eye and shook his head. "Maybe later. I've got too much to wrap my head around already without worrying about having drunk the eye of a bat, nose of a goat, and the blood of a virgin." He didn't notice everyone stiffen. Reaching for the wine, he refilled his glass. "Those details can wait until after we've ended this damned excursion. Ended it for real this time." He lifted his glass. "To that!" He gulped the glass empty again.

♪

That night everyone packed for their return to St. Louis. Pursuant to Frank's orders, Ladso ran to a local hunting store and bought up all their scent covering supplies. They would leave after breakfast the next morning and arrive in St. Louis early afternoon and in full sunlight.

Ladso drove and the miles passed easily. Quietly, too, until Nikki asked in a wistful voice, "I wonder… what life will be like after we destroy Sharon? How do we just pick up where we left off?"

"I've wondered about that too." Frank partially turned in the front seat. "Nighttime calls on found bodies will bring different thoughts to mind for me. Just being out at night will be different too." He paused as her turned forward again in his seat. "I'm not ready to retire yet, so I'm going to have to get used to this new normal. Not let it affect my work." He chuckled. "The truth is, I don't really know how to relax and I'm not interested in learning. I'm happiest when I'm working despite it providing a multitude of irritations. The department recognizes my ability to do my job, even if they don't often want to admit it." He chuckled again but this time it had an edge to it. "I won't be retiring until they push me out of the damned building. They haven't managed it yet."

Britt sat beside Nikki in the back as they'd all agreed to let Frank have the front passenger seat. He turned to face her. "Nikki, I hope you'll continue staying with me. Your help training the dogs is invaluable. I couldn't get along nearly as well without you. When we have clients, I'll put you on the payroll, but regardless, you'll have free room and board."

"You already offered. I'm grateful and, yes, I accept. I'll probably also pick up a part-time gig in a coffee shop somewhere. I think I might want to take some time to get back into music, too." Pi grinned on her friend's other side. "Bryant was always talking about getting gigs in Soulard." She took a deep breath. "What I was wondering about, though, is just living life while knowing the world has more and worse monsters than those identified on the nightly news."

"Pi, Ladso…" Nikki's voice now sounded more fragile. "You two are planning to continue as full-time Ghostbusters. I'm not sure I could handle that."

Ladso answered first. "I have been doing this for some time. While it is often difficult and always disturbing, I am accustomed to it. I hope Pi will still want to join me once this excursion is over, but I will certainly understand if she now, or later, wants to step away from its horrors."

With no hesitation, Pi responded. "I've got very personal reasons to want Sharon dealt with. Ladso and I have that in common, both of us lost someone dear to us because of those nasty things. I don't think the end of this excursion will change that." She tipped her head and smiled. "I admit, I wouldn't mind a little vacation before we move on to our next ghoulie, though."

"I'm sure that can be arranged." Ladso smiled into the rear-view mirror. "Perhaps England?"

Wide eyed, Pi grinned back. "That would be great fun, but I don't have a passport."

Ladso smiled. "The Embassy branch in Chicago is one of a dozen that expedites passports, for a fee, of course. We can have a passport for you in 72 hours, my dear."

Pi laughed, then. "Holy shit. I'm going to England!"

That kept the conversation alive for several more minutes. Then the vehicle quieted again as thoughts turned inward. After a pit stop for the dogs, and others, Britt and Nikki talked dog training for a short time, but then quieted again well before the St. Louis Arch peeked over the horizon.

The day was bright as they neared the city. Heavy breathing from Frank up front, the back seat, and the cargo area suggested that some of both the two- and four-legged passengers were sleeping. Ladso peered at Pi who grinned right back with that gamine smile he so loved.

"Let's make a pit stop soon." Pi wiggled in her seat. "Bathroom breaks and hot coffee will make this girl happy. I suspect our fellow passengers will forgive us for waking them up."

"Excellent notion. There is an exit coming up." Ladso used his turn indicator, although he was the only vehicle on that stretch of road, and merged smoothly into the right lane. The change of movement woke the dogs, and Ray's excited yip woke up the passengers.

"Break time!" Ladso announced.

"Hot coffee." That was Frank.

"Bathrooms!" Nikki and Pi echoed one another.

Britt responded to Ray's noises. "And a doggy potty break."

After Ladso parked, Nikki put leads on the dogs' collars, and they happily jumped out of the vehicle. Britt led the happy dogs to a nearby grassy verge.

He included a short walk before putting them in the back of the SUV. He then went into the station for coffee but also to do a little business of his own. As he exited the restroom, he saw Nikki carrying a six-pack of water. "For the dogs," she explained. Britt nodded his approval.

After getting his coffee, Britt joined the group at the vehicle and waited while Ladso hung scent covering wafers in the car. He grinned, seeing that Frank had a bag of his beloved donuts and two coffees. "Good to have you back, Frank." His mouth full of sweet dough, Frank saluted, licked his thumb and then waved the damp digit toward Britt.

As everyone climbed back in, it surprised Britt that Frank took the back seat with Nikki and Pi. As he climbed into the front seat, he realized that having him in front allowed him to easily direct Ladso through the city to their respective destinations. *That Frank was always thinking. So good to have him back.*

As Nikki looked at the Gateway Arch, she remembered her past drives on this stretch of highway. The first time, she was full of naïve dreams and ambition. The second time, she was full of crushing grief and guilt. This third time, what she felt was… righteous. They were doing something important, something to help make the world a little safer.

166

"Where to first? Frank's or Britt's house?" Ladso looked at Britt, reminding, "All we're doing is a drive by, no matter what we see."

Britt didn't need to think on it. "It makes more sense to go by Frank's house first. Both of my properties are in Soulard."

Everyone agreed, so Frank provided directions from the back seat. Soon they were driving side streets with tidy brick houses and neatly manicured lawns. It looked like a neighborhood from decades past, with few visible signs of decay. Ladso made a right turn and slowly drove down a street that looked like all the others.

There were few people out. Most, they presumed, were at work. Frank pointed out his house "Everything looks fine. Let's head to Britt's."

Ladso surprised them all by driving unerringly to Soulard. As they drove by, everyone got a good look at Britt's house. All looked normal. Ladso kept the car moving.

"Northeast for two more blocks, then turn left." Britt pointed as they continued on. "I'll guide you after that. It's best to take the alley. The garage is behind the property."

Britt navigated them directly to the alley having Ladso stop at the garage. Britt climbed out of the SUV, unlocked, then opened both garage doors. Simultaneously, Frank hopped out and unhooked the trailer. Frank began maneuvering the trailer into one stall while Britt gestured for Ladso to pull into the other. Once the SUV and trailer were parked, Britt quickly closed the doors behind them, locking them again from the inside.

Everyone climbed out with Nikki leading the two dogs on their leashes. Britt unlocked the door leading from the garage to the back yard then turned to Nikki. "The yard is completely fenced, so you can turn them loose. They'll both enjoy the fresh air and the exercise."

Britt then led the team up the wooden steps to a large deck. He unlocked the back door with the keys which had been secured in the garage and they entered the kitchen. Britt shut off the security alarm as Frank looked sadly at the small kitchen table. Seeing Frank's expression and its cause, Britt pointed over the kitchen island, where a sink was installed. "Fear not Frank, the dining room table will allow us to eat and gather in the manner we are accustomed to."

After stepping over to see the table, Frank smiled.

Pi was exploring the house room by room. Soon she returned to join them all in the kitchen. "I picked Ladso's and my room. The rest look nice, but you all decide where you're sleeping."

Ladso shook his head. "I have been rethinking. Sleeping all together in the den would be best, Britt says it is spacious. I suggest we drag the mattresses in there. Being separated at night worries me. If Sharon does find us here, she could use our separation against us. Together, we are far safer."

Nikki's voice wavered. "But we have the scent hiders, and she doesn't know about this place."

"She can't know about this place." Britt was confident. "There's no paperwork in my house; the only documentation is in a lockbox at my bank, and she can't track us through Frank anymore, either. But Ladso is right; we don't want any of us to be alone."

Nikki and Pi went to help Ladso unload the vehicle, while Britt hung the scent blocking wafers on every window and exterior door. He also checked to ensure that all the security cameras were engaged, inside and out. There were ones in every room but the bed and bath rooms.

Ladso entered, carrying the first two crates of books. "Where would you like these Britt?"

Britt thought for a moment. "I'll take a bedroom since they aren't being used for sleeping. Put them in the smaller of the two. Thanks."

Ladso grinned, tipped his head, and carried the crates away. Luggage was put in the larger bedroom which would serve with the bathroom as a changing space.

Next was a trip to the grocery store. Britt stopped Ladso at the door. "The refrigerator and freezer are much smaller than what you're used to. I'm sorry but there is also a lack of both good cooking utensils and spices."

"I will make it work." Ladso eyed the kitchen. "I will also need to adjust my shopping habits, but I could use an open fire on a moor to whip up a feast. This will be an easy challenge to overcome." Everyone proclaimed their confidence in him.

Ladso sprayed himself down with the scent blocker and drove away in search of a nearby grocery store outside of Soulard.

An hour later, he returned with several bags. As Ladso began unloading the groceries, Frank sat at the dining room table and checked his watch. "It's getting late. We've got daylight left and I'm starving. Who else thinks going out for some dinner is a good idea?"

"Food does sound great, but I don't think going to a restaurant is a good idea." Britt wore a concerned expression. Sharon could be nearby and we couldn't get somewhere, order, eat, and get back before sunset." He looked at Frank. "We're also in your jurisdiction. I didn't think you wanted anyone on the force to know you're back in town."

"Yeah, you're right, although it pains me to admit it," Frank paused to think and in seconds had another plan. "There's always take out!"

Ladso nodded agreement. "I do need to organize the kitchen before attempting a meal." Ladso gestured with containers of salt and pepper in his hands. "Take out sounds like an excellent solution."

"Anyone have a restaurant to recommend?" Britt's brows were raised in expectation.

Pi and Nikki immediately suggested Tucker's Place. Britt nodded but frowned. "They are good but that's close to my house. We'd have to pass close to where Sharon might be." The ladies cringed and rethought their suggestion. Frank cleared his throat. "South Grand has a variety of cuisines and isn't near either Britt's or my house. Most of those restaurants allow call-in orders for pickup, too."

Britt checked the time. "We'd best decide and get our orders in. Ladso, since you're unscented already are you willing to pick up the food? You can easily be back before sunset." Ladso said yes, then asked Pi to put away the food.

"Least I can do to get some cooked grub." Pi followed her words with a blown kiss which Ladso caught and gobbled down.

Choosing not to comment on the love birds, Britt looked to the team. "What does everyone want?"

The group chose Thai food, and selected *The King and I* as their destination. Britt phoned in the order and turned to Ladso. "It'll be ready in 30 minutes." Ladso went back to the SUV as the others worked together to get the place ready for their extended stay.

When Ladso returned, the groceries were all put away, the table was set, and everyone was ready to eat.

♪

At Britt's home, Sharon was also thinking about having a meal. On her makeshift bed in the cellar, she considered going out a day earlier than had become her habit. Sunset was moments away as she rose to her feet and dematerialized into her smoke form. Swirling up to the basement door, she paused, sensing the sun. *It is low enough. I'm not waiting.* When she snarled, the smoke that was her body appeared to vibrate. Moving forward she slipped through the openings around the door and solidified on the other side.

As she retook solid form, she noted that the faint glow from the setting sun was visible at the windows. Sharon squinted as she studied it from the shadows. As she did, she remembered standing in bright sunshine before she became a full vampire. *I'll never comfortably feel the sun on my skin again, but the blood makes it worth the sacrifice.* Opening her mouth, she licked her lips.

Her eyes lost focus as she remembered an earlier, bright, sunny day over two centuries ago. She'd still been fully human and had finished a day at school. Sister Chastity, a Sister of The Sacred Soul, had approached her on the field that bordered the school building and convent. "Your meeting with Mother Eugenia has been arranged for tomorrow night."

Sharon had been so happy. "To serve is my greatest desire," is what she'd told Sister Chastity, but what she'd truly wanted was the security, comfort, and respect the Order supplied. Her family was poor. She'd have never gotten an education without the nuns, but she wanted more.

Mother Eugenia had given her so much more. *I would have been forgotten dried bones long ago if not for the Mother's gift of the blood.* In gratitude Sharon had dedicated her extended life to Mother and the Order.

Blood tinted tears glistened in Sharon's eyes as she remembered the nights of the attacks. *So many died in the fiery pyre in our school.*

*Then fire took the rest of the Order in the cavern by the river.* The green glow in her eyes dried her tears as she pictured the blood chattel who'd taken her Sisters from her. *They almost killed me too, but this time it is they who will die. I will spill their blood and leave them to rot!*

With the sun fully down, she walked to the window and then bared her teeth when an alarm suddenly sounded. Across the street the front door burst open and two young men exited carrying sacks. Moments later, another came to the door. A man in pajamas. He looked fearfully down the street, stepped back in and shut the door tight.

Criminals. They deserved their role as chattel. With the alarm still blaring she prepared to take smoke form once more but stopped as two police cars with lights flashing stopped in front of the house. The officers jumped out and ran to the house across the street. After speaking to the man inside, two stayed while the other two ran up the street in the direction of the two with the sacks. The police cars were left blocking the street, their lights bright and flashing.

Sharon frowned. Exiting through the front door now might attract attention. She considered her secondary exit but turned away from the window. The green light in her eyes had faded as her thoughts returned to her days in the sun. Deciding to spend time reminiscing on those long-ago days she took her smoke form and returned to the basement. *I will feed tomorrow as I'd planned.*

By the time the team's plates were empty and bellies were full, it was well past sunset. Britt had let the dogs in before dinner. Now he double-checked the locks, alarm points, and security cameras. The outside cameras had their motion sensors engaged. On the side and back of the house they were programmed to alert Britt's phone if triggered. The one inside the front door was similarly programmed.

Turning toward the den, Britt stopped, his eyes bulging. "God, I must be going senile." Moving down the hall he crossed paths with Pi and Frank hauling mattresses into the den. Squeezing by, Britt barely slowed. "I've got to check something" Pi watched as Britt ducked through the smaller bedroom's door and shrugged at Frank.

Nikki also saw him. She frowned then yawned. "I'm going to go change for bed"

Pi called out from the den. "Wait!" Nikki stopped, looking puzzled.

Pi stepped back into the hallway. "I'll go with you. We're not supposed to be alone, remember? It's after dark now, so we need to be careful." Nikki agreed and both women went into the larger bedroom.

Pulling out loose pants and tops that would be appropriate to wear while sleeping in a room full of men, the women were half dressed when Britt called out to the team. "Everyone come in here! Hurry!"

Everyone did, although the women arrived last, still straightening what was going to serve as their pajamas.

Britt was sitting on a chair, pale and with his laptop on a stack of book crates. As the team gathered round him, he looked up. "I was checking the alarms and cameras when it occurred to me. In Chicago, I'd been so distracted over Frank's being bitten, caring for him, and trying to find a cure. His episodes kept me focused on him and I wasn't sleeping well either. Then we redirected to how to kill Sharon. Damn, we've been wondering where she was... I just didn't think of it until now."

"Didn't think of what?" Ladso, Frank, and Pi asked in unison as Nikki stood beside Britt, hoping to calm him enough to start making sense.

"I found her!" Britt looked up at them, his eyes bulging. "The filthy bitch is in my house. She's been there for days!"

The next several seconds were deafening in their silence.

# 12

The team had moved to the dining room where there was more space to view the screen. Britt first brought up the familiar scene of his front door. The whirlwind of smoke appeared, solidified into Sharon, then de-solidified again before dwindling, as it passed through the crack above the front door. There was only the sound of the team's heavy breathing as Britt switched to the inside videos. Her movement turned the cameras on and as she moved out of range, they shut down again. This allowed them to see only when there was action in the house. Britt flipped from room to room and they saw her walk through, damaging or destroying things again.

Sharon always appeared angry at those times. Other times she merely sat as though in thought. Sometimes her mouth moved. Those episodes often preceded periods of varying levels of anger and additional destruction. Her de-solidification occurred with some regularity, but it often occurred before the smoke filtered through gaps around the door to the cellar. "Is she staying down there during the day?" Nikki leaned away from the screen as Britt nodded. Without noticing Britt's movement, Nikki stared at the screen which blanked for a second then showed Sharon reforming. "She is. She's living there. Using our place to hide in!"

An hour later, they'd gone through all the videos. Seen the further destruction of Britt's table, which is where Sharon seemed to concentrate most of her many periods of frustration and anger.

Noting the times, they compared them to activities with Frank in Chicago. Most of her interaction with Frank occurred at night. Her struggles to control him were clumsy and therefore obvious to the team. After the first transfusion, she was particularly enraged. The second accompanied his receiving his cure which seemed to mostly confuse her. She spent periods solid and pondering on the first level.

They also saw her go into Britt's room for clothes. Britt paled as she selected pieces of his clothing for her to wear.

Additional viewings revealed she had a schedule. Every seven days she left the house. After one angry period, she left out of sync with her schedule and returned covered with blood. A check on recent local news revealed multiple deaths that night. Deaths that now had an identified culprit, but identified only by this team.

Ladso turned to using her schedule against her. "This is how we can force our schedule on her, by using hers against her as well. We plan our attack for the night she hunts."

Sleeping that night was easy for none of the team, but they were all happy to be gathered into the one room, and not in a room alone during what turned out to be a long night.

The morning began with Britt apologizing again. "That it never occurred to me…"

"It didn't occur to any of us," Ladso repeated.

"Yes, I know, but I should have kept tabs on my own place. What's the point of all that equipment? I just…"

"We all knew you had it." Nikki felt bad for Britt. "There has been so much going on. You thought of it now and none of the rest of us can say that."

Britt was connected again with his household server. "Her weekly going and coming looked like a glitch at first, a loop, or something. It certainly creates an opening for us."

"I was hoping for something like this." Ladso looked over the kitchen island to the rest of the team who were seated in the dining room. "We have her, but that said, how do we deal with her?"

Nikki gave Britt a sympathetic look. "I'm so sorry you have that thing in your house."

Britt shrugged but turned to Ladso. "You said, 'Now we have her.' How do we have her?"

"We know her daytime lair. We can choose our time and hunt when she is most defenseless."

"It's dark enough in my cellar that daylight won't hurt her. She's fast as a snake, and twice as mean. And we don't know what other tricks she's capable of."

"So we plan carefully, and we do not move until we are all certain of success." Ladso nodded for the team's agreement and got it.

"Again, though, how?" Britt's eyes shifted back to the screen. Sharon was on his table making new gouges in the hard wood. "She is so strong!"

"Should we just blow her up?" Pi looked at Britt. "I know it would also destroy your house, but during the day she'd be trapped. Either the fire or the sunlight, she'd be toast."

"I'd happily give up my house, but the floor of my cellar is dirt. She could dig into the dirt to protect herself. First, we wouldn't know if she'd died. Second, we'd have lost the advantage of knowing where she is. If she escapes, we will have to find her again. We must be certain she is destroyed!"

Ladso agreed vehemently. "We have been blessed by lady luck again. We dare not squander it." He walked around the kitchen island and joined the team. "Fighting her hand to hand would be suicide, even though we have her outnumbered." He looked to Britt. "Remember the vampire that attacked you those years ago. Murray's team was ineffective despite our number and the strength of our men. And that creature did not have the speed and dexterity of these vampires. Torches and fire bombs are our surest weapons, but in Britt's home it would be almost as dangerous to us to use them. When she erupts, she could take us all with her."

"Then how do we use our advantage?" Frank held his cooling coffee and looked puzzled. "My service pistol had a lot of punch, but we saw that it was only good for knocking them back temporarily. It did not knock them down."

"A head shot would," Ladso did not look confident. "But in the relatively tight space of Britt's largest room, without hitting someone else, and without missing... it is a great risk. The torso is a much surer target, but a bullet would not get the job done."

"A hollow tip?" Frank countered with his brows raised.

Ladso nodded uncertainly. "Depending on where it hit, possibly, but I've seen these creatures continue attacking with devastating wounds. No, we have to use their known weaknesses against her."

"Fire is out. Large caliber or special ammunition is dangerous and not guaranteed." Britt stood and began to pace. "We know wood kills them but wooden stakes or even Nikki's wooden knives with the metal edge would require hand to hand which is not our advantage, but is hers."

Ladso's eyes widened as he looked across the room. "Britt, you have done it!" Clearly lost as to what he'd done, Britt stared back. The rest of the team did the same. "Wood! That is the answer. Well, part of it."

"We're going back to the wooden stakes?" Nikki looked doubtful.

Setting his cup on the table, Ladso almost shivered he was so excited. "It is back to the hunters' supply store my friends." Blank stares were the only responses he got. Holding his hands as though he was holding what was on his mind, Ladso asked, "Have any of you ever fired a crossbow?" Understanding bloomed on his team members' faces but it was followed by despair as each shook their heads. "I have!" Ladso countered.

That afternoon, Ladso returned to the house, smelling once more like the woods. At least that's how the label on the can of de-scenting spray identified the odor. In his arms were two large, flat boxes. Over his shoulder was one quiver of wooden arrows.

"Only one quiver?" Frank looked disappointed.

Ladso nodded. "The quiver came with the arrows, of which, due to her strength and speed, we will only have the opportunity to use two. One for each of us. If we both miss, Sharon will have won."

"Fortunately, we have an alternative use for the others." The team looked at Ladso. "Practice. There is a target in the back of the SUV. I propose we set it up in the basement. I will take a few shots. It has been a few years since I used a crossbow." He looked at Frank. "You may want to take a few as well."

Dry mouthed, Frank nodded in reply.

In the basement, they set the target against a wall and on top of an ironing board. "Loading the crossbow is the most difficult, but we won't be loading under pressure. The pressure will be with taking the shot. We must not miss."

Frank was pleased to have only missed with his first attempt. After that, he was prepared for the jump as the mechanism released and the arrow leapt from the bow. His last shot was almost a bullseye. "That's twenty feet away. About as much distance as Britt's dining room will allow and as close to her as we dare approach. Again, a miss may mean our failure, our deaths, and the deaths of many more if Sharon survives."

Frank went to the target to collect the arrows and try a few more times. Loading the crossbow was difficult. He was confident that with practice he would be able to do it faster, but he put that thought aside. *If I miss, I won't get the chance to reload. If I pierce her evil heart, I won't have any need to load again.*

Britt was pained over his inability to take a more active role in the upcoming battle. Even the pistol Ladso had brought, because of its caliber, would require two hands to operate. He had been a fairly good shot before, but he was out of practice and short half the necessary equipment. Still, he was interested in the plan. "So, the dining room then."

"The cellar is not the location to fight her." Ladso frowned over his lunch. "If we go in during the day, she would come for us in the cellar, but the space is tight. She enters your house in her mist, or smoke form. We have to assume she could detect us despite the fact that, in that form, she has no eyes. We must give her no warning of our presence or our advantage will be lost." Upstairs we will have light from outside, but we will also have the light switches. In the cellar, you have already said that the only switch is at the top of the stairs. That is not a position we can take while waiting to surprise her, and if she is already in the cellar, turning on the light would leave us vulnerable during our descent of the stairs. Yes, the dining room gives us the space we need to keep our distance and the visibility to use our weapons."

"We also need to bring the dogs." Nikki frowned, but to Ladso's surprise did not object. "I realize Britt's cameras will be running, but Trooper and Ray will sense Sharon immediately. Those extra seconds of warning may make the difference between our success and failure." He looked back at Nikki. "You will need to control them once Sharon enters. We don't want Sharon to hurt them, but we also don't want them between us and our attacks." He held his gaze on Nikki. "I will want you, once Britt turns on the lights, to throw a handful of beans at Sharon's feet. One more opportunity to use Arithmomania to our advantage."

Ladso now looked at Frank. "The crossbows will be our first line of attack. They allow safe distance for our team and take advantage of the vampire's weakness regarding wooden weapons."

"Will we take the wooden knives with the metal edges?" Nikki was disappointed that her role would not directly injure Sharon, but she accepted that Ladso and Frank were the best able to operate the crossbows.

"Yes, we will carry the knives. I will also bring a machete. Pi will have her smaller version of our flame-throwers as well." Ladso looked worriedly at Pi. "Those are all weapons of last resort, particularly Pi's. If our other tactics fail, her smaller flame will be effective in destroying Sharon. The smaller flame will increase our chances of escaping the resulting fire alive."

"Finally, entering during the night, while she is out hunting, gives us the opportunity to surprise her when she returns. If she's feeding only once a week, she will be full and hopefully slower and less aware because of it. Britt will take us in through the kitchen door which we have seen Sharon does not use."

"Newer and clearly better insulated." Britt spoke with his eyes on the table.

"As we have seen, she solidifies after coming through the front door and then Britt will turn on the light. Pi will stand ready with her thrower, and Frank and I will drive our wooden arrows into her heart, or at least her body. As long as she is impaled, the advantage will remain on our side of the battle."

"Of course, our plan is contingent on Sharon's leaving to feed. Tomorrow night is the seventh day since she last went out, so we should follow our plan.

"Sounds like a winner." Pi's smile was confident and sincere. The room quickly became somber.

Dinner that night was simple. No one had much appetite despite their stated confidence in tomorrow's mission.

With no one ready to sleep, Nikki suggested a movie, maybe something funny would distract their thoughts, at least for a short time, from the difficult task ahead. With reservations, everyone agreed, but Nikki's plan had been only partially revealed. Asking for help in the kitchen, she took Pi with her as the others moved to the front room. Once through the kitchen door, Nikki closed it and, stepping up to her friend, made a suggestion. The two hugged for several seconds before Pi walked to the sink and called through the opening to Ladso.

When Nikki came to the front room alone, Britt and Frank noticed but said nothing.

Everyone was distracted but only occasionally by the film. Nikki just wanted this over and to have herself and her friends safe from Sharon and her horrors. Britt wanted Sharon out of his home with a visceral, savage desire. *Almost as much as I want her destroyed,* he realized with surprise. Frank wanted his city protected and didn't mind some revenge on Sharon for biting and attempting to do worse than kill him.

♪

Detective Mike Gently sat at his desk. In front of him were files on nine separate homicides. A total of fifteen dead. Most horribly mutilated. Several appeared to be drained of blood. Only one had punctures in their neck. Every time Gently looked at them, he knew he'd seen some like them before. He looked at the ceiling for over ten seconds before lowering his chin and voicing a curse. The rest of the victims' throats were slashed. Remnants of what might have been the same kind of puncture marks were found but neither the coroner nor anyone else he asked knew what they were..

Gently flipped through the folders hoping that something would catch his eye and give him an idea of where to go with the case. As he set down the last folder he cursed and leaned back in his chair. *What in the hell is happening in our city? And how am I going to put a stop to it?*

Looking up from the files, his gaze settled on the door to Frank Bolden's office. The man had never been away from the office for so long and he hadn't returned any of Gently's phone calls since before he left town. "Chicago. Who in the hell does he know in Chicago?"

He looked back down on the files. *I hope he's doing okay. Last time I saw him he looked pretty...* Gently's eyes widened. He picked up all the folders and looked at the names on the tabs. Finding the one he wanted he pulled it, dropped the others on his desk, and opened the one in his hands. On the inside of the front flap was a clear sleeve with a collection of pictures. The picture on top was there because Gently had placed it there. Each time he looked at it, he got a flash of a memory that sadly burned out as quickly as it had flashed. But not this time. He looked at the pictures of the punctures on the victim's neck and remembered where he'd seen them before. *On Frank's! I have got to find him! He's got answers that I need. I hope he's doing well enough to help.*

The next morning, everyone awoke early. During the night, Ladso and Pi had returned to their mattress on the floor and amongst their team. Good mornings were passed around as though all was normal, but Pi did grab Nikki's hand, gave it a hard squeeze and gave her a bright smile.

Knowing they'd need energy for the long day and night ahead, Ladso made one of his signature breakfasts, using most of what he'd bought at the store. Scrambled eggs, and omelets. Some were filled with veggies, others with cheese, sausage, and bacon. There were also pancakes and toast as well as sliced and fried apples in a sugary syrup.

The day was overcast. Ladso turned from the kitchen window. "Good. A gloomy day will make it easier for us all to take a nap later. We will need to be well-rested and at our peaks tonight."

After eating and with a long day filled mostly with waiting ahead of them, Frank looked at Nikki. "Let's work the dogs. Clear our minds and work our bodies."

Nikki was more than glad to follow Frank's suggestion. She grabbed her jacket while Frank was already buttoning his then had a thought and hurried to the bedroom where their luggage was stored. She raced back out with two thick canvas sleeves. Frank puzzled, "What're those for?"

"I'm going to finish some training today." Nikki smiled at Frank. "The boys might get a little rough and we don't want you hurt do we?" Frank nodded agreement as she whistled for the dogs.

Britt picked up his laptop. "I'll be in the small bedroom. Thanks for that breakfast." He waved to Pi before disappearing down the hall.

Pi looked at Ladso and grinned smugly. "Look who's left to their own devices." She batted her eyelashes at him. "Any ideas for something we could do?"

He laughed. "After your idea last night, I need a shower. Would you care to join me?"

She beamed. "I like the way you think!" They left the room, hand in hand.

♪

That afternoon, up from their naps, the group sat around the dining room table with a simple, but filling meal of burgers and salads. Everyone had beer, but it didn't loosen their tongues. There was little conversation; everyone was lost in thought.

After dinner and dessert, Ladso cleaned the kitchen alone, using the time for extra thought.

"Tonight is the night." Everyone looked up as Ladso came out of the kitchen. "We will enter Britt's house after Sharon has left to hunt. The videos have verified her timing, and that she did not go out last night. Thank you, Sharon, for being remarkably consistent. She is always gone for several hours. Britt will monitor the video feeds. When we see her leave, we move. Everything we need is already in the SUV which awaits us in the garage. When she enters, she should be unaware that we are there. Before we leave, we will all spray ourselves well with the de-scenting spray, the dogs too. I have checked that what we have is safe for them. Sharon should not smell us until it is too late for her."

"When she enters the dining room, Nikki, you hold the dogs back, Britt will turn on the lights and Frank and I will fire our arrows before she can react. Pi, with her lighter and can of spray, will stand by. If things go dreadfully wrong, she will torch the bitch. If things go as we have planned, that will not need to happen."

"Everyone have your knives ready. I will have my machete. After Sharon is hit with our arrows, I will move in and swing for her throat. Then we will drive one of the wooded knives through her heart and drag her into the yard where the sun will burn her away."

"This will be a dark night's work. All of us must be prepared to act immediately when the time comes. Sharon wants nothing less than our pain and death, which is exactly what we must deliver upon her."

♪

Everyone was sitting in the living room. The TV was on, but no one was paying attention to it when Britt looked up from his laptop. "There she is!" He looked back down. "She just appeared outside the door, walked down the steps and toward the street. Just like she owns the place." He didn't keep the bitterness from his voice.

"Pi has brewed a fresh pot of coffee." Ladso frowned at the laptop screen. "Everyone have a cup, then we can get ready. As long as we are there by midnight, we will be fine. Sharon will be home well before dawn, but we will have time to prepare before she returns."

Gathered in the kitchen, Ladso raised his cup. "Victory. Deus vult." Everyone took a drink of their coffee but Frank, who finished his and went for his second cup.

Nikki asked Ladso. "What did that toast mean?"

"It goes back at least to the crusades. 'God wills it' is the translation."

She looked thoughtful. "I hope he does."

After getting dressed and armed, Ladso met the team in the kitchen. "Grab another cup of coffee for the road. We can't take it into the house because Sharon might smell it. Don't forget to spray yourselves. Have a partner get your backs. We don't want to miss any spots."

Once everyone was ready, they went to the garage and left without a backward glance.

Britt's house was dark and empty when they slowly drove by. Britt pulled out his phone to check the video feeds. Other than Sharon leaving, there was no motion triggered. They were clear to continue with their plan.

Quietly, everyone climbed out of the SUV which Ladso parked a block away. De-scenting wafers hung from little hooks that extended over the tops of the closed windows. The dogs were on leashes and were also quiet, detecting tension from their humans. As the team entered the side yard, Trooper growled once, low in his throat, then quit.

Britt disarmed the security alarms and unlocked the side door. Cautiously, they slipped into the house which sat stale and musty.

It also contained an earthen smell that brought graves and dead things to mind. Most of the furniture was overturned and damaged. Britt opened the cellar door, and the musty, dead smell became far stronger. There was no doubt that Sharon was spending most of her time down there. Britt shut the door again and joined the team for final preparations.

"We will wait for her in the dining room as planned. As soon as she appears, Britt will turn on the lights and we will begin our attack."

"Nikki, throw your beans as soon as Sharon appears." Nikki's eyes tightened as she nodded.

"One-armed, I won't be much good in a battle with a knife or much else." Britt spoke with a minimum of bitterness. "After I've turned on the lights, I'll throw the beans."

Ladso nodded. "With the beans at her feet, she should stay still long enough to give Frank and me time to fire our arrows. After that, we'll still need to be careful, but the rest of the plan should run smoothly, though it will be gruesome."

They didn't know exactly how long they would have to wait before Sharon's return. Turning the lights off, they each found something to sit on and began their period of suspenseful waiting.

Britt sat with the bag of beans in his coat pocket, ready for him to grab and throw. He also had one of the metal-edged wooden knives tucked in his belt. Ladso and Frank sat with their crossbows, each loaded with a single arrow, in their laps. Ladso also had a machete, while Frank had a pistol. Pi had her mace and lighter and one of the knives, but things would have to go very, very badly for her to need it. At worst, her mace and lighter should be all she would end up using.

The minutes ticked on, slowly dragging the team closer to dawn. Ray's soft growl suddenly alerted them. At the same time, Trooper got to his feet, the fur on his spine rising. "Sharon," Ladso whispered in the dark. Nikki stroked Ray to keep him quiet, then whispered a command to both dogs. They sat silent as statues.

Britt checked the app on his phone. "The camera out front hasn't triggered!"

Despite Britt's announcement, the rest of the team focused on the front doorway. Britt continued to look at his phone. None of the team noticed when Trooper and Ray turned their heads to the window behind Nikki. Ray growled again, but Nikki signaled for silence and both dogs unhappily complied.

# 13

A swirling but silent smoke began rising from above the drapes between Nikki and the window. It hovered there for several moments, taking in the scene and preparing to do its worst.

Although Sharon currently had no mouth, she smiled. Her eyes, now little more than swirling smoke, surged with the power within her. If she'd been in her solid state, they would have been glowing the putrid green color that the team knew so well. She could not control others' minds while in this form, but that did not concern her. She wanted them alert and responsive to her when she killed each of them, one by one.

She paused, looking down on Nikki. *This girl child was in the school. She entered the hall where my Sisters slept. She was at the concert where dear Mother Eugenia and many of my other Sisters were destroyed. It is appropriate that she be the first to die tonight.*

She looked across the room at Britt. *The wounded one. He will suffer seeing the girl die, but this suffering will be nothing compared with what he will feel before I have finished with him.*

She looked at Frank. *My slave. You will learn the cost of denying my power over you.*

Finally, she looked at Ladso and Pi. *You both will suffer as well, for my Mother, for my Sisters, and for the pain I've suffered. Tonight, my revenge we be on all of you and you will know my power.*

186

Suddenly, behind Nikki, the blackness coalesced. As the dogs got to their feet, Sharon grabbed Nikki from behind. She pulled her head back to expose her neck.

Nikki screamed and Britt turned on the light. Weapons came up but no-one could make their planned attack as Sharon held Nikki before her like a shield. A guttural, inhuman laugh burst from Sharon's throat as she pulled Nikki tighter against her. Both dogs barked but held their positions as Nikki was locked in a position that only benefitted Sharon.

"You puny creatures have the gall to hunt me! No longer!" She looked down on Nikki's bared throat. "I knew you were here as soon as I approached this house." Sharon turned toward Britt and laughed again. "You will lose more than your arm tonight. You have killed all my Sisters and twice have tried to kill me as well. Tonight, this injustice ends. I will be the final victor and all of you will die!"

A glistening string of drool slid down her chin. Sharon looked at Nikki's neck, then into her eyes with an evil glare, and finally back to the others. "This fresh girl smells perfectly delicious. I will make you watch while I feed on her." Her gaze shifted back to Nikki. "Say your goodbyes to your friends."

Sharon eased the pressure on Nikki's throat and Nikki gasped for air. She pulled against Sharon's arm as she reached under her coat. Before Sharon could tighten her grip again, Nikki called out, "Trooper, Ray! Prieti! Pulti!"

The two dogs were instantly in motion. Following Nikki's command, they flanked Sharon, and snarling, they launched an attack, one from either side. Stunned, Sharon released her grip on Nikki and threw the dogs off. As she did, Nikki whirled around and planted her wooden knife into Sharon's eye. Sharon screamed in pain as Nikki dove away.

Blood pumped out of Sharon's ruptured eye socket, her hands grabbing at but unable to grasp the wood to pull it from her eye. She twisted in pain and effort as from the floor Nikki shouted another command to the dogs, to clear and stay back.

With their aims clear, both men fired their crossbows, but Sharon's movements thwarted them from hitting her heart directly. Ladso's arrow caught in her shoulder while Frank's almost passed through her arm. Now blood was spraying out of all of her wounds as Sharon writhed. She screamed ancient curses as she tried to dissolve into her smoke form. Twice she almost accomplished it, and the second time, both of the arrows fell to the floor.

She took solid form again, and her hands grabbed for the wooden knife once more. Her hands slipped off the handle once again as a thunderous blast suddenly filled the room. Sharon's head whipped back as her forehead exploded. Blood, brains and bone splattered the wall behind her before she fell to the floor twitching.

Ladso turned to see Frank holding the large caliber pistol he brought with him from Chicago. He'd known that Frank trusted his gun in a pinch and both Ladso and Frank feared that they might find themselves in just such a position. He turned back to the writhing Sharon as Pi stepped over to him with her knife. She handed it to Ladso. "Her heart. Put it deep into her heart."

Taking the knife, Ladso hurried across the room and stood over Sharon. She continued to writhe on the floor, her remaining eye open. It glared from the ruin that moments before had been her head.

Dropping to his knees, Ladso grasped the knife in both hands and raised it over his head. While Sharon's arms twitched, temporarily helpless at her side, he said, "For Murray, Delta, Bryant and James. For Mikka. For all those you and your vampire kin have killed." With a powerful cry, he thrust the knife deep into her chest. A sudden gush of blood sprayed around the knife's entry point, letting him know he had hit her heart.

Ladso stood and staggered back as Sharon quickly bled out. In what was only seconds, her corpse began shriveling and aging before their eyes. In just a few moments more, she looked like the remains of an ancient, poorly preserved mummy. The blood beneath her and on the wall turned black and grew tacky as it too died. In less than a minute, like ash, it stirred in the gently moving air.

Nikki's knees gave way beneath her. She collapsed to the floor, gasping for breath. Trooper and Ray came over to her, whining and pressing against her to deliver comfort. The rest of the team stepped over and they held one another as Nikki's knife, still impaling Sharon's dry, empty skull, tipped and broke through the decaying bone.

The team moved away from what remained of their defeated enemy. Stepping on and around the ruins of Britt's property that littered the floor, they retreated to the table in the kitchen. Sitting on chairs or leaning against counters, the team began their recovery from their months-long ordeal.

Ladso looked at Frank. "I am glad I gave you that pistol."

"I'm not upset about it either, but you were the one who wondered what would happen if she got hit by a large-bore gun at close range. Put that into one of your journals."

Ladso managed a smile, but Nikki was not yet up to that. She shivered as she held her head in her hands. As Pi prepared to step over to her friend, Trooper beat her to it. He walked over and put his head against her leg. Nikki's hand immediately was on the dog, congratulating him, drawing the comfort she needed.

Across the room, Ray scooted up next to Britt. His hand dropped to the dog just as quickly as Nikki's had.

Shaking his head, Frank looked at Nikki and the dogs. "That was amazing. You only finished their training on that attack command yesterday, with me as their attack dummy! Those dogs are as brilliant as you are."

Britt looked over at Nikki. "Frank's right, they are brilliant dogs, but you're a brilliant trainer! Not only did you teach them 'flank' and attack,' you delivered the command in the Lithuanian command words. The student may have surpassed the teacher!"

Pi came over and said nothing, just hugged her tightly. Ladso joined her and drew them both into his embrace. "We have done it!"

Looking toward the window, Nikki said, "Here comes the sun!" They all stepped outside to stand in the growing light.

After several moments, Frank looked toward the team. "Anyone hungry?"

# EPILOGUE

Again, saying goodbye to Ladso and Pi who were leaving for Chicago, the team gathered for a farewell meal.

There were no dark jokes this time, only happy thoughts and words. Sharon was dead. No other vampires had surfaced. St. Louis was safe again. "Well, let's not go overboard." Frank shrugged toward the large windows at the front of the restaurant. "But she is as safe as she was before. That's a big step up."

They had learned of the many deaths that occurred between Frank's journey to Chicago and the team's return. Sharon had done her damage, and they had returned the favor. Saint Eugenia Ravasco Academy was no longer, and neither were any of the cursed nuns that ran it.

"So, I hear you two are off to England for a month?" Frank raised his wine glass. "To safe travels and better adventures." The rest of the team raised their glasses as well.

Ladso smiled. "Pi has her passport. We will be leaving in a week. An extended vacation with no work. I love new experiences."

"New experiences! "Pi repeated. "I've never even had a passport before, never been out of the country either, of course, and a whole month! I won't know how to act." Her laughter was childlike in its glee.

Britt was curious about their travel plans. "Have you figured out your itinerary?"

"I have many wonderful ideas. Together we will decide what sites to visit, and when to just enjoy one another…"

Pi grinned. "You flirt. I guess I need to learn a little more about England or you'll be so focused on me that we won't see anything." Ladso wiggled his brows and this time Nikki didn't have to blush for either of them.

Britt got the group's attention. "Our waiter has been patient, but I think he'd like an opportunity to earn more tips tonight. We need to decide what we're ordering."

When the waiter returned everyone was ready. Ladso started by ordering a round of mojitos for the table. Pi took over listing the plates they wanted, explaining they were all going to share. Evidently, it was a common practice in the restaurant. The waiter didn't blink an eye. Instead, he encouraged sampling everything they could.

Their order placed, Britt tapped his glass with his spoon to get everyone's attention. "Nikki has accepted my offer to work with me as a co-trainer. We'll be taking on more clients, from basic obedience training to guard dogs. Clients will be lining up in no time, I'm sure."

Nikki grinned. "And it looks like I'll make enough working with Britt, that I don't need another job. "She looked at Pi and smiled. "That will give me more time to work on music and my singing."

Pi beamed. "Nikki, that's incredible news. I knew you couldn't give up music altogether. It makes you and everyone listening so happy. You have to let us know when you have your first gig. We'll be there, I promise you!"

The waiter brought their drinks and everyone held their icy glass up in a toast. Ladso stood. "To Britt and Nikki's collaboration. To Nikki's return to music…" He leaned forward and lowered his voice. "And to a vampire-free future for all of us!"

Everyone raised their glass, nodding their heads. Each then, made salutations of good luck and a long life for the entire team. After they tasted their drinks, they all cheered again, delighted by the mojito's mix of tart sweetness.

Britt lifted his glass again, looking through the cocktail. "Did you know that Hemingway practically lived on mojitos? He drank them like water, and I never understood why, until today."

"Like water? Like firewater, you mean!" Frank lifted his glass. "These things are lethal. They taste so good you don't notice the rum until wham, it hits you. You're right though, they are mighty tasty. Still, I'm driving myself home tonight and I don't want Cat to have to sleep alone again. He's so glad to be back in his house. I'll be stopping after this one. Hemingway was a weaker man than I."

The food arrived and everyone loaded their plates. Frank had quickly tasted several of the dishes. "I'm stopping at one mojito, but I'm definitely having seconds, maybe thirds of this delicious stuff." He looked at Ladso. "Don't get your feelings hurt over the cooking. I won't eat any more of this than I've eaten of yours."

Despite the sumptuous flavors, the chatter between the team members continued, each of them recognizing that their time together was soon ending. They all knew that being together as a team would not be the daily occurrence to which they'd grown accustomed.

The meal ended and inevitably, coffee was served. This time, no one argued about paying the bill when Ladso stopped the waiter.

With the evening and their long time together drawing to a close, Frank stood and cleared his throat to get their attention. Taking a deep breath, he set down his cup and attempted to put his feelings into words. "Meeting you all, and everything we've been though… as awful as some of it was, has changed me. I've always been a loner, by choice. Our time together has been very important to me, and now it's ending." Everyone shook their heads, but Frank did not give up the floor. "I'll go back to being another overworked detective for the City, knowing that there are far darker things than most people know. Britt and Nikki will be busy with their dog training business. Ladso and Pi will be off jet-setting, and then will be living a life that, even after my experiences with the team, I cannot truly imagine."

Frank's face pinched, his eyes developing a little shine. "What I'm trying to say is, I'm going to miss all of you. I'm going to do what I can, but I want your help in making sure we get together now and again. Deal?"

Pi jumped up from her seat, stepped over to Frank and gave him a big hug. Turning, she looked round the table and said, "Deal!" Everyone promised they would keep in touch with everyone else.

Britt guaranteed his promise to Frank by demanding they attend the Opening Day game together.

Nikki delighted them both by saying she'd join them. "You're going to have to give me some time to adjust to being a Cardinal fan. I've spent my whole life out east."

"The Cardinals will take care of that!" Frank nodded his head with certainty. Then he surprised himself. "After a lifetime of being a loner and as surly as my cat, I've found a family." He wasn't as shocked as he thought he'd be to realize he was totally thrilled about that. He grinned, an expression he'd find himself copying much more often. "You lot **are** family to me, which means, I guess, that I'm now your grumpy uncle who'll be showing up on holidays. That better sound good to all of you because I can guarantee, it's happening! You're all stuck with me. Just grin and bear it."

Everyone on the team was smiling. Ladso stepped over and threw out his arms. "Welcome to our family, Uncle Frank. You had better show up for holidays or I will be making complaints to your Captain."

"Oh, turning nasty already, huh?" Frank grabbed Ladso in a bear hug and Ladso returned it.

Nikki said, "That's fine for you 'lot'…" She pointed at Pi and Ladso while grinning about using Frank's term for the team. "…but we're in town. You aren't getting off with just holidays, Uncle Frank."

"In that case, I'm going to have to teach Nikki how to make a Cop-achino." Pi grinned as Uncle Frank followed that remark with a big hug for both of them.

## END

**First all is dark. Faint sound of breaths echo as dim light swirls, then brightens, revealing a room as envisioned in the author's mind.**

Enjoy this excerpt from a behind the scenes conversation with the characters due out in early 2023:

Initially, all is blank as he imagines the space he wants for his friends' gathering. The walls dim and the floor blurs and then sharpens into old vinyl tile, alternating dark and light. Countless dark heels have left scuffs on the lighter tiles. One wall swirls and dark panels of glass form windows with nothing visible outside. A wooden door with a glass panel appears opposite the windows, but the hallway beyond is dark.

A collection of desks large enough for high schoolers pops into view. First in rows, then they blur and reappear in a circle. Then, like a popped bubble, they disappear. Finally, there is a single, large, round table centered in the room. Three initially, then, one by one, chairs are added until there are ten. An urn and coffee cups move into place on the table.

A cooler appears on a small table beside the door.

The door opens revealing a woman and two men.

Oblivious at first, they move toward the table, then stop and seem to notice their companions for the first time. After hugs and tears, Nikki and James go to the table as Bryant heads to the cooler. "I need one of these." He pulls out a beer. "Anyone else?"

Both at the table nod.

# ABOUT THE AUTHORS

Joseph Hagen was born and lives in St. Louis, Missouri. Joe has published a pair of contemporary werewolf novels: *Moonrise* and *Wolf Hunt, in the Risen and Hunted Series.* He also has a collection of supernatural short stories, *Reasons to Leave a Light On.*

T.M. Kehoe was born and raised in St. Louis, Missouri. She grew up reading Stephen King, Bram Stoker, H.P. Lovecraft, and every horror book she could find.

These days she spends her time gardening, cooking, painting, writing, taking care of husband, dog, and chickens, and spoiling her grandson.

She has been writing her entire life, but this is her first attempt at publishing: "Never give up!"

T.M. and Joe hope you enjoyed the complete Night Hunters Series: *Dark Requiem, Darker Hunts* and *Darkest Vengeance!*

Join our mailing list here: https://BookHip.com/PMBGPMM

We have found that some of these characters have more story to tell. T.M. has several spin offs which will be available in early 2023. Stay tuned!

## Other books by Joseph Hagen

*Moonrise: Risen and Hunted Book 1*, <u>A Contemporary Urban Fantasy</u>

*Wolf Hunt: Risen and Hunted Book 2,* <u>A Contemporary Urban Fantasy</u>

*Reasons To Leave a Light On:* <u>A Collection of Supernatural Short Stories</u>

Made in the USA
Monee, IL
24 March 2023

30432672R10116